... Knitting Mystery series has it all: Friendship, knitting, murder, and the occasional recipe create
the perfect pattern. Great fun."
—*New York Times* bestselling author Jayne Ann Krentz

Praise for *The Silence of the Llamas*

"Maggie and her group are as efficient with their investigation as they are with their knitting needles."
—*Library Journal*

"Small-town crafty ambience. . . . This enjoyable
tale is similar in style to the work of both Sally
Goldenbaum and Cricket McRae."
—*Booklist*

"The antics of Maggie and her friends will keep readers
turning the pages. Tempting recipes round out the volume."
—*Publishers Weekly*

Praise for *Till Death Do Us Purl*

"An entertaining mystery."
—*Kirkus Reviews*

"[A] smooth fourth knitting cozy."
—*Publishers Weekly*

"Intriguing mysteries and a slew of interesting characters."
—*Single Titles*

"Enthusiastic, engrossing, and exciting."
—*The Mystery Gazette*

Praise for *A Stitch Before Dying*

"Sure to hook cozy fans."
—*Publishers Weekly*

"Congenial characters and a mystery that keeps you guessing."
—*Kirkus Reviews*

Meet the Black Sheep Knitters

Maggie Messina, owner of the Black Sheep Knitting Shop, is a retired high school art teacher who runs her little slice of knitters' paradise with the kind of vibrant energy that leaves her friends dazzled! From novice to pro, knitters come to Maggie as much for her up-to-the-minute offerings like organic wool as for her encouragement and friendship. And Maggie's got a deft touch when it comes to unraveling mysteries, too.

Lucy Binger left Boston when her marriage ended, and found herself shifting gears to run her graphic design business from the coastal cottage she inherited. After big-city living, she now finds contentment on a front porch in tiny Plum Harbor, knitting with her closest friends.

Dana Haeger is a psychologist with a busy local practice. A stylishly polished professional with a quick wit, she slips out to Maggie's shop whenever her schedule allows—after all, knitting is the best form of therapy!

Suzanne Cavanaugh is a typical working supermom—a realtor with a million demands on her time, from coaching soccer to showing houses to attending the PTA. But she carves out a little "me" time with the Black Sheep Knitters.

Phoebe Meyers, a college student complete with magenta highlights and nose stud, lives in the apartment above Maggie's shop. She's Maggie's indispensable helper (when she's not in class)—and part of the new generation of young knitters.

A Dark and Stormy Knit

Anne Canadeo

G

Gallery Books

New York   London   Toronto   Sydney   New Delhi

Gallery Books
A Division of Simon & Schuster, Inc.
1230 Avenue of the Americas
New York, NY 10020

Copyright © 2014 by Anne Canadeo

First Gallery Books trade paperback edition January 2014

GALLERY BOOKS and colophon are registered trademarks of Simon & Schuster, Inc.

For information about special discounts for bulk purchases, please contact Simon & Schuster Special Sales at 1-866-506-1949 or business@simonandschuster.com.

The Simon & Schuster Speakers Bureau can bring authors to your live event. For more information or to book an event contact the Simon & Schuster Speakers Bureau at 1-866-248-3049 or visit our website at www.simonspeakers.com.

Manufactured in the United States of America

10 9 8 7 6 5 4 3 2 1

Library of Congress Cataloging-in-Publication Data

Canadeo, Anne
A dark and stormy knit / Anne Canadeo. — First Gallery Books trade paperback edition.
    pages cm
Summary: "The Black Sheep Knitters are initially amused by the antics of the Knit Kats, a local knitting graffiti group that applies its stitching to public protest. Like covering the new parking meters along Main Street with knitted hoods that have silly cat faces. The amusing act of civil disobedience causes a stir in quiet Plum Harbor. But it's not the first time the Knit Kats have made local news. . . . The Black Sheep know about killers, who always leave behind a tell-tale thread. With clever detection skills and their own, irrepressible curiosity, Maggie and the knitting friends soon uncover the truth about the Knit Kats — and snag the guilty stitcher."— Provided by publisher.

  1. Messina, Maggie (Fictitious character) 2. Knitters (Persons)—Fiction. 3. Knitting—Fiction.
4. Massachusetts—Fiction. I. Title.
PS3553.A489115D37 2014
813'.54—dc23
2013027090

ISBN 978-1-4516-4480-7
ISBN 978-1-4516-4482-1 (ebook)

Three can keep a secret if two of them are dead.
~ *Benjamin Franklin*

The clever cat eats cheese and breathes down rat holes
with baited breath.
~ *W. C. Fields*

ACKNOWLEDGMENTS

Many thanks to my dear friend Kathleen Caputi, for sending me a news article that set me on the path to writing this story, for her support and encouragement of my literary efforts, and most of all, for her cherished friendship—definitely Black Sheep quality.

CHAPTER ONE

Maggie left for her shop earlier than usual on Thursday. She faced a full schedule—teaching a new sock-making class, sorting out the picked-over winter inventory, and hosting her weekly knitting group in the evening. She wasn't even sure yet what to serve her friends for dinner and considered swinging by the market to grab some ingredients for the slow cooker—conveniently stashed in the stock room.

Better to get to work and figure out the menu later, she decided. A good dessert would go far. Something chocolate to cheer everyone up.

Dense gray clouds hung low in the sky, and the forecast predicted flurries. She hated these long, bleak weeks after the holidays were over and spring was far from view. She hoped it *would* snow a little. The village streets, now dotted with dirty, melting patches, could use a fresh coat of white.

Her assistant, Phoebe, called this in-between season "the butt end of winter." Not a term Maggie would repeat, but the image fit, she had to admit. The town was so quiet and still, it seemed as if all of New England was hibernating. All of Plum Harbor anyway.

She didn't notice anything unusual as she turned onto Main Street. Did she have enough quarters handy for those infernal new parking meters? That was her main concern.

She checked the cup holder next to her seat, where she stashed them. Just enough to get through the morning. Unless some eccentric customer hauled in a piggy bank to pay for a purchase, she'd have to run to the Schooner Diner later for more change. Edie Steiber, who owned the eatery, was testy at everyone coming in just to feed the meters lately.

"Do I look like a casino slot machine to you?" Edie had complained only yesterday. It didn't take much to get on the diner owner's churlish side. Maggie thought it best to avoid that option for a few days.

She could always shake down her friend Lucy and see if some quarters rolled out. Her good pal stopped by almost every morning while walking her dogs to town, to share gossip and get advice on her knitting dilemmas . . . and real-life problems, too.

Maggie expected to see the trio trotting down Main Street any minute.

The meters were such a grand nuisance. Most business owners in the village, herself included, had protested the proposal. Village shops had enough trouble competing with the big-box stores on the turnpike and at the mall. People didn't like to shop where there were meters. The Plum Harbor Chamber of Commerce had even collected a petition to ban them with more than a thousand signatures.

But a stalwart faction for raising town revenue had finally won, pushing the parking meters through by a narrow margin.

None of the village trustees owned a business, Maggie had to assume.

Main Street was practically empty at this hour except for a slow, rumbling school bus, a few parked cars, and a delivery truck down near the deli. Maggie could see all the way to the harbor, mesmerized for a moment by a swaying ribbon of gray-blue water that came into view. But as she pulled up in front of her store, she realized something about the street definitely looked . . . different.

A round bag-shaped cover had been dropped over the top of each meter. Like a wrapper on a lollipop. Up and down the street, as far as she could see. Had the town finally given in to some protest she hadn't heard about?

Maybe it was a holiday she wasn't aware of. I could save my stash of quarters, she thought with a smile.

But no . . . the coverings were not village issue. She realized that as soon as she parked her car. She turned off the ignition and jumped out. Then examined the nearest meter with sheer amazement.

The coverings were knitted, made of brightly colored yarn. A purple feline face—complete with a pert pink nose, red whiskers, pointed ears, and glowing yellow eyes—stared back at her. The jagged smile—stitched in blood-red yarn—was a comical, yet somehow unsettling, detail.

For some reason, Maggie didn't want to touch it.

She stood back, gazing at the cat-face meter cover, taking in the variety of stitches and fibers. Then she pulled out her phone, snapped a picture, and sent it with a text to Lucy.

Are you coming this morning? You have to see this. Before someone takes them all down. Me-ow-sky!

Maggie walked a bit farther down the street and took a few more photos. Then she sent another text and photo to two more friends who also worked in town. Dana, a psychologist, had an office on Main Street just above the bookstore. She was also on staff at a nearby hospital, and her hours in town were scattered. No telling if she'd be in this morning, though Maggie hoped so.

Suzanne worked for Prestige Properties on a side street off the main thoroughfare. She often worked from home or was driving around, showing houses to clients. But she might get a peek at the display this morning. Maggie knew they'd both be upset if she didn't alert them.

She heard her phone beep, signaling a text coming in. Lucy had answered first:

Already on the way. Will jog last lap. This better be good.

Maggie didn't reply. What could she say? Yarn bombers had struck during the night, and the parking meters were covered with knitting graffiti . . . a parade of cat faces. Lucy was more of dog person but would appreciate this prank, though it looked like the unsanctioned decorations would not last very long.

A dark-green pickup truck, marked with the official seal of Plum Harbor Incorporated Village, stood at the far end of the avenue alongside a blue-and-white police cruiser. Two men in hard hats, gloves, and matching tan jackets jumped out of the truck and chatted with a police officer through his car window.

Did it take an armed law officer and two brawny guys in protective gear to handle the equivalent of teapot cozies? Yes, apparently.

She heard another vehicle approach from the opposite end of the street, and she turned to see a large white van. Some apparatus on top looked like a satellite dish, and the lively red logo on the side left no mistake about who was inside. *News Alive 25!* was chasing down this hot story.

Oh dear . . . let me out of here . . .

If she didn't beat a hasty retreat, some cheerful woman with fluffy hair and lots of lipstick was bound to hop out of that van and chase her down for a "person on the street" interview.

"And I am *not* ready for my close-up, Mr. DeMille," Maggie mumbled.

She quickly gathered her knitting bag and purse from the backseat and scurried up the walkway to the front porch of the shop. She unlocked the door and jumped inside, taking care to leave the sign turned to the closed position: "Sorry . . . Resting Our Needles Right Now. Please Come Back Soon."

The Black Sheep Knitting Shop covered the first floor of a Victorian house and was a perfect, cozy haven for knitters— and, very often, shopkeepers—hoping to hide away from the world for a while.

Maggie felt instantly at ease as she dropped her belongings on the counter near the register and headed to the storeroom to make a pot of coffee. Her usual morning routine. Lucy would be expecting a cup . . . or two. That was for sure.

The storeroom, formerly a kitchen, was still equipped with a stove, a fridge, and other culinary necessities. Maggie had considered pulling it all out when she'd opened the shop about three years ago. But she was soon glad she had not. She often held events at the store—book signings, afternoon tea, and even "Friday Night Stitching & A Movie." Her own knitting circle, the Black Sheep Knitters, enjoyed sharing a good meal almost as much as stitching together. Maggie was sure now that if the shop had not come equipped with a kitchen in back, she would have been obliged to add one.

A stairway in the storeroom kitchen led to an apartment on the second floor. There was an outside entrance as well, but the upstairs tenant—Phoebe Meyers—was Maggie's part-time assistant and most often used the inside stairs for her coming and going. Maggie listened a moment for Phoebe's footsteps but didn't hear any signs of life. Nothing but the coffeemaker dripping and hissing.

She was not surprised. It was not quite eight o'clock, the crack of dawn for Phoebe, who rarely appeared in the shop until ten. Maggie didn't begrudge the college student her sleep, though she did wish Phoebe would lead a healthier lifestyle. Phoebe was up all hours, either studying for her courses or out with her boyfriend Josh's band. Her second—unpaid—job was as unofficial manager, roadie, and number-one fan of the Big Fat Crying Babies. Phoebe had hinted that her romance with Josh had hit a few snags lately. But she hadn't offered any details.

Maggie wondered if the friction had to do with all the grunt work Phoebe did for the band. She wasn't sure Josh appreciated Phoebe's efforts, and maybe that had dawned on Phoebe, too. But last night Phoebe had helped with a gig out in Gloucester, and Maggie knew she wouldn't be up for a while.

Too bad. Phoebe, of all people, would love to see the meters tarted up in such a clever fashion. She would appreciate the absurdity and the artistry . . . and the subversive, radical attitude behind the display. Maggie appreciated that as well, having come of age in the 1970s . . . peace, love, and revolution. And all that. But she was still sure it was better not to wake Phoebe.

A sharp knock sounded on the door, and Maggie looked out the bay window at the front of the shop, peeking around the winter display. Yes, it was Lucy . . . and not some early-bird customer or—heaven help her—the crew from *News Alive 25!* She hoped that group had worked their way down to the harbor by now.

Maggie spotted Lucy's dogs first. Mainly their big wet noses, fogging up the glass. She could not understand why the dogs needed to sniff and drool all over the shop window every morning. What possible scent there could be of any interest to them? Windex?

She grabbed her coat and stepped out on the porch to talk with Lucy. "Did you see the meters? Isn't it wild?"

Lucy looked winded from her sprint and sufficiently shocked, two pink spots on her cheeks, her blue eyes bright.

"Totally and completely wild. It's absurd. And amazing. But creepy, too . . . in a way."

She unzipped the top of her jacket and pulled off her knit cap. Her long, wavy hair had been gathered in a hasty ponytail, and dark-blond strands came loose, curling around her face. "A little creepy, I agree." Maggie nodded as they headed back down to the sidewalk to take in the bizarre needlework.

"Someone . . . a group of people, most likely . . . went to some trouble knitting these things and sneaking out here in the middle of the night to cover the meters. I wonder if anyone saw them."

Lucy considered the question while staring at one of the cat faces. They weren't all purple, Maggie realized. Some were blue or green or black as well. And on some, the ears were a different color from the face. As if several knitters had interpreted the same pattern. She'd taught enough knitting classes to recognize that result.

Lucy was looking them over, too, stretching out the black whiskers that graced a dark-red cat. "Main Street gets pretty deserted at night. All the shops would have been closed. Even the restaurants close early during the winter. And there are only a few apartments on this street." Lucy looked over at Maggie again. "Who do you think it was?"

"I'm not sure . . . but I have a good guess." Maggie paused. "The Knit Kats. Who else could it be?"

"Oh . . . right. They would do something like this." Lucy smiled. "I never thought knitting graffiti artists would strike in our quiet little town. But you never know."

"Me, either. But you never know where the Knit Kats will strike next. That's part of their mystique."

The Knit Kats did have a certain mystique. The group could be called fiber artists, but they displayed their work anonymously, in public places, always with a clever flair. They often poked fun at somber public works—statues or monuments. Or brought attention to wasted tax dollars, like an unsightly and unnecessary pedestrian footbridge that arched over a turnpike in Peabody. The crafty knitting circle had hit the news about two years ago, Maggie recollected, and had not been caught yet, their targets ranging from the city of Boston all the way out to Rockport, at the tip of the Cape Ann peninsula.

Maggie pulled off the nearest cat face to check the stitching.

"Nice work. Whoever did this is very accomplished. And creative. Looks like they took a pattern for a stuffed toy or child's hat and just altered it here and there."

Lucy had pulled one off, too, and was looking it over. "Yes, it is nice work . . . Are the identities of the Knit Kats still secret?"

"I took a look at the group's website once, a year or so ago. They were anonymous then, and I've never heard that they'd come out of the closet."

Lucy dropped the cover over a meter again. "Perhaps the right term would be 'bag'? As in cat is out of one?"

"Right . . . or maybe even 'knitting bag.' But the Knit Kats have managed to maintain their anonymity, as far as I know. I'm sure the press has tried to unmask them. Every time they do something like this, I'll bet some ambitious reporter tries to track them down."

"Speaking of reporters, here they come . . ." Lucy turned from the meters and pointed toward the end of the street.

Maggie turned to see the same TV crew she'd spotted earlier whipping around the corner. "I saw that van a few minutes ago. They must have made a big circle through the village."

She hoped the van would pass. But it swung into a parking spot a few feet from where they stood. A woman in the passenger seat pointed at the knitting shop, then looked out the window, smiling and waving as she scrambled to release her seat belt.

Maggie stared down at her boots, still holding one of the cat faces. She quickly put it back on a meter.

"Oh dear . . . looks like the paparazzi have us cornered.

Let's make a run for the shop and lock the door." She turned, about to do just that.

Lucy grabbed her arm. "What do you mean? You're the perfect person for an interview. A knitting expert who also knows about the Knit Kats? It would be great publicity for the shop. Andy Warhol once said everyone will get fifteen minutes of fame."

"I'd rather have some warning before my minutes. So I can plan a better outfit."

She shook off Lucy's hold, determined to take cover with or without her friend. "You could be interviewed just as easily as I could. Really, I don't mind."

Lucy smiled and started to follow with her dogs. But before she could reply, another voice called after them.

"Ladies? Hello there! . . . I'm Chelsea Porter, from *News Alive 25!* I'd love to get your thoughts about these cat faces on the parking meters."

Maggie had made it to the porch, but the newswoman was right behind her. Chelsea Porter had dark-red hair. A thick wedge of bangs fell straight to her eyebrows, and a white down coat matched a supernaturally bright smile.

A brawny guy in an orange ski jacket followed like a loyal pet—a big video camera balanced on one shoulder.

Lucy had jumped out of their way and now stood on the lawn just below the porch, her two dogs sniffing tufts of winter grass and bits of snow.

Maggie stared at the duo like a deer caught in headlights. The reporter prattled on. "Are you waiting for this shop to open? It's adorable."

"I'm the owner of this adorable shop. And we open at nine."

Chelsea Porter was unfazed by Maggie's tart tone. "The owner? Fantastic! You must know a lot about knitting."

"Yes, I suppose I do," Maggie admitted cautiously.

"Could you spare a minute? You're the perfect person to interview. Can I have your name, please?" Chelsea Porter pulled out a pad and pencil.

Maggie's first impulse was to escape into the shop, like a mouse darting into a familiar hole in the wall.

She hesitated. Then sighed. Lucy was right. This could be good for business. Didn't people say any publicity is good publicity?

"Maggie Messina," she said finally, spelling her last name while Chelsea wrote it down. "This is the Black Sheep Knitting Shop . . . on Main Street, Plum Harbor. We carry a vast array of yarns. Knitting and spinning tools . . . and lessons for all—"

Chelsea quickly cut off Maggie's promotional pitch. "I'll tape a nice intro later. We can shoot with the shop in the background. This porch is a little dark."

Better to hide my wrinkles, Maggie thought. But she followed the reporter, then allowed herself be set in place by the cameraman—like some large lawn ornament—about halfway down the walk with her shop in the background.

"Is the sign showing?" Maggie glanced over her shoulder, hoping the shop's name would be in full view. What was the point of putting herself through this torture otherwise?

"We'll get a nice shot. No worries . . . I'm just going to ask you a few questions, Maggie. It won't take long." Chelsea positioned herself alongside Maggie and angled herself toward the camera with practiced flair.

While she and the cameraman worked out a few more details, Maggie felt around her coat pockets and came up with . . . a ChapStick. She could have sworn she had a lipstick down there, but this would have to do. She swiped some on, then rearranged her scarf—one she had knit herself—at a more fashionable angle.

Just goes to show, you never know what's going to happen when you wake up in the morning, Maggie reflected.

"You look great, Mag," Lucy called out. She stood nearby, smiling very widely. Too widely, Maggie thought. I'll get back at you later for talking me into this, my friend, she silently promised.

"Ready to roll, Chel." The cameraman's face was now obscured by the camera, which was pointed straight at them.

Chelsea turned to her. "We're talking to Maggie Messina, owner of the Black Sheep Knitting Shop, here on Main Street, Plum Harbor. So, you had quite a surprise when you arrived at your shop today, Maggie. Didn't you?"

"I'll say. Got out of my car, and there they were. Cat faces covering the parking meters. Up and down the street. I've never seen anything like it," she said honestly.

Chelsea nodded. Maggie could tell she was doing well.

"Do you have any idea who could have done this? Or why?"

"Well . . . that's a good question. This knitting is high-quality work, no doubt," Maggie answered vaguely. She hesitated to continue. She wasn't sure why. She'd so freely given her opinion on that very same query moments ago.

"And you are an expert on that topic," Chelsea prodded her.

"I know something about knitting. You might say that," Maggie agreed warily.

"So . . . who done it, Maggie? Any knitters you know?"

Chelsea's tone was half joking. But a tingle of apprehension crept up across Maggie's skin, like a tiny insect that had somehow gotten under her sweater. She crossed her arms over her chest. Chelsea was staring at her, nodding in encouragement. Was she worried about the Knit Kats? Afraid there might be some sort of retribution if she mentioned them by name to this reporter? If the young woman did two minutes of research on the Internet, she was bound to arrive at the same conclusion.

"I do have a guess," Maggie said, finding her voice again. "There's a group of knitting graffiti artists active in this area. Around Boston and out here in Essex County. They call themselves the Knit Kats. It may have been them," she said, hoping to sound as if she were putting forth one possibility of many. When, as far as she knew, there were no others.

"The Knit Kats," Chelsea repeated. "What were their motives? Why would they do this?"

"Installing parking meters on this street created quite a controversy in town. Many people think they're unnecessary and a nuisance. Especially the shopkeepers," she added. "Perhaps the Knit Kats are trying to protest by mocking the meters?"

"Mocking the meters, of course," Chelsea echoed. Maggie could tell she liked the turn of phrase. "Can our viewers find out more about this group of outlaw knitters?"

"Oh, yes, the Knit Kats have a website. It's all there for anyone to see. Though their identities are secret. They each have a pseudonym and wear masks and makeup in their photos. That sort of thing."

"Fake names? Masks and makeup? Sounds a little . . . extreme."

The young woman was trying to build this up, make it more newsworthy than perhaps it really was.

"I think it's all very harmless. They display their work in public to amuse and entertain. To make a social comment. In a clever way. They've covered telephone booths, taxis, school buses. On the Fourth of July one year they went into Boston and covered all the statues of colonial patriots—George Washington, Paul Revere, and Samuel Adams. Red, white, and blue yarns, of course."

"Of course." Chelsea nodded, looking pleased. Maggie could tell that was all the information she needed. More than she needed, probably. The reporter turned to the camera, her long hair whipping perilously close to Maggie's cheek.

Her voice was suddenly deeper. "That's the story from Main Street, Plum Harbor, on this mysterious and odd incident of vandalism. This is Chelsea Porter . . . for *News Alive . . . 25!*"

"Great, Chelsea. Cut," the cameraman called out.

"How was that? Want to take it again?"

"We're good," he answered. "Let's get another long shot of the street. Then a few close-ups on the cat faces."

Chelsea turned and offered Maggie her hand. "Thanks again, Maggie. You were great."

"Thank you, Chelsea," Maggie said politely. "You were . . . super," she added with a small smile.

A few minutes later, Maggie and Lucy were safely inside the shop, sipping coffee at the long oak table used for classes and group work. Maggie still felt a bit shaken.

Lucy's dogs were tied on the porch, and she sat across

from Maggie with her coat still on. She worked at home, as a graphic artist, but still had to be at her desk by nine.

"I can't wait to see the segment. You should tape it, and we'll watch it tonight. At the meeting."

Maggie wasn't nearly as eager to see herself interviewed. "I'll ask Phoebe to set her DVR. But I'm going to look just awful. I didn't have on a drop of makeup, and I really should have washed my hair last night."

"You look fine. Don't be silly. I hope she mentions the shop. These things get trimmed down to a few seconds. A tiny sound bite."

"Let's just hope so." Maggie had already begun setting out the needles and yarn for the sock class, which was due to start at half past nine. "You'd think if a reporter was sent on an assignment like this, they would do a little research beforehand. She didn't seem to have a clue about the Knit Kats."

"She didn't. But you filled her in nicely. I think those mobile units just drive all day and producers back at the network tell them where to go. The reporters don't have much time for research unless it's a big story."

"Knitted cat faces on parking meters is not exactly a world crisis, I agree." Maggie counted out the pairs of needles she would need and copies of the pattern. A former art teacher, she was organized and detail-minded.

"No, not a crisis. Amusing, though," Lucy granted the group.

"Definitely. And true to the Knit Kats' style. Though I didn't mean to accuse them without any proof."

"You didn't sound like that," Lucy assured her. "Who else

could it be? A copycat knitting graffiti group? Could there be such a thing?"

Maggie glanced up at her mirthful tone. She could tell Lucy was hoping she'd notice her silly pun.

"Very funny. Yes, they might call themselves the Copy Cats."

"But spell it with *K*s." Lucy sipped her coffee, watching Maggie sort out some balls of yarn the weight and color required by the pattern she was using to start off the group.

Maggie arranged the yarn in a basket and set it in the middle of the table. She never tired of looking at yarn, the varied colors and textures. Lucky for me, she thought. I'm surrounded by it all day.

"Well, I just might search the Internet for the Kopy Kats later today, when I have a spare minute," Maggie teased her friend. "Perhaps a new group has sprung up."

Lucy tilted her head. "Maybe we should start one here."

"I wouldn't go that far," Maggie said quickly. "That's the sort of publicity I don't need. But I do think that reporter should have more of a sense of humor about it. She seemed to be portraying the prank and the entire group in a sinister light. I think it's all in good fun. It's good to give people a jolt from their everyday routines. Make them think outside the box. I don't see any harm in it."

"Any harm in what?" Phoebe stood in the doorway of the storeroom. They hadn't heard her come downstairs, Maggie realized. She looked as if she'd pulled on her outfit in a hurry, a huge, loose sweater and tight black jeans. Her long dark hair, with its distinctive pink streak, was pulled back in a tight ponytail, and her large eyes were unusually makeup-free.

She came toward them, a big mug of coffee in one hand tilting at a perilous angle.

"Take a look outside. You won't believe it," Lucy promised.

"If the town hasn't taken them down by now," Maggie added.

"What are you guys talking about?" Phoebe trotted to the front of the shop and looked out the window. Lucy's dogs jumped up, barking and wagging their tails.

But Phoebe had no interest in her canine friends this morning. She leaned against the glass, looking up and down the street, then headed to the door.

"Wow . . . it looks awesome . . . Be right back," she called over her shoulder as she ran outside.

"Oh good. They're still there. I didn't want her to miss it. But I didn't want to wake her up, either. You know how she can get." Maggie rolled her eyes.

"Wise choice." Lucy nodded sagely.

Phoebe returned a few moments later with her phone in hand. Maggie guessed she'd taken pictures, too. "That is so amazingly cool. I can't believe it. I'm going to post it on Facebook and Instagram."

Maggie nodded, though she wasn't sure what all of that meant. Phoebe often urged her to join the twenty-first century and learn the basics of social networking. So far, the most Maggie had managed was to put up a simple website for the knitting shop. She'd glanced at Facebook . . . but couldn't see the point. She was a friendly person, quite social in real life. But she really didn't need to read a running stream of personal information and thoughts from myriad personalities. The many photos of children and vacations e-mailed to her by her friends more than filled that quota.

"Some TV newspeople were here. They interviewed Maggie," Lucy told Phoebe.

"They did? Why didn't you guys wake me up?"

Maggie shrugged. "I thought you got in late last night and needed some extra sleep."

Phoebe looked flustered and shook her head. "I did get home late . . . but I would have gotten up for that, Mag."

"That's sweet. But it wasn't much. Honestly. Lucy provided plenty of support . . . pushing me into the spotlight." Maggie gave her other friend a look.

"She tried to wriggle out of it. But the reporter was pretty tenacious."

"In a cheerleader-ish way," Maggie clarified.

"Maggie was very good," Lucy added.

"'Super,' I think, is the correct term. I guess we'll see tonight," Maggie said. "Could you set your DVR, Phoebe, so we can watch it at the meeting?"

"Already thought of that. What was the interview like?" Phoebe asked eagerly.

"She just wanted my reactions. A person-on-the-street sort of thing."

"A knitting expert on the street, you mean," Lucy corrected. "She asked Maggie who she thought was responsible. Maggie said the Knit Kats. Then had to explain because the reporter didn't know there was such a thing as knitting graffiti."

"Many people don't know that. Even a lot of knitters," Maggie pointed out.

"Maybe they've posted a message on their website about it. Don't they usually do that after they strike?" Lucy asked.

"That would make sense . . . I'm really not sure."

"Let's check and see." Lucy opened Maggie's laptop, which was sitting on the table, and began typing. "Do you follow the Knit Kats, Phoebe?" she asked as she searched for the site.

"Not really . . . I mean, I know who they are. I've heard of them." Phoebe shrugged and sipped from her mug. Maggie noticed that she had on fingerless gloves, white with little pink skulls stitched on top. She smoothed a cuff over her thin wrist.

"Ah . . . here's the home page." Lucy smiled and sat back, pushing the laptop to the middle of the table so they all could see. "You were right, Mag. Here's a photo of the meters and a comment: 'Pesky parking meters in Plum Harbor got your fur up? Here's one solution. Purr-fect, right?'"

Maggie leaned over Lucy's shoulder to get a better look. "Interesting. They don't take responsibility outright," Maggie noticed. "They say, 'Here's one solution.' Not 'our' solution."

Lucy looked back at the screen. "Good point. But it's obviously their handiwork. Otherwise, how could they get the photos up so quickly? We live here and we just noticed it."

Maggie had to agree. "Very true. At least I didn't lead the media astray."

The photo on the Knit Kats home page showed the scene right outside the shop door and then a close-up of one of the cat faces. Maggie couldn't put her finger on why it wasn't *exactly* cute.

A little ominous-looking, weren't they? Or was she projecting something onto it? Maggie wasn't quite sure.

Lucy looked back at the screen and scrolled down to read more. "It says over fifty meters have been covered. That's a lot of knitted cat heads."

"And ears, eyes, and whiskers," Phoebe noted.

Maggie glanced at her. "It was a while in the planning, no doubt. Good work, too. At least the piece I looked at. They're quite skillful. I was impressed."

"Maybe you should leave a comment on the site. Tell the Knit Kats how impressed you are," Phoebe suggested.

"Oh, you know I don't go in for any of that Internet stuff. You leave a comment if you like."

"How many Knit Kats are there?" Lucy peered at the screen. "I forget." She scanned the screen again. "I think there's a page with the members on here somewhere."

But before Lucy could find the right tab, Maggie noticed the time. She'd spent enough of the morning on knitting graffiti. Time to get going with the real thing.

"My students will be here soon. I'd better unlock the door and turn the sign. We can look at that later."

"I'll go." Phoebe picked up her mug and headed for the door. "Is the sock class starting today?"

"At half past nine. We still have a few minutes to get our act together. I hope you'll sit in and show them some examples of your work, Phoebe. To inspire the novices," she added.

Socks were Phoebe's specialty. She had a vast collection, many her original designs. It was Phoebe's obsession that had given Maggie the idea for the class. She'd hoped Phoebe would teach it, or at least co-teach with her. But her assistant did not feel comfortable in that role. Yet.

Under her flaky Goth-girl exterior, Phoebe very bright and extremely creative. But she did lack self-confidence and self-esteem. Maggie had seen it countless times as a high school teacher. It all went back to the family, or the lack of one. Phoebe unfortunately fell into the latter category.

Maggie had known Phoebe for more than two years and had watched her shed some of her shyness and attitude. She hoped her encouragement and friendship—and the affection of their knitting friends—had helped in that direction, and would help more, as time went on.

"Okay. I'll do a star turn in your sock class, Mags. Let me see what I have upstairs to show . . . Do sock puppets count?"

Maggie looked up at her. She'd never thought of that. "Well . . . maybe. But let's bring them in at the end. I'd love to start off with that purple pair you made last week. With the self-striping yarn and the fringe? But maybe you gave those to Josh," Maggie recalled.

"No way. That pair is classic. I'm keeping them for myself. I just blocked them the other day. I'll see if they're dry." Phoebe grabbed her coffee mug and headed for her apartment.

"I'd better get going, too." Lucy stood up and closed the laptop. "Can't wait to see you on TV tonight."

"That's sweet. But I'm not about to get an Academy Award. It's a two-second interview. Probably one second."

Lucy smiled at her over her shoulder. "This could be the start of something big. First a bite . . . then a blip. Then a TV news consultant. Then . . . who knows? Lunch with Anderson Cooper?"

Maggie shook her head. "Don't you have a deadline or something?" Lucy laughed and pulled her cap on low over her forehead. She looked very cute, Maggie thought.

"Okay, brush me off. But you're going to need a good agent. Think about it."

She snuck in the last teasing line as she zipped up her jacket and slipped out the shop door.

Right. All she really needed now was more coffee and a clear head to get this class organized in time.

The cat faces had definitely been amusing. But the realization that a clandestine clique had been prowling around the village in the middle of the night, totally undetected by the police, was actually disturbing.

No damage done this time. But what if the Knit Kats got it into their feline brains to take more malicious action?

Maggie brushed the unsettling thought from her mind and tried to get on with her day.

CHAPTER TWO

A vision of leering cat faces remained stuck in Maggie's head, distracting and unsettling her. She couldn't say why. Luckily, the day passed even faster than she'd expected. While Phoebe watched over the shop at noon, Maggie ran to the store and bought some ingredients for the slow cooker for tonight's meal. She also picked up some hummus and olives as starters.

Suzanne had called and offered to bring dessert. Her daughter Alexis had come home with a ton of leftovers from a charity bake sale at school. Maggie could only imagine a mound of squashed brownies, crumbled cookies, and mashed cupcakes. But sometimes that sort of treat tasted the best.

The knitting group officially met at seven. Dana strolled in a few minutes early. Maggie had just managed to ring up the last customer and clear off the worktable and the sideboard.

Phoebe usually helped her get ready, but Charlotte Blackburn, a friend of Phoebe's from school, had dropped by, and the two young women ran upstairs to check the DVR.

Charlotte was another student in the art department and also a very able knitter. She had come to a few knitting group meetings since last fall, when she and Phoebe had met in one of their classes. Maggie was glad that her knitting circle was so open and welcoming. Not like some she'd heard of. They were happy to include anyone who liked to stitch, or even wanted to try. The Black Sheep were all about spreading the joy of knitting, not judging the results.

Just the way she'd like to be in real life, though she didn't always meet her own standards. That was for sure.

Maggie was rolling utensils in big cloth napkins when Dana found her.

"Something smells good in here." Dana walked over and gave Maggie a hug.

"I hope so. I'm calling it Moroccan Stew. With chicken, not lamb," she quickly clarified. Dana didn't eat red meat, and Maggie tried to accommodate.

"Sounds good to me. How can I help?"

The two women worked together and soon had the back room set for dinner and their meeting. Lucy arrived with her knitting bag and a bottle of Chardonnay. She opened it and poured them each glass.

"Did you get to see the cat faces on the parking meters this morning, Dana?"

"Made it just in time. Workers from the village had taken them off near my office, but there were plenty left on the other side of the street." Dana took out her knitting and stylish red-framed reading glasses. "Pretty funny, I thought. Though I did see Mayor Swabish out there talking to Chief Nolan. They didn't look amused."

Maggie brought in a bowl of yogurt dip and set it next to some pita chips and other appetizers. "There was no harm done. But I suppose the police are in some hot water since this happened last night, right under their noses."

"What happened under whose noses?" Suzanne Cavanaugh bustled in, balancing two plastic cake holders.

Maggie ran to help so the entire pile wouldn't end up on the floor. The dessert, she assumed, though it looked like enough for three meetings. "We were just talking about the cat masks on the meters this morning. Did you get to see them?"

"I did . . . I had to get to a closing and didn't even notice the darn things until I parked and tried to put money in the meter. It was like . . . what the heck is that?" Suzanne dumped her knitting bag and shrugged out her of coat. "By the time I came out, they were gone." She dropped her knitting bag on the table and sat down next to Dana.

"I wonder what the town did with them. Do you think they threw them out? What a waste of good knitting." Lucy munched on a pita chip, considering the question.

"And yarn," Maggie noted.

"Maybe the police are holding them as evidence." Suzanne's tone was leery and suspicious, though Maggie was sure she was joking.

"The Knit Kats pretty much admit to the prank on their website. We checked this morning," Lucy told Suzanne. "But what's the crime? Do you think it's really vandalism? I think it was an improvement. Certainly brightened up the town for a few hours."

Everyone glanced at Dana, usually the most well versed about legal matters. Her husband, Jack, had been a detective before becoming an attorney. He practiced in town and still had a lot of connections in the police force and district attorney's office.

"Well, the decorations may have prevented people from putting money in the meters. That's probably some sort of violation. And even though it wasn't as bad as spray paint, the knitting did deface public property and it might also be considered littering. Town workers had to take them all off, right?"

"Yes, and they wore special gloves. It was all quite official-looking. No wonder the Knit Kats remain anonymous and cover their trail . . . and tail," Lucy quipped.

Lucy had taken out her knitting, too, Maggie noticed. She was working on a baby blanket for a friend who was expecting. She spread it out on her lap and carefully checked the stitches. While Lucy did seem very cheerful with the project, Maggie had to wonder if she felt any secret twinges of baby longing. Lucy and her boyfriend, Matt, had been living together now for almost a year and there was still no talk about a wedding . . . much less starting a family.

But these days couples didn't necessarily follow the traditional order—first comes love, then marriage, then the baby carriage. It was mixed up in any number of configurations, she reflected.

"Where's Phoebe? Did she see the meters?" Dana glanced at Maggie.

"Oh, yes. She loved the display, as you may have guessed. She's upstairs with her friend Charlotte. She's going to knit with us tonight. They're checking the DVR . . . I might be on the news," Maggie admitted shyly.

"I'm sure you made the cut," Lucy chimed in. "The reporter talked to her forever," she told the others.

Dana and Suzanne had abruptly looked up from their knitting and were now staring at her. "You didn't tell us that." Suzanne sounded hurt.

Maggie shrugged and busied herself at the sideboard. "It was too much to explain in a text."

Before she could change the subject, she heard Phoebe running down the stairs. She bounded into the room.

"Your interview is cued up and ready to roll, Maggie. And I cleaned up my place in honor of your TV debut. Follow me for a special edition of *News Alive 25!*"

Maggie squinted at her. "Do we have to watch it now? I was thinking maybe after dinner . . ."

Too late. Her friends dropped their knitting and jumped up from their seats, practically knocking her down as they hurried into the storeroom and up the stairs.

"Did you see it? How did Maggie do?" Suzanne followed close behind Phoebe, wineglass in hand. Dana and Lucy were next in line, and Maggie pulled up the rear.

"She was smooth. They might sign her up as one of those talking head consultants," Phoebe predicted.

"That's what I said," Lucy shouted out.

"A knitting consultant . . . on the local news? Is there much call for that?" Maggie mumbled at the end of the line.

Apparently no one heard her. Or, if they had, didn't feel obliged to answer. They stepped up into Phoebe's attic apartment, an open studio space with eave ceilings, decorated mainly with furniture found on the sidewalks around town.

Phoebe had a good eye and was handy with a glue gun and

a paintbrush. You'd never suspect it, but Maggie knew a mini–Martha Stewart was hiding under those piercings and streaked punky hair.

Charlotte sat in the big armchair re-covered with flowery pop art fabric.

Phoebe's own hand-knit decorating touches dotted the apartment—pillow covers, a mobile of small knitted birds that hung near a window, and a colorful, hip-looking afghan on the double bed, which was tucked behind a gauzy curtain partition.

The slanted ceilings made the space seem very cozy. Lucy and Suzanne jammed together on the love seat. Dana and Phoebe took kitchen chairs, and Maggie sat on the desk chair, mindful of not rolling away on the wavy wooden floor. A small television sat on a stand opposite the love seat and already displayed a picture—the *News Alive 25!* logo frozen on the flat screen.

"Ready, everyone?" Phoebe held out the remote like a magic wand.

"Yes, yes. Get on with it," Maggie urged her. This interview thing got under her skin.

Phoebe clicked, and the tape started. The anchorwoman, Trish Beasley, appeared, sitting at her desk, accompanied by jaunty music.

"Residents of Plum Harbor woke to a curious sight. Did it rain cats and dogs last night? Maybe just cats. Or maybe someone is mocking the new parking meters?"

"Mocking the meters? They stole my line!" Maggie told her friends.

"That's showbiz, Mag. Get used to it," Suzanne advised.

". . . Chelsea Porter was on the scene and logged this report . . ."

The picture changed to familiar sights: the village in the early morning, the harbor, and the shops on Main Street. The camera swept over the cat cozies on the meters, then zoomed in on one cat face in a tight close-up.

Chelsea Porter appeared, standing beside a parking meter, her expression very somber. *"No one seems to know for sure where they came from. But residents of Plum Harbor woke to a strange sight—the newly installed parking meters decorated with colorful, carefully knit covers. Each one, a cat face."*

"She makes it sound so dramatic and mysterious," Suzanne murmured.

"That's why she gets the big bucks, ladies," Lucy said quietly, making them all laugh.

". . . I spoke to local residents to learn their reactions," Chelsea continued, *"including Maggie Messina, needlework expert and owner of the Black Sheep Knitting Shop."*

"'Needlework expert'? I thought 'knitting expert' was a stretch. There's a lot about cross-stitch and even crochet I don't know," Maggie pointed out.

"Look, the shop!" Dana bounced in her seat. "They really zoom in on the sign. That's great advertising . . . and there's Maggie!"

Maggie cringed. She suddenly didn't want to see the alleged "needlework expert" being interviewed. Finally, she took a peek. "Oh dear . . . do I really look like that? My hair is just insane."

"You look great," Charlotte assured her. "I like that scarf."

"You're crazy. The camera loves you," Suzanne chimed in.

Maggie was feeling a bit better when Phoebe added, "Your hair always looks like that, Mag."

"Shush—I can't hear a thing." Lucy waved her hand.

". . . *a group of knitting graffiti artists active in this area,*" Maggie heard herself say. "*They call themselves the Knit Kats. It may have been them.*"

"*What were their motives?*" Chelsea asked.

"*Well, installing parking meters on this street created quite a controversy. Many people think they're unnecessary . . . Perhaps the Knit Kats are trying to protest by mocking the meters?*"

The camera switched back to Chelsea standing with the village's chief of police. "*I also spoke with Chief of Police Rusty Nolan. Here's what he had to say.*"

Chief Rusty Nolan stood near a police car, his crested cap pulled down low over his forehead. "*This is vandalism, pure and simple. Whoever did this better not come back. There would be serious consequences,*" he added, a hard edge to his New England accent.

"Good old Rusty sounds hot under the collar," Lucy noticed.

Suzanne sipped her wine, thoroughly enjoying the show. "It makes the police look really silly. Someone just crept around and put up all that stuff right under their nose."

"*We did a little investigating of our own,*" Chelsea Porter continued, "*and found the Knit Kats website. You can see why the police have a problem bringing these renegade knitters to justice. They appear with fake names and disguises.*"

The page of the Knit Kats website that showed the profiles of the group members came on the TV screen. Three close-up photos showed mainly just eyes and a bit of a cheek or nose. The rest of each face was covered in fibery concealments and knitted masks, one even covered with buttons, though each looked distinctly feline.

One of the faces had a big red X drawn through it, and something about that struck Maggie as quite ominous.

"We checked the website this morning. But we didn't get to that page," Maggie told the others. "Those disguises are pretty wild."

"Looks like they're trying out for a school production of *Cats*," Suzanne murmured. Maggie had to laugh . . . and agreed. The disguises were sort of tongue in cheek, she thought. But also, they gave her an eerie feeling. As if she'd just walked into a dangling cobweb. She shook it off and focused on the news report again.

"While it remains a mystery," Chelsea Porter summed up, *"it's not exactly a cat-astrophe for Plum Harbor."*

Phoebe hit the pause button and glanced at Maggie. "Well, that's it. Good publicity for the shop."

"I bet zillions of people saw it," Charlotte added.

"Thousands, at least. You were great, Mag. You sounded very expert," Suzanne said.

"You sounded just right," Dana chimed in. "The reporter was lucky to find you."

"Well . . . thanks. I was in the right place at the right time." Maggie sighed, glad it was over.

"Want to watch again? We were talking so much, I hardly heard a word." Phoebe held out the remote and hit the rewind button.

"Once was more than enough for me," Maggie quickly answered. "Let's have dinner. I don't want the food to get cold . . . and I have a project to show you."

That was enough prodding to get them going. Maggie rose quickly from her seat and headed for the stairs. Her friends stood up and followed her. "Thanks, Phoebe. That was fun," Lucy said.

Feeling greatly relieved to have the entertainment portion of the evening over, Maggie quickly set up dinner, with her friends each grabbing a dish to help.

The slow cooker was set on the sideboard, next to the rice and salad, and everyone stepped up to help themselves.

Suzanne was first in line. "Did that kitty caper give you any ideas for a class, Maggie? Maybe you could parlay this for some publicity. Those meter covers must be good for something."

"Possibly . . . I just can't think of what."

"I'll tell you what they remind me of. Remember those toilet tissue covers everyone had in their bathroom when we were growing up?" Lucy laughed. "When I moved into the cottage, I found one my Aunt Claire made. It even had jiggly eyes. I think I saved it somewhere."

Lucy lived in a cottage that she had inherited from her mother's sister, Claire. She and her own sister had spent many summers there as children, so Lucy knew Plum Harbor well and had always loved it. She'd been living in Boston, emerging from a difficult divorce and ready to leave office and city life behind, when it was time to decide what to do with her aunt's property. She'd come out to spend the summer a few years ago and ended up making the move permanent.

Suzanne nodded happily. "I remember those. My nana made them, too. I think everyone in the family had a few. But they were mostly poodles, weren't they? I don't remember cats."

Maggie was last in line and helped herself to stew and salad. The dish did smell appetizing, or she was very hungry.

"Cats, poodles. Porcupines . . . I'm not running any classes on kitschy toilet-paper camouflage. I'd close the shop before I got that desperate. I already teach animal-face hats for kids. But I would like to do a real fiber art class sometime. The Knit Kats have done some amazing big installations covering statues and even a city bus. They did that to protest a hike in the bus fare."

Phoebe and Charlotte finally came downstairs. Maggie had heard them moving all the furniture back in place. "Ready for dinner, girls? Help yourselves. There's plenty." She stood by the sideboard, making sure there were two plates and place settings left for them.

Charlotte had her coat on, a big leather tote hooked over one shoulder. "It looks delicious, Maggie. But I just got a text from someone at school, and I've got to get back to campus."

"Charlotte's artwork was chosen for an exhibit in the gallery on campus. The opening is Sunday night. So everything has to be ready," Phoebe explained.

"What kind of artwork do you do, Charlotte?" Lucy asked.

"I'm working with fiber and found objects right now. The pieces are sort of conceptual settings . . . That doesn't really explain it, right?" Charlotte laughed.

She was so pretty, Maggie noticed, though not for the first time. Tall and thin, with long, naturally blond hair, large, luminous eyes, and fine features. Charlotte often reminded Maggie of the ethereal beauties in works by Botticelli.

"Charlotte's work is really good. You have to see it," Phoebe said quickly.

"I'd love to," Maggie replied. "May I come to the show?"

"Oh . . . wow. Sure. That would be great. It's Sunday night.

I'd love you all to come." Charlotte glanced around at the knitting circle, her gaze resting on Phoebe. "Phoebe's going to be there. She can tell you what time it starts and all that. Just let her know if you can make it, and I'll put you on the guest list."

Looking pleased to have more friends at her reception, Charlotte waved good night, then slung her long purple scarf around her neck twice. Phoebe walked her to the door but soon returned.

"You might get ideas at that show for a fiber class, Maggie. There will be work by other artists, too. But Charlotte is the star." Phoebe stood at the buffet and returned to the table with her dinner—a few bits of salad, some lonely-looking pita chips, and a dab of hummus.

"I'm free on Sunday. Count me in." Dana flipped her knitting to the other side and smiled at Phoebe. "Jack has poker night. I was just going to hang around the house and do paperwork."

"Matt will be watching the Patriots with his pals. He'll never miss me," Lucy told the others.

"It's a little tough for me to shake loose on Sundays," Suzanne admitted between bites of stew. "But if you're all going, I will, too."

With three children—a daughter and twin boys—and a full-time job in real-estate sales, Suzanne was a classic juggling mom. Her husband, Kevin, ran his own construction business, and his hours were fairly flexible, so they somehow worked it all out.

"Great. I'll tell Charlotte to put us all on the guest list. Done," Phoebe added.

"Stick with Phoebe. She's our ticket to the hip events in this town," Lucy told the others.

"Charlotte is jumping-out-of-her-skin excited . . . but she didn't have too many people to invite," Phoebe added. "Her mom died when she was in high school, and her dad lives in Arizona with a new family. Charlotte will like seeing us all there."

Maggie nodded. She'd always had the sense that Charlotte was a lot like Phoebe that way—no strong family ties and not a large circle of friends at school, either. An artist and a loner. It made sense that they'd connect and be close friends.

"Mmm . . . this stew is really good. What's in it besides chicken?" Suzanne took a second taste of her dinner, savoring the forkful.

"Some white beans, carrots, and onions. A little chopped tomato. Garlic, of course. Oh, a handful of raisins and chopped almonds. I just sort of winged it," Maggie said honestly. "I'll try to remember and write it down for you sometime."

"Very tasty. I like the spices," Dana agreed.

Maggie was pleased her experiment had worked out. "And we have Suzanne's dessert to look forward to. Must be good, it took up two cake holders."

"Was that what you carried in? Did you make a cake for each of us?" Dana asked with a laugh.

"One of Alexis's school clubs ran a bake sale today, and she brought home the leftovers." Suzanne had finished her dinner and picked up her empty plate.

"What was the charity?" Lucy asked curiously.

Suzanne shrugged. "I'm not sure . . . Carbs for a Cure?"

Maggie laughed. "I'm sure it's some worthwhile project. We should make a donation. I don't mind helping Alexis's club."

The rest of her friends agreed and helped to clear the dinner dishes. Maggie soon served the brownies and cupcakes—just as crumbled and squashed as she'd expected—with coffee and tea while her friends settled down to work on their knitting in earnest.

Maggie sat down again and opened a folder she'd brought over from the sideboard. "All this dreary weather gave me an idea. The next bright spot on the calendar seems to be Valentine's Day. I thought that was a worthy knitting goal, small gifts for your valentine?" Maggie showed the group pictures of projects she'd found. "Here are some little felted hearts and a knitted greeting card. A cup warmer, very cute, and a case for a phone or iPod. Everyone needs those. Oh, there's a heart scarf, and I found two choices for mittens, moderately challenging and this very simple pair. You can sew a heart as an embellishment. The pattern was created by Eleanor Roosevelt. She was an avid knitter," Maggie noted.

"If they were good enough for FDR, they're good enough for Matt," Lucy said decidedly, looking over the instructions.

"Just what I thought." Maggie smiled at her. "And how about two-hour fingerless gloves and heart-covered socks?" She slid the pages directly to Phoebe. "Hard to resist."

Her friends passed around the pictures and patterns. "I think Kevin would use the mug warmer. It's a fast one, too." Suzanne was fairly slow and easily distracted from her projects. The mug warmer did seem a good choice. "And every time he sips from a travel mug, he can think of his sweetie pie." She made a silly romantic face.

"Same for Jack . . . though I think I'll sew the top and turn it into a golf-club cover," Dana decided with a laugh. "Do you think he'd be embarrassed on the course?"

"It might make him feel better after he hits a bad shot to remember somebody loves him anyway," Maggie replied.

"Oh, this one is cute." Lucy held up the picture of a pink bear with a red heart sewn on its chest. "Too bad Isabel and Regina are past the stuffed-toy stage," she said, mentioning her nieces, whom she often knit for.

Phoebe took the page and looked it over. "It is cute. And doesn't look hard, either."

"It's fairly simple," Maggie said. "I stuck that one in because I thought we might make some extra gifts and share the love . . . and the knitting. There's a shelter for homeless women and children in Newburyport. I thought we could make some bears and other things, and drop them off for the residents."

"What a lovely idea. I'd love to do that." Dana was the fastest knitter in their group. Maggie knew she could churn out a few of these projects by Valentine's Day.

"I'll try to make at least one extra," Suzanne offered. "That is a nice idea."

Suzanne was generally slow with her work, short on time and patience, Maggie knew. But she did a lot better with a goal, and Maggie knew she'd come up with something.

Lucy and Phoebe quickly agreed to make gifts for the shelter, too.

"So, heart-covered socks for Josh? Or maybe you've already made him a pair?" Maggie teased Phoebe.

Phoebe looked confused for a moment, then blinked and shrugged. "Yeah, he's stocked with socks. He's not getting any more out me, that's for sure."

Phoebe seemed upset. She and Josh must have had a fight. But before Maggie could decide if she should probe any further, the shop phone rang—the loud, shrill sound catching the group's attention.

"Want me to get that?" Lucy was sitting closest to the counter and about to jump up.

"Oh, no . . . let the machine get it. Some customer checking on an order or something," she guessed. Her friends sat quietly, waiting to hear the message.

But there was only silence. A long, empty silence. Then a very strange sound . . .

It sounded like a cat—an angry cat yowling. Then a muffled voice said, "Maggie Messina? Needlework expert? We have our eye on you!"

Then an odd laugh and a loud click.

"What in the world was that?" Suzanne's brown eyes bugged out.

"It sounded like a . . . a cat. And some sort of prank caller?" Dana's voice was calm and even, but Maggie could tell from her expression she was as surprised and chilled as the rest of them.

"Whoa . . . that gave me the creeps." Lucy turned to Maggie.

"Me, too," Maggie admitted. "Dana is right. Some sort of silly prank. See? I told you I didn't want to be on TV. Now every nut job in town is going to call me."

"Let's check the number. You have caller ID, right?" Suzanne jumped up and picked up the receiver, then turned back to the table. "Restricted. I should have guessed."

"It does give new meaning to the term 'catcall,'" Lucy suggested, making them all laugh.

Dana looked up from her knitting and glanced at Maggie. "Maybe the Knit Kats saw you on the news, and that's their review."

"I don't know . . . That was weird. Maybe you should tell the police," Suzanne said quietly.

"The police? Don't be silly. It's just a stupid joke." Maggie shrugged and picked up her knitting, trying to shake off a creepy feeling. "If I get any more calls like that, I guess I will," she added. "Someone saw the news and is acting silly. Let's get back to knitting, shall we?"

Her friends nodded, all quietly agreeing.

What a strange day this had been . . . from start to finish. Time to shake off these odd feelings and wind down on a comforting, familiar note. Chatting and knitting. Even the mysterious Knit Kats could not possibly enjoy themselves more than she and her own knitting pals did on these Thursday nights together. Or anytime, for that matter.

As she picked up her needles again, she glanced at the phone, sitting innocently on the long counter.

No reason to think about that silly call twice. Was there?

CHAPTER THREE

L ucy had offered to drive everyone to Charlotte's art exhibit on Sunday night. Maggie sat up front; Dana and Suzanne were in the backseat. Phoebe had left earlier in her own car, but promised to meet them at the gallery before six. The reception ended at eight, but they planned to leave before that and go out to dinner.

Phoebe had also invited Charlotte to dinner with them. Charlotte had a lot of friends on campus, but none very close, Phoebe told them. Charlotte had recently broken off with a boyfriend, and Phoebe was worried she had no one to celebrate with.

"Of course she can come with us. We'd be honored," Maggie had replied immediately.

It was only half past five as they drove onto the campus, but the sun was already low in the winter sky. A rosy hue tinted the horizon, just visible through bare branches.

The Stimson Art Center, named for a wealthy benefactor of the school, was located at the edge of the Whitaker College campus, a few minutes north of Plum Harbor.

A mixture of old buildings and new, Whitaker College was quite pretty, Maggie thought. The grounds had once been the estate of a prominent New England family. They'd owned a foundry or textile mill in the area. Some dark industrial enterprise, she recalled. In the early 1900s, the family set up a college for the children of their local workers and eventually donated the estate to Essex County, along with an ample endowment so the school could be expanded.

The tuition was reasonable, and Phoebe had been enrolled as a part-time student for a few years now—though she did not seem any closer to earning her degree, Maggie noticed. But she was happily finding her way. Majoring in philosophy one year and art the next. She was still quite young, only twenty, and had her whole life ahead of her.

Young people rush themselves so much these days, Maggie thought. Racing toward some invisible finish line with blinders on. So focused and directed, they miss all the scenery, the simple joy of the journey. When the truth of it is, there is no finish line. No final goal to life. Just important stops and milestones along the way. That was her impression anyway.

"Looks like we turn left here," Dana said from the backseat. Maggie noticed a sign on a lamppost, advertising the exhibit.

"I think the gallery is in that building up ahead," Lucy announced. A large warehouse-like building came into view. She parked nearby.

Lucy led the way as they walked together up a gravel path. "I think Phoebe said the gallery is on one side and some art studios are on the other."

"I see a lot of lights on. I think we're in the right place," Dana added.

"And there's our own little Phoebe . . . right on time." Maggie spotted her assistant standing just inside a set of glass doors in the middle of the building.

Phoebe stepped out and waved. "Hi, guys. You made it."

"Wow! Look at you . . . I didn't know this was such an elegant affair. Should I run home and change?" Suzanne leaned back theatrically, taking Phoebe in from head to toe.

Phoebe wore a sweeping black maxi skirt, a lace tank top with a long, lacy pink knitted scarf around her throat, and black fingerless gloves that extended up her slim white arms, over her elbows, though the gloves did not cover a small heart-shaped tattoo on her slim upper arm. Her hair was gathered in a puffy washer-woman-style knot that seemed about to tumble down very stylishly at any second. Her eyes were ringed with liner, shadow, and mascara, and sparkling studs dotted her ears, matching the tiny stone in one nostril.

"No worries. I think you'll see mostly jeans and hoodies in there. I just felt like glamming it up a little."

"You look very glam to me," Maggie assured her.

Phoebe smiled shyly and led them inside. The large entrance, painted pure white, was decorated with a smooth white stone sculpture on a black pedestal. A large poster, balanced on an easel, announced the opening of the exhibit. The photo of a piece of fiber art was featured on the sign—tarnished spoons and half-broken teacups dangling from a colorful tapestry.

"That's one of Charlotte's pieces, *Granny's Parlor*. It was chosen for the poster," Phoebe said proudly.

"Very interesting. Can't wait to see the rest." Maggie shrugged out of her coat. The group left their things at a checkroom and followed Phoebe to the gallery entrance.

Another student, also dressed in black, though not quite as dramatically as Phoebe, checked a list for everyone's name.

As she stepped into the gallery, Maggie decided she'd surrendered her coat too willingly. The vast, open space was quite chilly. With ceilings as high as an airplane hangar, it was, she guessed, a hard space to heat and not often occupied. But as these events often went, a throng of warm bodies would soon fill in the emptiness and quickly raise the temperature.

The floor was wood, bleached white, the walls white-washed as well, covered by artwork. A few partitions, painted pearl gray, broke up the area, making it look less like a gymnasium sans basketball hoops. Waiters, who Maggie strongly suspected were more dressed-up students, circulated with trays of white wine and sparkling water in plastic cups. Others offered bits of cheese and crackers.

"We're a little early. But you can get a better look at the artwork without a crowd here. And talk to Charlotte. She's around here somewhere . . .."

While Phoebe gazed around for her friend, a woman about Maggie's age sailed up to them. "Phoebe . . . you look lovely. Are you helping out here tonight?"

"Hello, Professor Finch . . . No, I'm just here to see Charlotte's work. She invited me and my friends."

Not very tall and a bit stout, the professor made the most of her assets with her outfit, Maggie thought. She wore slim black pants with a billowing chiffon top, a blue-gray color that matched her large eyes, dramatically kohl-lined and shadowed. Her short hair, a shock of white, stood out in stylish spikes. Large silver earrings, studded with random stones, matched a pendant and thick cuff bracelet. A tag on her blouse revealed her name: Professor Sonya Finch.

Phoebe turned to the group. "Professor Finch is one of my teachers this semester."

Maggie introduced herself and extended her hand. "Maggie Messina. Very nice to meet you, Professor."

"My pleasure. I think Phoebe mentioned that you own a knitting shop in the village? Where she works?"

Maggie nodded. "Yes, that's me."

"I saw you on the news the other night. That little prank really stirred up the town, didn't it?" Professor Finch laughed, sounding very amused. At the Knit Kats, Maggie hoped. Not her interview.

Was the art professor poking fun at her—or someone—for making such a fuss over the knitting graffiti? Chelsea Porter should take the flak for that, Maggie thought.

"It did cause a stir. But we've kept calm and carried on," she replied drily.

Sonya Finch had a loud, bold laugh and obviously appreciated the volley. "I'm sure you have. You look like the calm type . . . Phoebe is so talented," she added, suddenly changing the subject and resting her hand lightly on Phoebe's shoulder. "I'm so glad she's in my sketching and painting studio this semester. She's doing some fine work."

"Is that your area of expertise?" Dana asked curiously.

Sonya shrugged. "Not really . . . but in a small department you have to be flexible. I just jump in wherever needed. I usually know enough to push them in the right direction," she added with a smile.

Before Maggie could ask the teacher more, Charlotte

appeared. She usually dressed down in jeans, adopting the tattered, drab look that was the local art-student style. But she was quite glammed up tonight, too. A knockout in a beaded black minidress, lacy stockings, and high black boots. She looked very much the guest of honor and arrived at their circle flushed and breathless.

She was nervous, Maggie realized, and not at ease in the spotlight. It had to be stressful, having your artwork on display for all to judge and critique. Especially at that tender age, Maggie reflected.

"Charlotte . . . there you are. Everyone has been asking for you." The art professor smiled warmly at her star pupil. "Time to mingle and meet your fans," she encouraged. "I think there's even someone here from the Plum Harbor newspaper. That will be good publicity for the gallery."

Charlotte glanced at her teacher and nodded—though she didn't smile, Maggie noticed. "Thanks, Dr. Finch. I'll catch up with them."

"Time for me to mingle, too," Sonya Finch added. She took in the knitting group with another smile. "Thanks again for coming. I hope you all enjoy the exhibit."

"I'm sure we will," Maggie replied.

Professor Finch sailed off to greet another group of art lovers. Phoebe turned to Charlotte. "Hey, Charl, what's up?"

Charlotte drew close to her. "I just got a text from Quentin . . . I told him not to come. But he said if I don't . . ."

Charlotte's words trailed off. She looked over at the gallery entrance; her fair complexion turned pale as paper.

Maggie looked over, too, and saw the girl with the guest

list arguing with a young man in a leather jacket. Another student, one of the male waiters, had trotted over to help her.

"Oh no . . . he's here. Don't let him see me . . ." Charlotte turned to Phoebe with a fearful expression.

Maggie could tell the leather-jacket guy was trying to talk his way into the exhibit, but the other boy had hold of his arm. The argumentative intruder had dark hair, a super-close buzz cut on the sides with a thick, spiky section sprouting down the middle of his skull. He wore the leather jacket over a black T-shirt and tattered jeans. A blue-and-red tattoo climbed up one side of his neck, like a colorful lizard.

Maggie saw Professor Finch heading toward the fracas. She had an uneven gait, moving along in a rocking motion, Maggie noticed. Not exactly a limp, but perhaps one leg was shorter than the other? She looked down at the professor's shoes and saw that, indeed, one black boot did look different, the heel and sole much thicker.

Charlotte cowered next to Phoebe—which Maggie found quite ironic since Phoebe herself was such a slim little waif. Not exactly a fortress of protection. Both of them ducked behind a gray partition.

"He's totally crazy . . . I wish he'd just leave me alone . . . He just doesn't get it . . . not even the order of protection . . ." Maggie couldn't hear every word, but Charlotte's tone—angry and frustrated—was clear enough.

Obviously the boy was harassing her. Hadn't Phoebe mentioned that Charlotte had just ended a relationship? This must be the aftershock.

Maggie glanced back at the entrance. Voices were growing louder and more insistent. Even though Professor Finch had extended her hands, gesturing for the uninvited Quentin to go, he roughly pushed her aside, shook off the hold of the waiter, and headed toward Charlotte like a lovesick heat-seeking missile.

"Oh God . . . here he comes . . ." Charlotte tore away from Phoebe and took off, the clicking heels of her high boots echoing in the empty space.

Phoebe stared at Maggie a second, then chased after her friend.

"Phoebe? Wait . . ." Maggie called out, but it was too late.

Quentin quickly cut across the gallery, heading straight for a black metal door at the far corner of the room. Maggie could see the two girls aiming for the same door by a more circuitous path.

Luckily, they reached it first, pulled it open, and ran through. It slammed shut, the sound echoing in the empty space.

Quentin bumped into a cluster of visitors, spilling their drinks and tipping paper plates of crackers. He quickly pushed past them, reached the door, and ran through, only a few seconds behind Phoebe and Charlotte. The door slammed for a second time, as if sealing off a portal to another dimension.

"What's going on? Where's Phoebe?"

Maggie turned to see Dana, Suzanne, and Lucy, who had left to view the exhibit.

"Charlotte's ex-boyfriend just crashed the party. He's after Charlotte. Phoebe is trying to protect her." Maggie paused, the realization sinking in. Could Phoebe even protect a . . . fly? "Come on . . . before he catches up to them."

The friends dropped their glasses on a nearby table and joined the chase.

Sonya Finch followed, too. "I've just called campus security . . . they're on the way . . ."

She moved as quickly as her bulk and gait would allow. Maggie barely had time to glance back as she pulled open the heavy black door.

The door closed behind her, separating her from the rest of the pack. Maggie found herself in silent, pitch-black darkness. She paused, waiting for her eyes to adjust.

This had to be the studio space that she'd noticed when they were outside. It felt even chillier than the gallery and damp. She took a few steps forward; the floor was hard and cold under the thin soles of her dressy shoes, and Maggie took in a musty, earthy scent. As if she were in a basement. Then she realized it was the scent of damp clay; she must have wandered into the ceramics studio.

All she could hear were her own deep breaths and the hollow echo of heavy footsteps moving very quickly somewhere on the other side of a warehouse-sized space.

Before she could figure out which way to go, a piercing scream cut through the darkness. Then what sounded like a pile of dishes crashing to the floor. Maggie stood very still, listening. She held her breath.

Was that Phoebe . . . or Charlotte?

Neither choice was preferable.

"Phoebe . . . is that you? Answer me, please! . . . Are you in here? . . . Are you all right?"

Maggie ran toward the sound, though in the darkness it was hard to tell if she was moving in the right direction. Her eyes were more accustomed now to the dark, and a bank of high windows let in some thin, milky light from a distant street lamp.

Finally, she heard footsteps coming up behind her.

"Maggie? Wait for us . . ." Maggie turned to see Lucy and her other friends running toward her with their phones out, which they were using as flashlights.

Why in the world hadn't she thought of that? She was just too low-tech for her own good, that was the problem. She reached in her purse and took her phone out, too. "I'm here . . . Did you hear that scream? It came from back there." She pointed, hoping they could see her.

"Lead the way. We'll follow," Dana called out. Maggie nodded and continued toward the sound.

"Phoebe . . . where are you?" She strained to hear an answer. Anything. But there was suddenly silence. Not even the sound of footsteps.

Maggie stopped in her tracks and sighed aloud.

"Maggie . . . I'm over here," she finally heard Phoebe answer. Maggie dodged to her left, finding her way around a large partition. Using the light from her cell phone, she soon spotted Phoebe in a black puddle of fabric on the floor, huddled against a wall of steel shelves. Most of the shelves held pale white ceramic pieces. But quite a few more lay broken on the floor, jagged-edged shapes scattered all around Phoebe. Maggie sneezed from the dust, her shoes crunching on broken pottery bits, as she crouched down to check on her.

"Oh dear . . . are you hurt?"

"I'm all right . . . Quentin gave me a shove and my boot got caught in the hem of my skirt . . . so much for formal wear. I sort of hit my head on this shelf thing," she explained. "And a ton of stuff flew off and crashed on the floor."

"You're lucky none of these pieces fell on top of you. Does it hurt anywhere? "

Phoebe grabbed Maggie's arm and hoisted herself off the dusty floor. Her lovely outfit was coated with white dust. "I'm okay, I think. I just got a little dazed."

"Dazed? You might have a concussion," Maggie fussed. "Do you feel sick to your stomach, or dizzy?"

Dana, Suzanne, and Lucy appeared. "Phoebe . . . are you all right?" Lucy asked.

"Never mind me. I'm worried about Charlotte. She ran into the next studio. I tried to block the door, but Quentin pushed me down."

Maggie didn't like hearing that. She hoped the boy didn't have a weapon. He was certainly brawny enough to do damage to a little thing like Phoebe—or Charlotte—without one.

Phoebe limped bravely toward the next door. Maggie quickly followed. "Wait. You can't go after them alone . . . He sounds violent."

"That's why she's been trying to lose him. He gets crazy angry . . . and he's very jealous . . ."

Phoebe shouted the last few words over her shoulder as she pulled open the next door and disappeared.

Maggie quickly followed. "Phoebe . . . wait! I'm coming with you . . . That kid is dangerous." She turned back to her other friends. "Go back and make sure campus security knows where we are. Shouldn't they be here by now?"

"I'll go," Suzanne offered. "Dana might be needed for hostage negotiations—to talk some sense into crazy Quentin."

Maggie hoped that didn't happen. But it was certainly possible.

Suzanne turned and ran back toward the gallery while Maggie followed Dana and Lucy, who had run ahead, trying to keep up with Phoebe.

"Don't worry, Maggie. We can still see her . . . or at least hear her. She isn't too far ahead," Dana called back.

Maggie followed. The next space was also dark and cut up into sections with partitions that only reached halfway to the very high ceiling. Now she smelled the distinct odor of oil paints. Did students still learn how to paint in oil these days? That was encouraging. She thought the whole world had gone acrylic.

Passing halfway through the painting studio, she suddenly saw that big metal doors on the far side of the space had been pulled open. A section of the campus was framed in the opening.

Phoebe came into view, and Maggie's entire body sagged with relief. She was outside, near a walkway, her slim figure silhouetted in the light from a nearby lamppost.

Before Maggie could call to her, a motorcycle engine revved and roared, the sound deafening.

Maggie made it to the open doors just in time to see the shiny black bike fly down a sidewalk and swerve around a pair of shocked students. They dropped their books and ran for cover. Then the bike drove up on a snowy lawn, slipped wildly, bumped over a curb, hit the road on one wheel, and roared into the dark.

So much for Quentin, Maggie thought.

Where was Charlotte?

CHAPTER FOUR

Maggie stood alongside Phoebe on the walkway, catching her breath. She was so overwhelmed and overheated, she barely felt the cold, though each breath made a frosty cloud. Lucy and Dana were outside as well. Dana was on her phone. Maggie could tell she was talking to Suzanne, asking what happened to the campus security.

Good question. Maggie was just relieved the chase was over and Phoebe had come out of it safe and mostly sound.

"Some driving. That kid should be in the movies," Maggie finally said.

"Quentin is out-of-his-flipping-mind crazy. Charlotte has an order of protection against him. But he doesn't get it." Still breathing heavily, Phoebe checked her hair with her fingertips. Her upswept hairdo had flopped to one side, and she pushed it around her head like a hat, then just yanked out the hairpins.

"Okay, never mind the movies, how about jail?" Lucy suggested as she and Dana joined them. "He's the very definition of a hazard and a walking, talking public disturbance."

"Totally," Phoebe agreed. "I never got it. I mean, why Charlotte ever hung out with him in the first place."

Maggie didn't, either. Charlotte was bright, talented, and a good student. Maggie would hazard a guess this boy was none of those things. Though opposites did attract, especially at that age. Maybe he seemed exciting, and she was curious about the bad-boy type. Or she'd been flattered by his attention.

"Where is Charlotte?" Dana glanced around. Maggie wondered, too, but assumed Phoebe knew.

"I just saw her like a minute ago." Phoebe spun around, looking for her friend.

The few students who had watched the chase and Quentin's dramatic escape had already dispersed. The nearby campus and walkways were empty.

Phoebe turned and cupped her hands around her mouth. "Charlotte? It's just me, Phoebe . . . and Maggie. Where are you?"

They stood together, waiting for an answer. Phoebe looked worried. "Maybe she ran back inside and hid somewhere?"

"Maybe. I didn't see her. But there was a lot going on, and it was pretty dark in there," Maggie replied.

Lucy started back toward the building. "Let's go inside and check."

"Good idea. I'm freezing out here." Dana rubbed her arms for warmth as she quickly stepped back into shelter.

Just as they passed through the doorway, the lights all over the building flashed on. Maggie blinked, the burst of light blinding her for a moment. Large metal fixtures high above made a dull, humming sound.

"Phoebe? Charlotte? It's Dr. Finch . . ."

"And Suzanne," their friend called out. "Are you guys still in here?"

"Over here, Professor . . ." Phoebe turned. There was a partition between the teacher and the doorway. Phoebe quickly stepped into a space where Professor Finch could see her.

Sonya Finch approached quickly with Suzanne and two security guards following close behind. Maggie noticed that a campus security car had also pulled up outside. Two more officers got out and walked toward the open doors.

"What happened? . . . Where's Charlotte?" Professor Finch looked flushed and nearly breathless as she hobbled closer.

"I don't know . . . I followed her through the last studio, and she ran in here. Quentin pushed me down before I could get through the door," Phoebe explained. "I thought she was right outside, hiding somewhere. But after Quentin flew off on his bike, she like disappeared into thin air."

"Oh . . . that's too bad." Dr. Finch stared down, clearly distressed. Then she looked up at Phoebe, taking in her appearance with grave concern. "Are you all right, dear? Do you need a doctor? We'll get you over to the infirmary right away."

Phoebe rubbed her forehead. Maggie hoped she didn't end up with a big lump or a black eye.

"I'm okay . . . I just wish I knew what happened to Charlotte. I hope he doesn't catch up to her," Phoebe said quietly.

Maggie was thinking the same. Charlotte seemed terrified. She must have run off to hide somewhere.

"I'm going to call her. Maybe she'll pick up for me," Phoebe told her teacher.

"Good idea. I'll tell security what happened. Maybe they can catch Quentin before he leaves campus."

At the rate he was moving, Maggie would bet that boy was long gone.

"Let's check that last studio," Lucy suggested. She and Dana went back inside the building.

Professor Finch went back to the group of officers talking together outside the open doors. Phoebe stood with her phone pressed to her ear, waiting for Charlotte to pick up. Maggie heard her leave a message. Then she started furiously texting.

Finally, Phoebe shrugged and put her phone away. "She didn't answer. I sent a text, too."

"It was worth a try." Maggie reached out and rubbed her thin shoulder.

"Maybe she'll answer in a little while. Give her time to catch her breath," Suzanne suggested.

Professor Finch returned. "The security guards found some students who saw a girl fitting Charlotte's description run into their dorm. Right after the motorcycle took off. Charlotte must have snuck past him somehow."

"That's good news." Maggie glanced at Phoebe, but she didn't look encouraged.

"They're going to alert the police in Plum Harbor. Don't worry, someone will find Quentin," she assured Phoebe. "Charlotte's a smart girl. I'm sure she will find a safe place to stay for a while."

"I hope so . . . I just wish she'd answer." Phoebe checked her phone again. "She could stay with me tonight. Quentin doesn't know where I live."

Maggie wouldn't count on that. If he was really stalking

Charlotte, he probably knew who her friends were. Even where they lived. Maggie didn't want Phoebe to put herself in such a dangerous situation. Not that she didn't want to help Charlotte. If she got in touch again, both girls could stay at her house, Maggie decided. But Phoebe's idea was definitely not safe.

Phoebe was still distressed, and Maggie decided not to debate the point. Without Charlotte in sight, it wasn't even a question.

Lucy and Dana returned. They had obviously not found Charlotte, either.

Dana put her arm around Phoebe's shoulder. "Don't worry, sweetie. Charlotte probably knows a place to hide from Quentin. I just hope she checks in with you soon to let you know she's all right."

Phoebe nodded, her expression bleak. "It just really stinks that she's missing her big night. She worked so hard for this. That jerk just totally ruined it."

Professor Finch gazed at Phoebe with sympathy. "I was thinking the same thing. It really is so unfair and unfortunate. But people are viewing and appreciating her work. If that's any comfort. I need to get back, too. I hope you'll all return. I don't believe you got to see any of the exhibit."

Maggie forced a smile and nodded. Once the professor left, Maggie turned to her friends again.

"I know you're probably not in the mood anymore for art viewing. But maybe we should take a quick look?" When no one answered, she added, "I think Charlotte will resurface unharmed very soon. I want to be able to tell her honestly how much I liked her artwork."

She watched her friends exchange glances. Lucy was the first to speak. "Good point. A quick look would be good manners. Then let's get our coats and get out of here."

"And go out to eat," Suzanne suggested. "Chasing down psycho boyfriends really builds an appetite. I had no idea."

The lights were on in all the studios now, and they found their way back easily. As they emerged in the gallery once more, the space was crowded and noisy. Phoebe steered the group through the mass of guests over to Charlotte's work. They wanted to see that most of all.

"Here it is . . . Isn't it great? I love the way she blends all the textures. Then sticks it together with all these random objects and sort of tells a story. Or makes you imagine one."

Phoebe was not the most eloquent or precise art critic, but Maggie thought her summation did capture a sense of Charlotte's work.

The artwork was constructed of sections of knitting, most of it ragged, even torn. Pieced and patched together from a blend of yarns—thick and thin and all sorts of colors. She brought together random objects with loose themes.

Time Flies was the name of the first tapestry, in a similar style to the one featured on the poster. Maggie examined it closely. Quite interesting, she thought, with bits of broken clocks and wristwatches dangling down from different spots, and colorful feathers and beads woven into the knitting.

Another, called *Date Night*, was centered around a department store mannequin, her head and arms mainly. The blankly staring figure held out a hand mirror, gazing at her reflection. A length of knitted lace, blended with some rougher-looking weaving, was draped around her body and chest. Pieces of rhinestone jewelry glittered on her neck and wrists, and on her head, a pert retro hat with a veil covered her eyes. A small silk handbag overflowing with play money sat on a dressing table, along with a big perfume bottle. She could have been a woman checking her appearance before going out for the evening. Except for a single disturbing element, a roughly knit swatch tied around her mouth like a gag.

Interesting, Maggie thought. Was this a feminist statement?

A sweeter-looking piece, called *Granny's Parlor*, had been featured in the exhibit poster. A large tapestry, what Maggie would call a parody of an afghan, was wrapped around a small white rocking chair. Broken teacups and tarnished spoons hung from the knitted swath. A pink cat made out of knitting sat next to a basket with needles and balls of yarn. Long scarves in bright candy colors were wrapped around everything, including a side table with a teapot and a dish of cookies, preserved by a covering of lacquer.

"Isn't her work amazing?" Phoebe seemed cheered for a moment, showing off Charlotte's pieces.

"It is," Maggie had to agree. "Though I must admit, I didn't expect some of these . . . dark images. Charlotte always seems so cheerful," she said honestly.

Of course, she didn't know the young woman that well. They'd only met a few times, Maggie reminded herself.

And she well knew artistic expression was often an outlet for a person's shadow side, for fears and anxieties. A way for some people to take control of complex feelings. Charlotte clearly had a few issues and used her art to work them out.

As it should be, Maggie thought.

"So, is this the type of fiber art you want to teach at the shop, Mag?" Maggie could tell from Suzanne's little smile that she was teasing.

"Not exactly. Though I do like the way she's blended all these yarns and random objects . . . and feathers and things," she added, examining a patch.

"I like the mannequin . . . She looks so surprised. That's supposed to be funny, right? I mean, a little?" Suzanne asked, glancing around at her friends.

"Maybe a little," Lucy agreed tentatively. "The gag is a bit disturbing. But I thought it was clever," she admitted.

"Quite clever . . . a provocative comment on feminine mystique," another voice offered.

Maggie looked up to see a stranger had joined them. A man in his forties dressed in a tweed sports coat, his denim shirt, simple black tie, and jeans offering a youthful look. She had already guessed he was a professor; the tag on his jacket lapel confirmed it.

Maggie recognized the name, too. Professor Alex Healey. Phoebe spoke about him often. He was her favorite teacher and had come to be her adviser and mentor. She'd taken several classes with him and hoped to enroll in more.

Phoebe had returned to *Granny's Parlor* with Suzanne, but quickly came toward them. "Professor Healey . . . did you hear what happened to Charlotte?"

"I did . . . What a shame. She worked so hard for this night. And everyone here is so impressed. I hope she'll come back. Have you heard from her?"

Phoebe shook her head. "Not yet . . . I wish she'd send a text or something."

"I hope so, too. Professor Finch and I are very concerned. Could you let me know if you hear anything?"

"I'll let you know right away. I'll send you a text or an e-mail," Phoebe promised.

He nodded, looking into Phoebe's eyes. He was not bad-looking, Maggie thought, in a soft, scholarly way. His dark-brown hair was thick and wavy, touched with a few gray strands that lent a distinguished air. He had a full beard, dark-brown eyes, and even features.

The type who encourages the crushes of female students to pump up his ego? Maybe, she thought. She hoped Phoebe didn't fall into that category. Those situations never ended well.

He looked as if he wanted to talk more but was distracted when a woman approached and touched his arm. She didn't spare a glance at the group but leaned toward him, speaking in an intimate tone. "Dean Klug is here. He's looking for you."

Professor Healey's eyebrows jumped. He had some explaining to do to the dean, Maggie guessed, about the way Charlotte had run off and the school security had been called. He looked like he dreaded the interview. Understandably.

"Right. Would you please tell him I'll be there in a moment . . . dear?" Suddenly remembering his manners he added, "This is one of my students, Phoebe Meyers. And a few of her friends. Ladies, this is my wife, Gena."

Gena Healey turned to greet them with a brilliant smile. She was petite, with bright dark eyes and delicate features. Glossy brown hair cut short with long bangs that fell across her eyes. Sort of sexy for a professor's wife, Maggie thought. But she was polished-looking as well. A black wrap dress, complemented by large, pearl earrings, was a perfect choice for the occasion and for her slim, lithe figure. She looked like a model—or former model—and at least ten years younger than her well-preserved husband.

"Enjoying the show?" she asked.

"Very impressive," Maggie said.

"The art department must be proud of their students," Dana remarked. "The work is very professional . . . especially Charlotte Blackburn's."

"Oh, yes, it is. Outstanding. I wanted so to meet her and congratulate her. But I understand she left early?"

Maggie cleared her throat. "Yes . . . she did. But she might be back. The instructors should be congratulated, too," she added graciously, trying to avoid any more gossip about Charlotte.

"Yes, they should be. Including my husband. The department works very hard to get these results. It's sort of his glory night, too," she confided.

"And well deserved." Maggie smiled back. She'd only taught at the high school level, but knew how much effort went into this type of event.

"Well . . . I'd better go find Alex. I'm not sure if he's looking for the dean . . . or trying to hide from him," she said with a laugh.

"We're going to see the rest of the show. It was nice to meet you," Dana said.

"Nice to meet all of you, too . . . and I hope Charlotte is all right and comes back to enjoy the party. Please let us know if you hear anything?"

"I will. Definitely," Phoebe promised.

Once Gena Healey was out of view, Maggie turned to her friends. "I think we've done our duty here. Ready to go?"

Her friends agreed they'd all had enough art appreciation for one night and only glanced at the work of the other artists as they headed out. Maggie didn't think any other pieces were as impressive or interesting as Charlotte's. She had clearly been the star.

They collected their coats but soon decided they were no longer in the mood to go out for dinner. It had begun to rain, an icy drizzle that collected on the car windows and caused Lucy to drive back to the village with care. Phoebe was driving her own car, a little VW Bug, back to town. Maggie watched her car disappear from view as they drove off campus.

"Quite a night. Not what I expected, I must say." Maggie turned to her friends in the backseat to gauge their reactions.

"Do you mean Charlotte's artwork . . . or chasing Quentin?" Suzanne asked.

"Both, I suppose."

"I didn't expect her artwork to be so complex," Dana admitted. "She always seems so sunny and sweet."

"Same here," Lucy said. "I wonder if the gag on that mannequin was inspired by her relationship with Quentin? Phoebe said he was very jealous and possessive."

"Could be," Dana agreed. "Either way, she's clearly done the right thing breaking up with him. He's totally out of control. I hope she's someplace safe. I'm going to ask Phoebe to give Charlotte my number, in case she needs any support. I'd be happy to help her without charge. Young women are so vulnerable."

Maggie listened to the windshield wipers swish and slap. "That's so true. These relationships can seem so romantic and passionate at first. They don't even realize what's really happening until it's too late."

Suzanne leaned forward, resting her hand on the back of Maggie's seat. "Charlotte's well rid of that guy. She woke up just in time. She has everything going for her—looks, personality, talent . . ."

"But inside, she must feel something is missing," Lucy cut in. "Otherwise, why would she have let herself get involved with a guy like Quentin in the first place?"

Maggie sighed. "We're all vulnerable in some way. We all have our confidence issues and blind spots. And some men can be so charming at first."

Lucy glanced at her. "Sounds as if you've had a Quentin in your own life, Maggie."

Maggie glanced at her. The darkness and patter of rain on the car roof invited confidences. "I did know someone like him once. Long ago. He was quite good-looking . . . and I was very flattered that he noticed me. I was sort of bookish and quiet back then. I know you all find that hard to believe," she added with a grin. "He even had a motorcycle, which my parents strictly forbid me to ride."

"So, naturally, you wanted to even more?" Dana prodded her.

Maggie smiled back. "Something like that . . . Luckily, he got bored with me. Too much of a goody two-shoes. Do people even say that anymore?" She laughed, recollecting. "He dumped me for one of my more adventurous friends. Which stung a bit. A blessing in disguise, I realized later."

Lucy glanced at her. "Let's hope Quentin gets bored chasing Charlotte and gives up on her, too."

"Or someone—like a police officer—lets him know that would be the smart thing to do," Suzanne added.

Maggie glanced back at her but didn't reply. She knew that they all hoped this situation would resolve itself without Charlotte being harmed in any way. She hoped so, too, though she knew that was not how it always turned out.

It was past nine when she finally got home. She took off her wet coat and shoes by the door, then went straight up to her room and changed into pajamas, slippers, and a flannel robe. She was hungry but wanted to warm up first.

She put on some water for tea and heated a can of soup on the stove. She'd put in her time cooking for her family—her late husband, Bill, and her daughter, Julie, who was away at college. Now that she lived alone, Maggie felt relieved to cook just for one . . . or not cook at all, if she didn't feel like it. Crackers, cheese, and a sliced apple were all she needed as a side dish.

She scanned a magazine while she ate, instructions for Valentine's Day cupcakes, quickly followed by the latest miracle diet and homemade wrinkle and cellulite cures—all from ingredients she could find in her own kitchen.

No wonder women fall prey to controlling relationships. We're brainwashed night and day into thinking there's something wrong with us. Something always needs improvement and fixing. Some reason we are not worthy of love and respect. From our crow's feet, to our saggy boobs and baggy thighs. As if a woman were a cellophane-covered package of chicken parts in the supermarket, to be critiqued and passed over. Or an old house always in need of repair and improvement.

Why do women give men this power? Let them judge us, define us? Why do we struggle so to feel lovable?

It was really sad in a way. Women had come so far in the last fifty years. She hoped to see the first woman president elected in her lifetime. But in some ways, women hadn't made any progress at all. How could young women like her own daughter and Phoebe throw off the shackles, when popular culture reinforced these ideas every day?

This Valentine's Day, she would send a card to all her women friends and tell them they were wonderful just the way they were. No improvement necessary. She didn't have a romantic relationship right now and someone to celebrate with. But this idea was even better.

A mystery show was just starting on television—an episode of Agatha Christie's *Miss Marple*. Maggie always enjoyed the subtle steps of Miss Marple's deduction.

She set herself up in her favorite chair, with a mug of tea and her knitting bag, jangled nerves instantly soothed by the British accents and smooth pace of the plot. No car chases or scenes of bodies on a coroner's slab. Miss Marple didn't need any of that. She operated in cozy parlors or blooming walled gardens. Over silver tea sets and the occasional glass of dry sherry. She simply chatted and listened . . . and observed.

Miss Marple was also a dedicated knitter, another reason Maggie appreciated her. Maggie had noticed that, at times, the act seemed to make her invisible. She had overheard many very private—and interesting—conversations while riding in a train or waiting for an airplane. Just because she sat in public knitting. Maggie knit and sipped her own tea, watching and listening as Miss Marple set about solving another murder. It was all so relaxing, she didn't even realize that her eyes had drifted closed.

Her cell phone was ringing. The sound was very loud and went on and on. Maggie woke with a start, and her mug toppled to the rug. The TV was still on, the digital clock on the cable box showing the time: 12:32. She must have fallen asleep before Miss Marple had caught her culprit.

The phone continued to ring, and she fumbled to pull it from her bathrobe pocket. Without her reading glasses she couldn't see who was calling.

"Hello?" Her greeting came out in a startled croak.

"Maggie? . . . It's me . . . Phoebe . . ."

Maggie sat up, instantly alert. The tone of Phoebe's voice was alarming. "Phoebe . . . what is it? Is something wrong?"

All she heard was a deep sob.

"Phoebe? . . . Are you hurt? Where are you?" Maggie stood up, a panicky feeling rising in her chest.

"I'm at Charlotte's apartment . . . I had to let myself in and I . . . I just called the police. Can you come here? I'm so scared. It's just horrible, Maggie . . ."

Maggie felt her heart sink with dread. As much as she wanted more details, she knew there was no time to waste talking.

"I'll be right there. I just need to throw on some clothes. What's the address?"

"Thirty-three Nutmeg Street. There's a pizza place on the corner." Phoebe managed to relate the information between her sobs. "Oh, Maggie . . . come quick. I can't believe it . . . I'm so scared."

Maggie was scared, too. What if Quentin had gone there and hurt Charlotte? He could come back and hurt Phoebe, too. But she couldn't leave. She had just called the police.

"Phoebe . . . get in your car and lock the doors. Don't get out until you see the police . . . or me," she instructed.

It wasn't a foolproof plan, but it was something, she reasoned.

"Okay," Phoebe said in a tearful tone. "I'll be all right . . . just hurry."

"I will," Maggie promised.

Maggie pulled on jeans, sneakers, and a sweatshirt over her pajama top, and slipped her down jacket over that. The rain had stopped, but the air was frigid. She didn't have time to wait for the windows to clear and drove along warily, wiping her breath from the windshield with a gloved hand until the defroster kicked in. Charlotte's apartment was on the outskirts of the village, less than five minutes' drive. Maggie drove along the side streets as fast as she was able.

What was Phoebe doing at Charlotte's? She must have gone over there to check on her . . . or maybe Charlotte had called her for help? Why did Phoebe say she'd called the police . . . and not an ambulance?

Maggie swallowed hard. A few possibilities came to mind. But she didn't like any of them.

CHAPTER FIVE

Maggie soon turned onto Charlotte's street and quickly found number thirty-three—a narrow two-story house with a flat roof. Something about the house just screamed that students lived there. Maybe the tired string of Christmas lights dangling around the door and the plastic flamingo stuck in the dirty snow. Or the flag of some distant nation that hung in an upstairs window in place of a curtain.

The windows in front were dark, but Maggie saw lights on in the back, where Phoebe had told her Charlotte lived. Two police cruisers were parked on the street in front, and Phoebe's car was in the driveway.

She walked up along the side of the house and saw a small back porch. The door stood ajar, and a uniformed policeman stood in a patch of light. Yellow tape, printed with the words "DO NOT CROSS—POLICE LINE," stretched across the porch and stairway, and from the house to a separate garage, sealing off the backyard.

Another officer stood at the bottom of the steps, talking

to Phoebe. She was facing him and didn't see Maggie approach.

"Phoebe? Are you all right? What's going on?" Maggie asked as she drew near.

Phoebe turned, her face streaked with tears and melted eye makeup. She burst into tears and threw herself into Maggie's arms. She was saying something, but Maggie couldn't understand a word. Maggie just patted Phoebe's back and stroked her long hair.

"Are you Phoebe's mother?" the officer asked.

Maggie shook her head. Mother *figure* at times, yes. But of course, she couldn't say that.

"A good friend. And her employer. What's going on, Officer? Where's Charlotte Blackburn, the girl who lives here?"

Phoebe heaved another sob and pulled back a bit, though she didn't let go entirely. Her eyes were filled with tears. "She's inside. In the bedroom. On the floor. Oh, Maggie, poor Charlotte . . . she's . . . dead."

Maggie couldn't breathe. Her heart skipped a beat. She stared at Phoebe and then looked back at the officer.

That beautiful young girl. Maggie couldn't speak. She couldn't get her mind around it.

"How can that be? We just saw her . . ."

The officer met her gaze but didn't reply. He took a pad out from his back pocket. "Your name, please?"

"Maggie Messina," she replied, watching him write it down.

"Did you know Charlotte Blackburn?" he asked.

"Not very well. But I'd met her a few times," Maggie replied.

"When did you last see her?"

"A few hours ago. At Whitaker College, at an art show on the campus," Maggie answered.

He nodded. "Detectives will be here in a few minutes. They need to speak to Phoebe and may ask you a few questions, too."

"All right." Maggie glanced at Phoebe. She seemed to be in shock, staring into space, blinking as the raindrops mingled with her tears. Maggie took her arm, thinking it would be best to wait in Phoebe's car until the detectives came.

But a dark-blue sedan had pulled into the driveway behind Phoebe's VW. A man got out of the driver's side, and a woman emerged from the other. The man wore a dark-gray trench coat and a baseball cap in lieu of a rain hat. Red Sox fan, of course. He was not very tall but had broad shoulders. Or maybe that was just the raincoat. Maggie guessed he was a detective from the county, but she didn't recognize him. She was simply relieved to see it wasn't Detective Walsh, who had once considered her a suspect in a case and made her life miserable for a few weeks.

She did recognize the woman, a tall, slim brunette, Detective Marisol Reyes. Her path had crossed with the Black Sheep Knitters on a few occasions in the past few years. Maggie liked and respected Detective Reyes. She was very professional, smart, and fair-minded. She still strongly discouraged Maggie and her friends from getting involved in her investigations, but Maggie sensed Detective Reyes didn't write off the knitting group as a bunch of cackling, vacuous women. The group had, in fact, helped her close more than one case.

Though we never get the credit, Maggie reflected.

"Look, Phoebe, Detective Reyes. She's easy to deal with."

Maggie could tell Phoebe heard her, but Phoebe was clearly in shock. Maggie put her arm around her friend's shoulder and felt her trembling.

A uniformed officer came down from the porch and spoke to the detectives for a few moments. Maggie heard snippets of the conversation: ". . . forced entry . . . window in the back . . . footprints . . . victim . . . bedroom . . ."

Detective Reyes looked over at Maggie and Phoebe, then finally walked toward them.

"Detective Reyes, it's so awful . . . Phoebe's friend from school, Charlotte Blackburn. We'd all just seen her this evening, at an art show . . ." Maggie's voice trailed off nervously.

Not like her to ramble on. But the situation was unnerving.

Detective Reyes gazed at Maggie in her calm, steady way, then looked at Phoebe, trying to catch her eye. But Phoebe was staring down at the ground, softly crying again and dabbing her eyes with a tissue.

"You found the victim, Phoebe?" she asked quietly.

Phoebe nodded. "Yes . . . I did."

"Tell me what happened. How did you get into the apartment?"

"The door was locked. But I knew where Charlotte left a spare key. I heard the TV and saw a light on. I thought maybe Charlotte was asleep and hadn't heard me knocking."

"Did you hear anything else? Any sounds from inside, besides the television?"

Phoebe shook her head. She took a deep breath. "No . . . I don't think so. I listened at the door a while, thinking I'd hear her coming to open it. But I just heard the television."

Maggie could see she was trying to settle herself. She tried to talk again, then squeezed her eyes closed and pressed her hand to her forehead. Maggie put an arm around her shoulder.

Detective Reyes waited a moment, then spoke again. "I know it's hard to talk about this. You're doing fine. Tell me, did you know Charlotte very long? How did you meet?"

"We met at school, last spring in an art class. Professor Healey's mixed media. We didn't have any classes together this semester. But we stayed pretty close and hung out a lot at the studios."

"When was the last time you'd seen her or spoken to her?" the detective asked.

"A few hours ago, at the school. Charlotte's work was in an art show on campus. Maggie came, too. With the rest of our knitting group."

Detective Reyes marked this on her pad and nodded. She was familiar with the Black Sheep, but Maggie couldn't tell if she was pleased to hear her friends were involved or not. Probably not, Maggie decided.

"So you and your friends went to the gallery at Whitaker College to see Charlotte's artwork. And she was there."

"She was . . . but the show hadn't even really started yet and her boyfriend, Quentin Gibbs . . . ex-boyfriend, I mean . . . showed up, and she's like totally terrified of him. So she just took off and Quentin chased her and we were all like chasing her through the art studios, trying to make sure Quentin didn't hurt her. I caught up with him, and he pushed me into a wall," Phoebe added.

"That's true. I was there. He pushed her down, could have hurt her badly," Maggie chimed in.

Detective Reyes glanced at Maggie. "Thank you, Mrs. Messina. We'll ask you some questions later. Just let Phoebe answer now." She turned back to Phoebe. "So Gibbs chased Charlotte. Then what?"

"She like ran outside, onto the campus, and just . . . disappeared. Into thin air. We were all watching Quentin. He made a big scene taking off on his motorcycle. When I turned around to look for Charlotte, she was gone. We stayed at the gallery a little while; then I went home. I kept calling and texting her, but she never called back." Phoebe took another deep breath. Detective Reyes nodded, but didn't interrupt.

"I couldn't go to sleep. I was too worried. I got dressed again and came over," Phoebe explained. "I thought I could get her to come back to my apartment. I mean, this is the first place Quentin would look for her. But maybe she didn't have anyplace else to go."

Detective Reyes nodded again. "What time did you get here? Did you notice?"

"I guess I left my apartment about half past eleven. I sent one more text, and she didn't answer. I can check my phone . . ." she offered.

"That's all right. We'll check later. Did you see anyone on the street or near the house when you arrived?"

Phoebe shook her head. "No . . . nobody. I saw lights on back here, and when I got to the door, I heard the TV. I knocked a few times. But no one answered." Phoebe paused and sighed, staring down at the ground again.

"I know this is hard, but you have to tell me everything, Phoebe." Detective Reyes's tone was firm. "What did you do next?"

"When she didn't answer the door, I called again and sent another text. I told her I was outside and I just wanted to know that she was all right. When that didn't work, I walked around the side of the house and peeked in the window . . . I didn't know what else to do. I thought maybe Quentin was in there and he wouldn't let her answer," she added. "But I didn't see him. I just saw the TV on in the bedroom. Which made me think she was there. I didn't know what to do," she said again, sounding overwhelmed. "I knew that Charlotte kept a spare key out here. In a flowerpot. So I let myself in."

Detective Reyes stopped her. "When you used the key, the door was locked?"

"Yes, it was definitely locked. I didn't want to be that obnoxious, so I just like stepped inside and called to her. She didn't answer, and I thought, well, maybe she went out and left everything on. Or maybe she was asleep. So I kept calling and walked toward the bedroom. Then I got to the bedroom door and looked in . . ." Phoebe paused and took a breath. Maggie noticed her chin start to tremble. "I saw her. On the floor. Wrapped in . . . it looked like a big afghan. But like patches that don't really match." Phoebe swallowed hard. "It looked like her own artwork. Her fiber art pieces . . . or . . . or some knitting graffiti," she added quietly.

Maggie felt a sharp stab in her chest. She hadn't heard that part of the story before.

Detective Reyes looked puzzled. "I'm not sure I understand you . . . but go on."

"I just stood in the doorway. I couldn't make myself go in. There weren't any lights on, except for the TV." Phoebe paused and squeezed her eyes closed. Maggie could tell the awful image was imprinted now in her mind's eye. She'd never forget it. "I could see her eyes. Wide open. Just staring. And her body was like frozen, one arm sticking up. I couldn't get close to her. I'm sorry . . . I could tell that she wasn't breathing. She was so stiff and just staring . . . I just knew what had happened . . ."

Phoebe broke down and started to cry again. Maggie slipped an arm around her shoulder. Detective Reyes waited, her expression sympathetic but also intense. Maggie suddenly wondered if the detective had any suspicions about Phoebe. Her job did demand that she consider every angle. But the detective also knew the knitting group a bit and had excellent instincts about people and probably sensed that Phoebe couldn't even kill a bug. She actually coaxed insects into cups or jars and then let them loose outdoors. And Phoebe had no possible motive. She loved her friend and had come here out of true concern.

"So you didn't enter the bedroom or touch the body?" Detective Reyes asked. "You're sure about that?"

"Positive. I started to go in. But when I saw her, I just stopped in the doorway and sort of backed out. I thought I might faint and pretty much ran out of the apartment . . . screaming," she admitted. "I'm surprised none of the neighbors came out."

Maggie was, too. But it looked like the sort of neighborhood where people kept to themselves.

Phoebe took a deep breath to steady herself. "I called nine-one-one. Then Maggie."

Detective Reyes nodded. She seemed about to ask another question when the other detective called down to her from the doorway. He had removed his cap to reveal a head of silvery white hair cut very short.

"Sorry to interrupt. But I think you need to see this."

Detective Reyes turned and answered with a quick nod.

"I have to go inside for a while," she told the two women. "I know it's been a long night. But you need to come to the station and make a full statement."

"Okay," Phoebe said, "but I know who killed her. It was Quentin. Had to be. He's like totally crazy and out-of-his-skull jealous of her. She told me the other night she got an order of protection against him. That's why she thought he'd never show up at that gallery. But he's been like stalking her . . ."

"We'll send officers out right now to find him and talk to him right away. But I also want you to think about anyone else who may have had a grievance with Charlotte—students at school. Or outside of school. Anything you can remember, even if it seems insignificant. Anything could be important."

"Phoebe isn't exaggerating about that boy," Maggie added. "Charlotte was truly afraid of him."

But if it had been Quentin, Maggie didn't see how the knitting graffiti fit in. He seemed the type to commit a crime of passion. But the elaborate wrapping suggested an intentional plan, didn't it?

The way Phoebe had described the knitted wrapping on the body also suggested the Knit Kats. Could the group be linked with this horrible act? Maggie recoiled at the thought. She also wondered if Detective Reyes was familiar with the term "knitting graffiti." But Maggie was sure Phoebe would explain that—and talk about the Knit Kats—when she gave her statement. Maggie decided to tell the police her impressions, too . . . and about that odd phone call she'd received the night of her TV interview. Probably not connected in any way, but as the detective had just said, any small detail could be important.

Detective Reyes met Maggie's gaze as she pulled a pair of plastic gloves from her coat pocket. "The medical examiner is on his way. We'll know a lot more once he looks at the body."

She headed up the steps to the front door of Charlotte's apartment. Her partner had already gone inside, and Maggie spotted him for a moment through a window.

Maggie imagined them going into the bedroom to examine the crime scene. A lump formed in her throat.

A gray-and-white cat sat on a windowsill, then paced from side to side, softly meowing. Phoebe was crying again but looked up at the sound. "One of Charlotte's cats, Van Gogh. He wants to go inside. He doesn't realize what's . . . what's happened."

She stared at Maggie, tears welling up in her eyes.

"Of course he doesn't," Maggie said quietly.

Phoebe walked over to the porch and stopped at the yellow tape. She called to the cat, "Come here, sweetie. It's me . . . Phoebe. Remember?"

Van Gogh clearly did remember. Or he was very hungry and sensed Phoebe was a cat lover. He turned and came quickly on delicate white feet. Most of his face and the tip of his tail were white, too. His fur was glossy and thick—maybe a little Angora mixed in with his alley-cat ancestors? He was a pretty cat and seemed very friendly and gentle.

Phoebe picked him up and held him in her arms. He seemed relaxed and obviously knew her.

Phoebe walked back to Maggie, holding the cat, his paws pressed to her chest and his head at her shoulder.

"I wish we had something to feed him. Maybe the police would give me some cat food from inside? I know where Charlotte keeps it."

"I doubt it. They're still looking for evidence. They probably aren't allowed to remove anything from here for days." She rubbed Phoebe's shoulder as she continued to stroke the cat.

"How many cats did Charlotte have?"

"I'm not sure . . . at least five. There was Frida and Georgia, Leonardo and Picasso."

All named for artists. That made sense.

"That's a lot of cats. That's practically a herd," Maggie noted.

"They just come and go as they please. But they always come back for food, and if it's really cold or wet. But now there won't be anyone around to take them in or take care of them," Phoebe said quietly.

As if on cue, the cat clinging to Phoebe's jacket turned and glanced at Maggie, his little head cocked to one side in a charming pose. She noticed that one ear was a little crumpled. A large portion had been bitten off, in a cat fight—or perhaps in the quest of winning over some female feline? His name fit well.

"Maybe a neighbor or two will take care of them. At least they might feed them."

"Maybe," Phoebe agreed with a sigh.

Maggie didn't say anything for few moments, then glanced back at Phoebe. "Maybe you should take Van Gogh and watch him for a while."

Phoebe looked surprised at the suggestion. She'd often asked Maggie if she could have a pet in the apartment, but

Maggie always stuck to the terms of their lease: no pets of any kind. "Really? But you always said—"

Maggie sighed, interrupting her. "I know . . . but this is an emergency. As long as the cat doesn't come in the shop. I think it will be all right. Temporarily," she clarified.

She wondered if that last caveat had even registered. Phoebe was gazing down at her new charge with a small smile, momentarily distracted by the idea of taking in Charlotte's cat, which had been Maggie's intention. She actually didn't want a cat in the shop, or even on the floor above, but she didn't know what else she could do to help Phoebe get through this.

"I guess I can put him in my car. He should be all right in there. I think I have a towel in back. I'll make him a little bed," Phoebe said.

Phoebe walked back to her car with the cat, and Maggie saw another car pull up and park across the street. Two men emerged. One took a large black bag from the backseat, and the other pulled some type of equipment from the trunk. It looked like large lights. She guessed that the medical examiner and an assistant had arrived. She watched them walk up to the apartment and show badges to the officer on the porch before they entered the house.

"I think the medical examiner is here. Maybe we won't have to wait that much longer," Maggie said when Phoebe returned.

"I hope they sent someone to look for Quentin," Phoebe replied. "I hope they find him and put him in jail . . . and never let him out again." Phoebe turned to Maggie. "Do you think it's wrong that I didn't check if she was breathing? I mean, I could see that she wasn't. How could she be alive, staring up that way? She looked like . . . like a broken doll or something . . .”

Maggie comforted her again. “There was nothing you could have done for her, Phoebe. Nothing anyone could have done. You did the right thing to call the police,” she assured her.

It was actually better that Phoebe had not touched the body or anything in the bedroom. Her fingerprints and DNA would have been all over the crime scene . . . and that could have caused complications. As it was, just finding poor Charlotte had dragged her into this.

Maggie saw Detective Reyes meet the medical examiner at the door. But instead of going back inside with him, she came out and walked over to Maggie and Phoebe.

She took them in with a serious glance. “We’ve identified the victim. I think you should know that it’s not Charlotte Blackburn.”

Phoebe stared at the detective, her mouth dropped open. She hugged her stomach, practically doubling over with shock. “Are you sure? . . . But I saw her . . . with my own eyes. How could that be?”

Maggie was afraid that Phoebe was getting hysterical. She took her arm and patted her hand. “Take a few deep breaths. Let the detective explain.”

She glanced at Detective Reyes while Phoebe tried to compose herself. She also wondered how this could be. One minute Charlotte was stone-cold dead, staring into space like a broken doll. And now . . . she was presumably alive and well.

But some other young woman was lying in there. That part of the story had not changed.

"I'm sure this is a shock, Phoebe. You sounded so sure it was your friend. But when we searched the apartment, we found a pocketbook with a driver's license and school ID. The photos match the deceased. Her name is Beth Shelton, and she's also a student at Whitaker," the detective explained. "Do you know her?"

"It's Beth? Not Charlotte?"

Detective Reyes nodded. "So you do know her. Are the three of you friends?"

Phoebe shook her head. "I just know Beth a little. She's also an art major. But Charlotte and Beth are good friends. They'd been roommates last year or something. Before Charlotte moved to off-campus housing. But Charlotte did say that Beth's roommates this year had gotten really weird and she wanted to move out. Maybe Beth knew where the key was, too, and she just came here to crash."

"Possibly," the detective replied.

Maggie still didn't understand how this mix-up had happened. "Beth and Charlotte must look very similar for you to have mistaken her, Phoebe."

Phoebe swallowed hard, remembering. "I guess they do . . . I never really thought about it. But they do have the same sort of build and the same color hair. And Beth's hair is long and gets wavy sometimes like Charlotte's. Especially when it's raining." She turned to Maggie. "I was so shocked and freaked out. And she was mostly covered up. I barely looked at her before I panicked and ran out." She turned to Detective Reyes. "I didn't mean to tell you the wrong thing."

"Of course you didn't," Detective Reyes replied. "But we still need your statement. Everything you can remember will help the investigation. I need to go back inside. This won't take too much longer."

As Detective Reyes left them, Phoebe looked over at Maggie. Her expression was blank, but her dark eyes were wide and bright. "I'm like totally . . . stunned. I don't know what to feel. I feel awful about Beth . . . but I am happy to hear Charlotte's all right. I mean, as far as we know."

Maggie didn't know what to say. The girl lying inside was not Charlotte. So could they safely assume Charlotte was alive and probably hiding somewhere after she'd run from the gallery because of Quentin? Maggie certainly hoped so.

Phoebe turned to Maggie, a new look of dismay crossing her delicate features. "But if someone came in looking for Charlotte and killed Beth by mistake, that means someone is definitely after Charlotte. No wonder she ran away."

"Yes . . . no wonder." Maggie had already thought of that.

Of course the police had to consider the possibility that Charlotte killed Beth. The body was found in Charlotte's apartment, and Charlotte was missing. She had to be considered, at this very early stage at least. Just as Phoebe is probably being looked at and needs to be eliminated as a suspect, Maggie realized, because she found the body.

But Maggie was fairly certain that the police would eliminate Phoebe quickly and also find no grievance between Charlotte and Beth. Phoebe's scenario was probably correct. Poor Beth had been in the wrong place at the wrong time and had been mistaken for her elusive friend.

Beth was having roommate troubles and either asked Charlotte for a place to crash or just assumed it would be all right if she stayed over. She let herself in, made herself comfortable in Charlotte's bedroom, turned on the TV, and didn't hear the intruder enter.

Maybe Beth had even fallen asleep by that point. Or maybe she thought Charlotte had come in. Either way, in the dim light cast by the TV, the killer assumed Beth was Charlotte.

As Maggie mulled over the sad situation, she saw another cat leap down from the porch railing, landing in a puddle of yellow light from the lamp near the apartment door. This feline had come from the other side of the house and landed with a thud. A much larger cat than Van Gogh, it strutted to the front door with a cocky manner, sounding a loud, demanding yowl.

"That's Pablo Picasso," Phoebe told her. "He's very bossy. He picks on Van Gogh."

"Just as well . . . rescuing one stray tonight is plenty. Charlotte might be back tomorrow. Or even sooner," Maggie pointed out. "Or maybe you'll get a message from her and she'll tell you where she went tonight."

"Yes . . . I guess I might," Phoebe agreed.

Or maybe the police would catch up with her. Maggie had to add that possibility to the list. They had probably begun looking as soon as they discovered the true identity of the poor young woman lying dead inside.

Picasso was startled by a sound inside the apartment and jumped back into the shadows. He was quick. Phoebe couldn't have caught him anyway.

An old saying came to mind—"All cats look the same in the dark." As Maggie recalled, it was Benjamin Franklin's nod to bedding older women.

A little coarse and very misogynistic, Maggie thought. But something in the phrase seemed to ring true here, too—in regard to poor Beth Shelton being killed instead of Charlotte. And in the dark sleek coats and flashing eyes of Charlotte's many pets melting in and out of the darkness.

CHAPTER SIX

Maggie rarely missed her scheduled hours at the shop. She felt that she owed it to her customers to be open as advertised. On various occasions through the years, she'd come in with a cast on her leg, a fever of one hundred and two, backaches, toothaches, and covered in poison ivy. Her friends teased her that she should have gotten a job at the post office. Neither snow, nor rain, nor gloom of night stayed her from her appointed knitting rounds.

But after dealing with the police department for hours and getting home at nearly three, she'd only had four hours of sleep when the alarm sounded at its regular time on Monday morning. She allowed herself a bonus hour in bed but tossed and turned, thinking about the grisly events of the previous night and the random, unfortunate death of Beth Shelton. She finally pushed herself out the bed and into the shower.

An hour late wasn't so bad, all things considered. She knew the local news was probably full of the story about the young woman's murder. But she couldn't bear to turn it on, and she didn't want to linger around the house anyway.

She wondered if any of her friends had seen the morning news today. If they had, they would soon be calling her.

Sure enough, when Maggie emerged from the shower, wrapped in a towel, there was a text from Lucy on her cell phone.

Did you see the news? Tried Phoebe. Not picking up. Hope she's OK. Call me.

Maggie quickly texted Lucy back:

Long story. Not a happy one. Phoebe is OK. Come to the shop @ lunchtime. Or call later.

Lucy often took a midday break if her work deadline wasn't too pressing. She liked to stretch those long legs of hers and might walk downtown to hear Maggie's—and Phoebe's—sad story.

After two mugs of coffee and some oatmeal, Maggie stood dressed and ready to go, her purse and knitting bag in hand. She peeked into the guest room, where Phoebe was still fast asleep; her newly adopted pal, Van Gogh, slept curled in a ball, his head burrowed into Phoebe's knee. He was either snoring or purring in his sleep. He sounded like a little furry motor.

Phoebe slept with a distressed expression on her fragile features. She certainly looked exhausted, and Maggie did not have the heart to wake her.

After waiting at the crime scene for more than an hour

and then sitting in the police station, giving statements to Detectives Reyes and Mossbacher for even longer, Phoebe was exhausted, alternating between free-flowing tears and a catatonic stare. When Maggie suggested that she come back to her house, Phoebe had only nodded numbly and allowed Maggie to care for her.

They were both very disturbed by Beth Shelton's death. Phoebe even more so, since she had known the girl a bit and discovered the body.

Maggie carefully closed the door and left a note for her guest on the kitchen table, then headed for town.

Maggie should have guessed. A few hours later as lunchtime rolled around, she was expecting not only Lucy but also Suzanne and Dana, who had learned the bare bones of the story from the television news and wanted all the gritty, inside details.

The police would be working on the case intensely, and Maggie guessed that Dana already had some inside information from her husband, Jack, who knew everyone on the force from his bygone days in law enforcement and heard a lot of inside gossip.

Phoebe arrived first, at about half past eleven. She carried a large paper carton and set it on the counter. Maggie could hear something moving around inside and occasionally offering a plaintive meow.

Maggie hoped this cat business worked out. She didn't want to think about it right now, though. "How are you feeling? Did you get enough sleep?"

Phoebe shrugged. "I guess so, but I had some really bad dreams," she added quietly.

"I'm not surprised." Maggie glanced at the box. "I think the cat slept well. He was cuddled up right next to you, snoring away when I left the house."

Phoebe managed a small smile, one that seemed to draw on all her energy. She looked so drained. Maggie was sure a week of sleep could not make up for last night's ordeal. Remnants of makeup ringed her eyes, and her dark hair, streaked with magenta and choppy on one side, was clipped in at the back of her head in an unattractive lump.

Maggie had loaned her some clothes—a pair of sweatpants and a sweatshirt she found up in her daughter Julie's room. Julie was smaller than Maggie, but Phoebe still looked as if she were wearing a collapsed tent.

"Everyone is concerned about you. Suzanne, Dana, Lucy. They're coming at lunchtime. But if you don't feel up to seeing them . . ."

"I want to see them. I want to stay down in the shop today and work. It will be distracting."

Maggie knew that was true. The steady stream of customers she'd dealt with so far had kept her from thinking too much about last night's crime scene . . . and where Charlotte might be.

Everyone wanted to know that.

Maggie wanted to ask Phoebe if she'd heard from Charlotte yet. But of course, she would have said something if she had. The police were waiting, too. Phoebe had promised to let them know if she'd had any contact with her friend at all.

Of course, the police weren't going to wait for a message from Charlotte to Phoebe . . . or anyone else for that matter. Detective Reyes had told them last night that the search for

Charlotte was well under way. Investigators were not only relying on the information from Phoebe and Maggie about last night but also looking for anyone on the Whitaker campus who may have spotted her as they tried to track her movements after the art show.

They would find her soon, Maggie felt sure of it. Isn't that the way it always went when you watched some detective show on TV?

Phoebe went up to her apartment to shower and change her clothes, and get Van Gogh settled in. Maggie returned to the task at hand, following up on special orders with a few different yarn companies. The morning rush had cleared off, and there weren't any customers in the shop, waiting for help. For once she hoped no one would come in. Not until her friends had come and gone.

She was glad that they all wanted to see Phoebe and rally around her. Phoebe needed their support and friendship now.

Maggie only knew a little about Phoebe's family and background. She'd grown up in New Hampshire, and her father had left the house when she was about seven. Her mother, who had died a few years ago, had faced her own demons. Phoebe and her brother had been shifted around to stay with relatives and had more or less brought themselves up. Phoebe was close to her older brother, Sam, growing up. But he was in the navy now and always out at sea somewhere. He sent e-mails and letters. Sometimes they Skyped. But she was lucky to see him in person once a year. If that much.

There may have been an aunt and uncle or a grandmother somewhere. Phoebe had never mentioned them. She seemed very much alone in the world for one so young. Maggie had realized that last night, at the police station.

Phoebe was very independent, to be sure. But sometimes Maggie wondered if that was her true nature or simply a survival skill she'd picked up along the way. Ditto for her sometimes defensive, even prickly attitude. Maggie gave her a pass for that as well.

Phoebe wasn't in any trouble, Maggie hurried to remind herself. The police just needed to rule her out. It was all very routine. But the situation had been stressful, and most people her age would have called a parent. Phoebe called me, Maggie reminded herself. It was a great compliment . . . and a responsibility.

No matter. She was happy to help Phoebe right now in any way she could, and she knew the rest of her knitting circle felt the same.

Dana and Suzanne arrived at the same time and, after a quick greeting, walked straight back to the worktable, where they set out their lunches.

Dana opened her blue thermal pouch and began to set out containers. Maggie would be willing to bet at least one contained seaweed salad.

"How's Phoebe?" Dana asked. "She must be very upset."

"Yes, she is . . . She called me right after she called nine-one-one. At first, we thought it was Charlotte."

"Good Lord . . . that must have been awful . . ." Suzanne had opened a brown paper bag and now took out a plastic spoon.

"She was very shaken . . . and only a little relieved to hear it wasn't Charlotte. She knew the girl who was killed—Beth Shelton—but not very well. Phoebe said Beth was a really nice kid. Another art student." Maggie sighed. It was all so sad and senseless. It was hard to ask the question, but Maggie wanted to know. "How was she killed? Was she smothered or something in all that knitting?"

Detective Reyes had made Maggie and Phoebe promise not to talk about the investigation, especially the crime scene. But Dana obviously already knew, and Maggie was finding it hard—well, impossible actually—not to talk about it with her friends. It couldn't be kept secret forever. It would soon be in the news, she rationalized.

"I'm not supposed to tell," Dana began, obviously wrestling with her conscience, too. "But they've pretty much pieced it together. Someone came through a back window while Beth was in the bedroom, watching TV. There were signs of a brief struggle, but the intruder overpowered her quickly with some fast-acting drug she inhaled, chloroform or something like that pressed to her face. Then the killer smothered her and . . . well, wrapped her in big sections of knitting. Most of her face was covered. That's why Phoebe didn't realize it wasn't Charlotte."

Maggie nodded but couldn't speak. The image was very unsettling. Poor Beth. What a tragic, senseless loss of life.

"That is so weird . . . Why was the girl in Charlotte's apartment?" Suzanne had unwrapped a container of soup and an apple but had put it aside. This conversation could take away anyone's appetite—even Suzanne's, Maggie realized.

"Phoebe thinks Beth was having roommate problems and Charlotte invited her to stay over," Maggie recalled.

"I think police have confirmed it. One of Beth's roommates told them Charlotte planned to leave town very soon and Beth was going to take over her apartment. Beth wasn't supposed to tell anyone. But Beth and her roommates got into an argument and it came out. Needless to say, the roommates are very sorry now that they'd been so mean and driven the poor girl out that night."

"As well they should be," Suzanne said huffily. "Alexis is quite a few years from college. But I'm already worried about her living on her own. My heart just breaks when I think of Beth's parents. Did she come from around here?"

Dana shook her head. She'd put aside her salad—seaweed, just as Maggie had suspected—and taken out her knitting. "No, she's from Maine. Carlisle, I think. It will be a few days before the police can release her body. Her parents are already in town. Of course they want to be close to the investigation."

"My heart goes out to them. It's a parent's worst nightmare." Maggie sighed. What else could one say? The very idea took your breath away. She sipped another cup of coffee. She'd had so little sleep last night, she'd need a whole pot by the time the day was through.

"Where's Phoebe? Is she still at your place?" Suzanne glanced at Maggie.

"She came back a little while ago. She should be down soon."

They heard someone at the shop door. Maggie was relieved to see Lucy walk in. She really didn't feel like taking care of a customer right now.

"Hi, guys . . . Did I miss much?"

"Not really. We were just talking about Beth Shelton and how sad it is for her family."

"What an awful shock. Have the police figured out yet if Beth was the intended victim or if the intruder had really been after Charlotte?"

"They have to investigate both possibilities at this point. Jack said they'll still have to rule Charlotte out as a suspect," Dana added. "They have samples of Charlotte's DNA in the apartment and can figure out if there's any on Beth's body. But so far, there's no report of any ill will between the two girls. So there's no real motive."

"Oh, I don't think Charlotte had anything to do with it. Do any of you?" Before anyone could answer, Maggie added, "I think she's running from someone who wants to harm her . . . not from the murder scene. And we already know Charlotte had plans to leave town and didn't want too many people to know about it."

Lucy found a chair and sat down. "She did? That sounds important. Where was she going? Did she tell anyone?"

"She didn't want Quentin to know," Suzanne cut in. "But she must have told Phoebe."

Maggie shrugged. "Phoebe said she doesn't know why Charlotte was moving or where she was going. Just that she wanted to leave Plum Harbor."

The sound of footsteps on the staircase in the storeroom drew everyone's attention. Phoebe was coming down, and they all turned at once to see her.

"Here she comes. Let's ask her," Suzanne said.

Phoebe appeared in the doorway a moment later, wearing one of her signature outfits—tight black jeans, laced-up boots that reached to the middle of her shins, and a large turtleneck she'd knit herself made of thick gray yarn flecked with black, purple, pink, and other colors. Lavender socks showed at the edges of the boots, and she carried Charlotte's cat in her arms.

The "no cats in the shop" rule had gone by the wayside already. But Maggie didn't have the heart to hold the line. Phoebe just wanted to show everyone the new pet, she guessed. Just this once would be all right, Maggie decided.

"Hey, guys . . . Maggie said you were all coming by."

"We wanted to see how you were. You had a terrible night." Suzanne's voice oozed with concern.

"It was horrible. I felt like I was trapped in a fright film."

Despite her improved appearance, Phoebe suddenly looked pale and shaky again. Dana rose and put an arm around her shoulder. "Come and sit down with us. You don't have to talk about it if you don't want to . . . Who's this?"

"Vincent Van Gogh. I'm just watching him till Charlotte gets back."

"Hello, Van Gogh." Dana was a big feline fan. She owned a rare but crazy Maine coon named Arabelle. Using just her fingertips, she gently massaged Van Gogh behind his chewed-off ear. His eyes closed to narrow slits. "I thought you had a firm rule about pets, Maggie?"

"I do. I mean, I did," Maggie insisted. "But Charlotte has all these cats, and they were roaming about last night, looking so hungry and forlorn. Phoebe was able to grab this guy, and we decided he could visit a while. Until Charlotte comes back," she added quickly. "I guess you haven't heard from her?"

Phoebe shook her head, biting her lower lip. "Not a word."

She petted Van Gogh in an absentminded way, but he didn't seem to notice. "I knew Quentin was crazy. I should have told her right away, before the show even, to stay at my place . . . Even though that wouldn't have helped poor Beth."

"Phoebe . . . you can't blame yourself for this. Not any part of it," Dana said quietly.

"If anything happens to Charlotte, I will," Phoebe insisted.

No one answered. They were all thinking the same thing, Maggie realized. Hoping Charlotte was all right . . . but wondering if whoever had killed Beth had somehow caught up with Charlotte, too.

"I think she's all right," Dana said in a very definite tone. "I really do. The police do, too," she added. "They've questioned Quentin. He has an alibi for last night. Though it isn't airtight."

Phoebe looked up from the cat. "One of his idiot friends standing up for him?"

"Not entirely," Dana replied. "After causing a scene at the art show, he went to work for a few hours. He cleans up at a little café in town that closes around eight. He claims he was working there from eight to eleven. Then met up with friends at a bar in Gloucester. He punches a time clock at the restaurant," she added.

"Yeah, and at the bar, too?" Phoebe shot back. She stared at Dana a moment, thinking. "He still could have gone over to Charlotte's house in between. Or left the bar for a while. As if any of his crew would ever tell the truth about where he was, or how long he was there."

"The police know that. I don't think they've ruled him out entirely yet," Dana assured her.

Phoebe still didn't look pleased, but she didn't argue, Maggie noticed. Neither did anyone else.

"Whether she was afraid of Quentin or someone else, Charlotte knew she was in danger," Suzanne pointed out. "That's why she went into hiding. Someplace where no one can find her."

"I think that's true, Suzanne. She's a smart girl. Very resourceful," Lucy added, turning to Phoebe. "I bet she's safe and the police will find her soon. They must have started tracking her credit cards and phone calls by now."

"They have," Dana confirmed. She seemed about to say more, then stopped herself. She looked down at her knitting, her lips pursed. Maggie guessed she'd heard something from her husband that she wasn't supposed to repeat.

Suzanne was the only one brazen enough to prod her. "Don't be a tease, Dana. Did they find out anything yet?"

Dana sighed. "All this is confidential. I'm not supposed to say, but . . . yes, they did find a transaction at a train station in New Jersey. Newark, I think. There were security cameras on the platform, so they know it was Charlotte, not someone using a stolen card. She left her car in the parking lot and bought a ticket. The ticket office was closed, and she couldn't pay with cash, so I guess she was forced to use her card. It's the only transaction they've come up with so far. But it does indicate she's all right and traveling under her own free will."

"What time was that? Do they know?" Lucy asked quickly.

"I'm not sure. I think around one a.m. Beth was killed between nine and eleven, so it doesn't quite eliminate her as a suspect."

"No . . . but . . . it does make it seem even more unlikely.

Even if Beth was killed at nine, it would be hard to drive from Plum Harbor down to Newark in four hours. And if she was killed later, it would be pretty close to impossible," Maggie noted. "At least we know Charlotte is alive and well." Maggie felt encouraged by the news. She glanced at Phoebe. "Feel any better?"

"I do . . . but why didn't you just tell us that when you walked in, Dana?" Phoebe gave Dana a look.

"I'm sorry . . . I wasn't supposed to tell. Jack made me promise. I figured you would hear it soon on the news, or from the police. But I should have just told you right away. That wasn't right." She leaned over and gave Phoebe's shoulder a gentle, affectionate squeeze. "Will you forgive me?"

"I guess I have to . . . You're the only other cat lover around here," Phoebe muttered.

"Thanks . . . I think," Dana answered with a smile.

"Where was the train going? Can they tell where she planned to get off?" Suzanne asked.

"Good question," Maggie added.

"The train was headed south, final stop Baltimore. The fare goes by zones, and she bought a full-fare ticket," Dana explained. "But she could have gotten off earlier, at any stop. Especially if she's trying to hide her trail. They're checking video from security cameras at all the stops on the route, to see if they can spot her. And they hope to find more credit card or cell phone use. But so far, she's been very careful."

Maggie thought the same. "If Charlotte really doesn't want to be found, there are ways around leaving a trail of transactions. She can even disguise herself when she gets off the train."

"She's been smart so far," Dana agreed. "But since she's wanted for questioning in regard to a murder investigation, this is more than a simple missing-persons case. I think our local investigators have reached out and the FBI is already involved, too."

"Charlotte has a lot of people on her trail now. They have to find her soon." Lucy glanced over at Phoebe, but their youngest friend showed little reaction.

"What about the Knit Kats? Have the police made any progress tracking them down?" Suzanne asked Dana. "And I know you probably promised Jack you wouldn't tell but—"

"How do the Knit Kats figure into it?" Lucy cut in. "Did I miss something?"

"The police don't want any details to get out," Maggie began. "That's why the news reporters don't even know. We had to promise Detective Reyes . . . and Dana promised Jack," she added.

She didn't care so much about herself. But she didn't want Phoebe to get into any trouble.

"Should we swear on a knitting magazine or something?" Suzanne held up her right hand and pressed the other to a recent copy of *American Stitchery*.

Dana glanced at her and shook her head, then turned back to Lucy. "The knitted wrapping on the victim, Beth Shelton, wasn't just a blanket or afghan. It looked frighteningly similar to the wrapping the Knit Kats use for their installations on statues and phone booths. That sort of thing."

Maggie nodded but couldn't speak. The image was very unsettling. And it sounded like the wrapping on the victim also looked like the knitted swathes in Charlotte's artwork. Another disturbing thought. She glanced at Phoebe, wondering if she should say anything. She knew the point would only make her more upset.

But before she could decide, Lucy was the first to answer Dana. "Ugh . . . how creepy. That gives me the chills."

"Me, too," Suzanne agreed. She shook her head as if to dislodge the dark image. "Phoebe, that must have been awful for you to see."

Phoebe looked down, still stroking the cat. She spoke very slowly and quietly. "I know I'm not supposed to say anything . . . but I just need to talk about it. It looked like an afghan, at first. Then I realized . . . it looked just like one of the Knit Kats' projects. Just like all the pictures on their website, all the different patterns and loose tangled yarn they tack on. It was exactly the same, and it just made me sick, thinking they had done that to a real live person. Well, maybe I guess she was dead first. But . . ."

Phoebe suddenly covered her face with her hands, her slim shoulders shaking as she muffled her tears. Van Gogh sat perfectly still for a moment in a tight, alert ball, then leaped off Phoebe's lap and disappeared into the shop.

Oh dear . . . just what I didn't want to happen, Maggie thought. But she couldn't worry about the silly cat now, and quickly rose and put her arm around Phoebe's shoulder.

"And you told the police that?" Lucy asked. "So they're looking for the Knit Kats now?"

Phoebe nodded. "I guess so."

Suzanne suddenly turned to Maggie. "Hey . . . how about that weird phone call you got the other night? With the cat yowl? Did you tell the police?"

"Detective Reyes made a note. I erased the message, but

they might look at my phone records and see if they can find the caller. I got a feeling they didn't think it was important." Maggie still had her arm around Phoebe's shoulder. She was crying in earnest again, and Suzanne handed her a box of tissues. "Phoebe . . . try not to think about it. I'm so sorry we reminded you." Maggie didn't know what else to say.

Dana walked over and sat next to Phoebe. "It's going to take time to get over this. You've had a terrible shock. We're all here for you, sweetie. We love you," she added, stroking Phoebe's hair.

Phoebe sniffed and lifted her head. Lucy handed her a bunch of tissues with a wordless gesture and a kind smile.

"Thanks, guys." Phoebe sniffed. "You're real friends. You're like my . . . my . . . family," she stuttered through her tears. "I love you guys . . . but I just feel so bad because . . . because . . . you're all being so great to me and . . . I . . . I really need to tell you something."

Maggie could hardly understand what Phoebe was trying to say between her tears and gasps for air.

She had to tell them something? About Charlotte? About Beth perhaps? She leaned closer, wondering what Phoebe was about to say.

The rest of her friends were quiet, too. All looking at Phoebe, waiting.

The most unholy racket broke the silence. Lucy's two dogs, tied on the porch, burst into a fit of barking and howling as they flung themselves against the window at the front of the shop. Maggie couldn't imagine what had gotten into them . . . until she heard Van Gogh answer with screaming cat yowls and hisses.

She ran to window. Phoebe and the rest of her friends followed. Maggie got there first and braced herself before glancing into the display.

Vincent Van Gogh stood with his back arched in full defensive cat mode, then sprang from one side of the window to the other, leaping around the Flexible Flyer sled and piles of fake snow. The dogs barked wildly, their faces and paws pressed to the glass as they tried to get at him.

The cat had gotten into the display area for some reason. Looking for a sunny, warm spot to sleep? That was Maggie's guess.

But now he couldn't find his way out. Maggie started to reach in to grab him, then decided that was a dumb idea. Her hands would be torn to shreds.

Meanwhile, his claws and hectic activity stirred up the fake snow into a mini tornado and tangled the skeins of yarn in her display. Hand-knit hats and scarves in the wintery scene flew in all directions.

"Maggie . . . I'm so sorry . . ." Phoebe stood beside her, looking almost as panicked as the cat.

"Don't worry . . . it's not your fault," Maggie consoled her. It was her own fault for breaking her rule and allowing the silly creature in the shop in the first place.

Lucy had taken one look at the scene and then run out to her dogs. Maggie saw her through the glass, trying to untie the knots in the leashes and pull the two dogs away.

"Let me go out and help her. Those wacky dogs are very strong," Suzanne said.

"And stubborn . . . and not very well trained," Maggie added under her breath.

Dana looked like she wanted to laugh but wouldn't dare. Now that the dogs were almost out of sight, the cat had calmed down a bit. But he was huddled in the corner of the window, look frozen and traumatized.

"Poor Van Gogh. He's terrified," Phoebe crooned.

"Should I go look for a treat in the kitchen? Do cats like crackers?" Maggie asked.

"They definitely like shrimp . . . and I happen to have a bite left over from my salad." Dana had gone back to the table and retrieved her lunch bag. She held out a large white chunk. "This should reel him in. What do you think, Phoebe?"

"Fast thinking, Dana." Without waiting for their reply, Phoebe climbed into the window and offered the scrap. Maggie braced herself. She expected to hear at least a few cat growls. But Phoebe's soft voice and gentle manner easily calmed the testy feline. She coaxed him out of the corner and into her arms, then emerged cradling the cat, who happily munched his fish treat.

Maggie did not think it was a good practice to reward animals that wrecked window displays. He might jump in there and do it again, expecting more seafood. But she decided not to offer that opinion, at least at that moment.

"I'm going to take him upstairs and make sure he stays there," Phoebe promised. "Then I'll help you fix the window."

"Good plan," Maggie said in a weary tone. "That window needed a redo anyway."

It did need a new look . . . though she hadn't planned on working on that today. She wasn't sure what she'd call it now. A cat-astrophic mess?

Suzanne came back inside, looking a bit winded. "Lucy's heading home. Those dogs are a handful." She yanked her sweater down over her ample bust and pushed back her thick hair with one hand. "Overall, this break sure beats eating lunch at my desk," she said, gathering up her purse and knitting bag.

"I have to run, too." Dana collected her coat and bags, too. She turned to Phoebe and gently touched her arm. "You've been through a lot, Phoebe. If you want to talk more, just give me a call. Anytime, okay?"

Phoebe stood holding the cat. She looked down and nodded. "Thanks, Dana. I just might."

Dana smiled and turned to Maggie. "If I hear anything more from Jack, especially about Charlotte, I'll let you all know. Even if it's classified info," she added in almost a whisper.

"Your secrets are safe with us," Maggie promised.

"I hope so, but you know what they say about secrets. 'Three may keep a secret if two of them are dead.'" Dana offered her friends a smile.

"Good one. I'll have to remember that." Suzanne laughed as she headed for the door.

Maggie smiled, too. Though she noticed Phoebe looked uneasy and started petting the cat again. She either didn't find the adage amusing or was still upset. About Beth and Charlotte . . . and everything. She had a perfect right to be, Maggie reminded herself.

After all their friends had left the shop, Phoebe took Van Gogh upstairs. She soon appeared downstairs again. "Sorry about the window. I'll clean it up right away."

"That's all right. We'll do it together." Maggie was putting some receipts in order but quickly put that task aside, grateful for Phoebe's help with the window. While she was perfectly able to maneuver herself in and out of the display space, it was a tight fit and she had to use the step stool. Phoebe jumped in and out like a bird, hopping from branch to branch.

They soon removed the props, the scattered skeins of yarn—which were headed for the discount bin, Maggie guessed without looking too closely—and Phoebe swept up some fake snow and took down the paper cutouts of flakes as well.

"What next?" Phoebe asked as she climbed out of the empty space. "Should we put up the 'Pardon Our Appearance' sign?"

"That was my original plan. But now I'm thinking, what about Valentine's Day? We can wrangle up everything pink and red, hang some hearts and cupids and such?"

Phoebe crossed her arms over her narrow chest. She usually got excited about any creative projects and would extend and amplify Maggie's ideas. Often waving her hands as she spoke.

"What do you think?" Maggie asked her bluntly.

"Valentine's Day is good. I have some red paper and stuff to make hearts for you to hang. That will be easy. And I have socks with hearts."

"I have a red-and-white striped scarf . . . and there's a pattern in a knitting magazine for a children's turtleneck with a big heart in the middle. We can display that page somehow. Let's gather up some possibilities while the shop's still empty."

Maggie took a basket and wandered around the store, looking for a selection of yarns that would suit the color scheme—pinks, reds, even some lavender and purple. She also found a pack of doilies in the storeroom, and Phoebe was soon settled at the worktable, applying her considerable artistic skills to constructing heart-shaped valentines to hang from the window's ceiling.

Maggie glanced over at her as she sat focused on the task. So creative, just this simple project, cutting the hearts in abstract shapes, freehand, and using the ribbons, lace, and paper doilies in inventive ways. Phoebe seemed a bit calmer and more focused. Sometimes a good old-fashioned arts-and-crafts project was just the thing to settle your nerves and distract you from stressful thoughts. Maggie had not proposed the job for that reason, but it seemed to be working out that way.

Maggie went back to the table with an ample selection of yarns. She pointed to the heart Phoebe was just finishing. "That one's very interesting. Maybe you should keep it and give it to Josh."

Phoebe glanced up from her work, then back at the glue stick. "Josh and I broke up."

"Really?" Maggie's head tilted back, as if she'd been sitting in a car that had just stopped short. "When did that happen?"

"Um . . . a few days ago. I broke up with him, actually. He's just being such a jerk. I got tired of it . . . I do all this stuff for him and the band, and he never thanks me. Or takes me out anywhere fun anymore. I'm like his slave or something. *Was* his slave," she corrected. "Let him find someone else to move his amps and sell his stupid CDs. I am so done with that guy."

"I see . . . Well, I'm surprised. But I understand," she added.

It was very understandable to Maggie. She actually didn't

like Josh very much and had always thought he was quite self-ish and self-involved. Phoebe was right. He didn't appreciate her. Or pay nearly enough attention to her. And she could certainly do better.

But Maggie knew it was best right now to keep these opinions to herself. What if it was just a fight and they made up? Phoebe would always remember how Maggie had trashed him.

Phoebe had mangled the lovely heart shape she'd been working on, and Maggie watched her crumple it and start another. "Oh, and by the way, his music like totally sucks. I always told him it was good. I just didn't want to hurt his feelings."

Maggie agreed but felt she was no judge of the compositions of the Big Fat Crying Babies. She was totally not the target audience, as Phoebe would say.

"It sounds like you've given this some thought and come to a firm decision. A good decision," she added. "It's hard to end a long relationship. Inertia sets in. Most people are afraid to be alone. They'd rather be with anybody than nobody. It's brave of you to say this isn't what you want. Very brave. I think you can do better," Maggie said honestly.

"Thanks, Mag. I do, too . . . though I'm not in any rush. I'm sort of mad at the entire male species right now. Except for Van Gogh," she added.

Maggie smiled. "Maybe you should make a valentine for him."

Phoebe laughed—the first time all day, Maggie noticed.

"Cute, Mag. Maybe I will," Phoebe replied, sounding serious.

Maggie sorted out the skeins of yarn for a moment, arranging them in baskets with balls of yarn and needles. "I did wonder why you didn't call him last night . . . and didn't mention him at all," she confessed. "I thought maybe he was just away, working somewhere."

Phoebe glanced at her. "He's away all right. Out of my brain. He's been living in there too long. Rent free."

Maggie glanced at her but didn't reply. There were stages of ending a relationship, and Phoebe would go through a lot more—anger, denial, depression . . . shoe shopping. But she would get through this. She was strong. It was a pity, though, that at a time when Phoebe could have really used some extra support, Josh was out of the picture.

"It must be very hard for you, to be in the middle of this breakup and then this horrible situation with Beth Shelton and Charlotte happens, too."

Phoebe shook her head. "The last two weeks of my life have been the absolute marshland of despair. Breaking up with Josh was just a squirt of fake cheese on a big crappy cracker."

Maggie nodded, taking in the image. "So how did it happen? Did you have a fight?"

Phoebe nodded. "Yeah, a doozy. I was late to his gig on Sunday, over in Essex. I have a life, too, you know? He got all hissy with me, and I said like this is so over. And I walked out and that was it."

"The straw that broke the camel's back," Maggie said sympathetically. She sounded terribly old-fashioned, saying that, didn't she? But she was stumped to come up with a modern equivalent.

So it had only been a week. No wonder she was still smoldering. But didn't she go to a gig on Wednesday night, in Gloucester? Maggie was confused. Not that it really mattered.

But before she could ask, Phoebe said, "Oh, Maggie, I'm such an idiot . . . a complete jerk. How can I live in the world? I'm such a stupid dope . . ."

Maggie stared at her, surprised at this bout of self-recrimination. She sat down and tried to catch Phoebe's eye.

"Because you dated Josh for so long before seeing his true colors? That happens all the time. You can't blame yourself. People always show their best side at the start of a relationship."

Phoebe sighed and shook her head. "He was a total waste of time, but . . . it's not that." She swallowed hard and couldn't seem to say more.

"Do you blame yourself about Beth? . . . Or Charlotte? You had no control over that, Phoebe. I know you think you could have helped Charlotte more. But it's starting to look like she'd already made plans to leave town."

Phoebe sighed and picked up her head, her shoulders sagging. She turned to Maggie, looking truly lost and forlorn. There was something else on her mind. Maggie couldn't seem to figure it out.

"Is there something you want to tell me?" she asked quietly. "You know I won't judge or criticize you. I just want to help. Honestly."

Phoebe sighed again. "I know."

She looked straight ahead and took a breath. She seemed to be centering herself, about to admit what was really bothering her, when the shop door opened.

Maggie stood up from her chair, automatically summoning her pleasant shopkeeper's expression, but quickly realized customers had not arrived. It was Detective Reyes . . . with Detective Mossbacher following close behind.

What were they doing here? Maggie felt indignant and protective as she took a step toward them. Putting herself between them and Phoebe.

Hadn't they asked her enough questions last night? Wearing the poor girl down to a shaking bowl of jelly? This had better be good. Did the police really need to come back here and scare her some more? Couldn't they just call?

"Mrs. Messina, I'm surprised you opened the shop today," Detective Reyes greeted her.

"If you mean because we were all up so late last night, well . . . you're both working." Maggie shrugged. "So here we are."

Mossbacher smiled at her comeback, but his expression quickly turned somber again. "We're actually here to speak to Phoebe."

Maggie had expected that. Phoebe had, too, she guessed, though she showed little reaction.

Phoebe looked over at the police officers through a veil of dark hair but seemed stuck in her chair. Her body was hunched over. As if she wished she could curl up in a ball. Or duck under the table.

"Here I am, too," Phoebe said quietly.

Detective Reyes walked closer to her. Detective Mossbacher hung back, standing beside Maggie.

"We've been looking at video taken here in town last Wednesday night and early Thursday morning. A few of the stores on Main Street have security cameras. Did you know that?"

Phoebe licked her lips, then shook her head. "Um . . . no, I didn't."

"That was the night the parking meters were covered. Well, the vandals actually struck very early Thursday morning," Detective Reyes clarified.

Vandals? What was she talking about, the sack of ancient Rome? Maggie was about to interrupt when Detective Reyes said, "But you already know that, Phoebe. Right?"

Phoebe looked straight at Detective Reyes, her mouth gaping open. Blood had drained from her cheeks, turning her skin chalky white. She glanced up at Maggie with eyes full of fear.

"Me? . . ." Phoebe finally looked up, staring at each of the detectives. "Why would I know that?"

"We saw you on one of the videos, Phoebe. Right outside Kroll's Hardware," Mossbacher answered.

"Your mask fell off right before you finished. Don't you remember?" Detective Reyes asked.

Maggie was stunned. Her mask? What were they talking about? She felt her heart beating painfully fast, and she could barely breathe.

"She was out that night. Helping her boyfriend's band. She was probably just getting home and unpacking her car," Maggie quickly explained. "That's why you saw her on the video."

Then she realized that, in fact, maybe Phoebe had not been with the band in Gloucester on Wednesday night. She'd just said that she'd broken up with Josh on Tuesday. Maggie hoped Phoebe had gotten her days mixed up. But something told her that was not the case.

"We saw you clearly, and the pink streak in your hair. There's no sense denying it," Detective Mossbacher said in a gentler tone.

Phoebe looked at each of the two detectives and then, finally, at Maggie. Then she burst into tears, covering her face with her hands.

What where they trying to say?

Was Phoebe . . . a Knit Kat?

CHAPTER SEVEN

"**P**hoebe . . . you don't have to say anything without a lawyer present," Maggie reminded her.

"Oh . . . what's the difference? Yes . . . I was there . . . I was
helping the Knit Kats. But it was just a stupid prank. I thought it
was so cool or something. I never even spoke to any of them . . .
I swear it."

Maggie felt her heart drop like a stone. So that's what
Phoebe meant about being an idiot. That's what she'd been
trying to tell her all morning.

Maggie was sure she was totally innocent. An innocent
dupe of the Knit Kats. But she was in trouble now. These
detectives were moving slowly, but they definitely meant business. Maggie still thought Phoebe shouldn't answer questions
without a lawyer, but she seemed determined to unburden
herself now that the dam had finally burst.

"I'm in trouble now, right? I didn't mean to lie to you, honest.
I was just so freaked. Are you going to throw me in jail . . . or
something?" Her last words melted into a plaintive whine, and

more tears fell. "You don't really think I hurt Beth . . . do you?"

Detective Reyes sat in the seat next to Phoebe. "Let's talk about the Knit Kats for now."

Maggie rested a steadying hand on her shoulder. "You never asked if she was involved with the Knit Kats. So, technically, she didn't lie to you."

Reyes looked surprised by Maggie's impudence, but Mossbacher pressed his lips together, as if trying to smother a shocked smile. They both ignored her comment—which was fortunate, Maggie realized. She certainly didn't want to make things any worse.

"You've held back important information, Phoebe. *Technically*, you could be charged with interfering with the investigation," Reyes told her. "And defacing public property . . . and littering. We can book you on those charges and continue this conversation in the police station."

Phoebe looked as if she might start crying again but was trying hard not to.

Maggie felt so torn. She didn't know if it was better for Phoebe to call a lawyer or just answer their questions. She knew Phoebe had nothing to hide except for this Knit Kats silliness. But the police did have a way of twisting things around when they wanted to.

Mossbacher stepped up to the table. He spoke in a deep, quiet tone. "You can help yourself—and help us—by answering a few questions. What do you know about the Knit Kats? How many are there? What are their real names?"

"I don't know who they really are. They sent me e-mails. I never saw any of them face-to-face." Phoebe was struggling not to cry. She spoke in a trembling tone.

"Not even the night the meters were vandalized?" Detective Reyes asked.

Phoebe shook her head. "I was assigned a certain section of Main Street and told to go out during a certain time period. I thought I'd see at least one of them out there. I even looked. But there was no one. I did see that some meters farther up the street had already been covered. So I knew at least one Knit Kat had been out there before me."

"What happened afterward? Didn't they get in touch again?" Mossbacher followed up.

"I never heard from them. I even tried the e-mail address they'd used . . . something like slinkytail@knitkats.com? But it came back undeliverable."

The detectives exchanged a look. Maggie wasn't sure what they were thinking. Mossbacher had a small pad on the table and was taking notes.

"How did you first make contact with the group? From their website?" Detective Reyes asked.

"No, nothing like that. I'd checked out their website a few times. Whenever they were in the news. But I wasn't like a fan or anything."

"So how did you connect? Did they get in touch with you?" Mossbacher persisted.

Phoebe took a deep breath and stared down at the paper hearts again. She didn't answer, and Maggie felt the tension in the room rise; she could tell the detectives were losing their patience again.

Detective Reyes was the first to speak. "Believe me, Phoebe, this is not the time to protect anyone."

Maggie knew that was true. Phoebe had to think of herself

now. If she didn't watch out, the police department was going to start making a case again her. Totally circumstantial, of course. But Maggie knew how easily that could happen. She'd once been the victim of ersatz evidence and flimsy theories herself.

When Phoebe finally glanced her way, Maggie said, "She's right, Phoebe. You need to tell the police all you know."

Phoebe sighed and nodded. "It was Charlotte," she said quietly. "Charlotte put me in touch with the Knit Kats."

"Charlotte Blackburn." Detective Reyes didn't sound surprised.

But Maggie felt surprised. She took a quick breath and blinked.

"Go on. What was her connection to the group?" Detective Mossbacher prodded.

"I'm not sure. Honest. She just told me she knew they were looking for a new member. She asked if I was interested. I know it was like stupendously stupid, but I said okay, I'll give it a try. I mean, I thought they were cool and did this interesting fiber art and had a lot of meaning and higher purpose to their graffiti installations. I didn't realize they're like . . . creepy and dangerous. I mean, nobody thought that even a few days ago . . . right?"

Maggie had to agree. The truth was nobody knew for sure if the Knit Kats were involved in Beth Shelton's murder. So far, it just seemed as if they might be, and it was all the police had to go on.

"Go on, Phoebe. Charlotte put your name forward. How long did it take before the group got in touch?" Mossbacher asked, pushing her back on track.

"Not long. I guess it was a day or so before I got the first e-mail. They said if I wanted to try out, I needed to knit twenty of the cat-face meter covers. They gave me about . . . oh, a week to do it, I guess."

"A week? That's all?" Maggie couldn't help herself. Those meter covers were small but complicated, with the trimming and everything. Phoebe had never knit any of their group projects that fast. Those Kats had certainly made her jump through some hoops.

"How did you know what to do? . . . And what to do with the knitting when it was finished?" Detective Reyes asked.

"A pattern was attached to the note. The note didn't explain what the covers were going to be used for. It just said I'd get instructions about what to do with them. Oh, and the note said everything had to be totally and completely secret. Or there would be 'very unpleasant consequences.' Those were the words they used." Phoebe paused. "I wasn't really sure what they meant, but hey, it doesn't sound like something you want, right?"

"Not at all," Mossbacher agreed. "And what if you didn't want to do it? Did they say there would be consequences then?"

Phoebe shook her head. "They just said if I didn't reply in twenty-four hours, they would assume I agreed." She sighed and bit her lower lip.

"What about the second e-mail? What did that say?" Detective Reyes asked.

"That one gave me instructions on what do with the cat covers. Oh . . . and they told me to make sure I couldn't be recognized when I went outside. I guess I screwed that up, too," Phoebe added.

"Your hood slipped off right at the end," Mossbacher explained.

"Let's go back a minute," Detective Reyes cut in. "How did you and Charlotte get on the topic of the Knit Kats in the first place? Did she bring them up, or did you?"

Phoebe took a moment, trying to remember. "We were talking about the art show. Charlotte said the Knit Kats had submitted a few pieces, but their work had been rejected."

"Rejected by who? Who does the choosing?" Detective Reyes asked.

"Three professors were working together to curate the exhibit. Let's see . . . Professor Healey, Professor Finch, and Professor Sylvan. He's on sabbatical this semester. I'm not sure if he saw everything."

Detective Reyes patiently heard her out. She turned to Phoebe. "So Charlotte brought up the group. Was Charlotte Blackburn one of the Knit Kats? Is she the face that's crossed out on the website?"

Phoebe stared bleakly at Detective Reyes. "I swear, Detective . . . I *really* don't know."

"You never asked her?" Detective Reyes persisted.

Phoebe shook her head. "No . . . I didn't, honest. I guess I thought the subject was a little touchy since the group is so secret. I figured if Charlotte wanted me to know, she'd tell me. I think I did ask her how she knew them. She wouldn't really say."

"What *did* she say?" Mossbacher cut in.

"Something like, 'Oh, they're around. You'd be surprised.'"

Mossbacher took quick note of that, Maggie noticed.

"How about Beth Shelton? Do you know if she was one of the Knit Kats? Did Charlotte mention that?" Reyes continued.

Phoebe shook her head. "Beth's name never came up. She was into ceramics. She never did any fiber art. I didn't know her that well. But I don't think she knew how to knit."

Phoebe is definitely doing the right thing by cooperating and telling all she knows, Maggie decided. But hasn't this informal interrogation gone on too long? She could slip up and say the wrong thing . . . and find herself a suspect. If she doesn't watch out.

"Doesn't Phoebe have the right to have an attorney present before she answers more questions?"

"Yes, she does," Detective Reyes replied. "We can continue this at the station, with your attorney present if you choose, Phoebe. And you'll have to make a new statement. We'd also like to look around your apartment," she added. "You can give us permission now. Or we can get a warrant."

"A warrant . . . you mean like a *search* warrant? . . . Why?" Phoebe's eyes were wide with shock.

"For evidence relating to the murder of Beth Shelton." Detective Reyes's voice was flat and matter-of-fact.

Maggie felt her blood run cold, and she saw the color drain instantly from Phoebe's face.

"But you don't think . . . You can't think I had anything to do with that. I already told you last night. I was looking for Charlotte because I was worried about her. I didn't even set foot in the bedroom . . ."

"Unfortunately, you didn't tell us everything. Your connection to the Knit Kats makes you a person of interest in the case."

A person of interest? That was ludicrous! Phoebe was an innocent pawn . . . and a totally harmless one, Maggie wanted to point out. But the less said the better right now, Maggie decided.

It was time to find Phoebe a good lawyer. Maggie had needed legal help years ago and remembered the attorney's name, Christine Forbes. She had an office right in town. Maggie was going to call her right away, no matter what Phoebe said.

Maggie heard a phone buzz, and Detective Reyes reached in her pocket to check a text, then looked at Phoebe again.

"Looks like we can get a warrant to search your apartment by the end of the day," Detective Reyes reported.

"You can look in my apartment right now. I don't have anything to hide," Phoebe said emphatically.

Maggie wasn't sure that was the wisest course. But it was Phoebe's call, and maybe being so cooperative did show she was innocent.

She suddenly realized that they might want to search the shop, too. She did have an issue with that.

"Do you intend to search the shop?"

"Not unless we have probable cause. Do you think we should?" Detective Mossbacher asked.

"Of course not. There's absolutely no reason. I was just wondering. And I'd hate it if you did," Maggie said bluntly.

That was dumb. Maybe I've just piqued their curiosity. But she suddenly realized Detective Mossbacher was teasing her. In a low-key way.

"Don't worry, Mrs. Messina. We have no need to search your shop. Not right now anyway," he assured her. "Everything is in such nice order. I can see why the idea would disturb you."

His reply made her feel a bit better. It was nice of him to say that. He didn't have to. Under his tough-guy act, she thought, he was probably a nice man.

Detective Reyes had taken out a form from the slim black binder she carried. She filled it out and asked Phoebe to sign the bottom. Consenting to the search, Maggie guessed.

"We'll need to take your computer, Phoebe. And anything else that seems relevant."

Phoebe sighed, her chin practically touching her chest as she nodded. "Okay . . . I understand."

Maggie was alarmed. "I'm calling an attorney for you. Right now."

Phoebe looked up at her. She looked scared.

Maggie headed over to the counter, where she kept her phone book. If this attorney wasn't available, Dana would help them find another. Of course she would go down to the police station again with Phoebe and help her through this latest fiasco. Once their circle of friends found out what was going on, Maggie was fairly certain she would not be alone waiting there, either.

"I'll go up and get the computer. It's upstairs," Phoebe said.

"Don't bother . . . we'll find it." Detective Mossbacher stood up from his chair and met Phoebe's gaze.

"I'll go upstairs with you whenever you're ready to get your purse and jacket," Detective Reyes said, as politely as if they were about to take a ride to the mall.

They didn't want Phoebe to tamper with her computer before she gave it to them. Or touch anything else up there. That was clear to Maggie.

She hoped with all her heart they wouldn't find anything more linking Phoebe with the Knit Kats . . . or Beth Shelton's murder. Detective Reyes started toward the storeroom, then paused and looked at Phoebe.

"One more question before we go. Do you have any idea where Charlotte Blackburn is?"

Phoebe stared at her bleakly and shook her head. Tears welled up in her eyes again.

"I swear, Detective . . . I *totally* don't know . . ."

CHAPTER EIGHT

It took several hours before Phoebe was finally released by the police. She submitted to many more questions and had to sign a new statement. Her attorney negotiated to have all charges dropped—even littering—in exchange for Phoebe's cooperation.

The police had her look at the photos of the Knit Kats, printed off the website and enlarged. Phoebe hadn't recognized anyone. Maggie was also asked to look at them, but she didn't recognize anyone, either.

Even with the images enlarged, the makeup and disguises held up well. But questions from the police had made her wonder if she actually had met any of the Knit Kats. They could be customers coming into her store from time to time, Detective Mossbacher had pointed out.

The notion had crossed Maggie's mind, too. But who? Some pleasant senior taking a class on easy projects for her grandchildren? Some mother-to-be learning how to knit booties and bibs? The truth was, you just never know. Case in point, Phoebe had been auditioning for the group right under her nose and she had not suspected a thing.

Maggie had been upset with Phoebe for not coming clean sooner about her Knit Kats connections. But she understood that she'd been trying to protect Charlotte. Still, she should have told somebody. They all would have advised her to tell the truth. The police always find out everything anyway, in their slow, methodical way. Now Phoebe had discovered that for herself and was suffering the consequences.

Maggie felt so sorry for her, she couldn't stay mad for long.

After they were done at the police station, Maggie took charge of Phoebe once more. Maggie decided to take Phoebe home again, where they would have a quiet dinner and go to sleep early.

They both knew that tomorrow would start with an onerous task: cleaning up Phoebe's apartment.

"Should we swing by the shop and check out the mess?" Phoebe asked as Maggie drove across town.

Maggie had been silently debating the same question.

"I don't think so. We're both a little tired for that right now. But maybe we should pick up your car," she suggested. "In case one of us needs to sleep in tomorrow."

Maggie was fairly certain of which one of them that would be. But didn't want to elaborate.

"All right, let's get my car," Phoebe agreed. She glanced at Maggie. "I hope Van Gogh is all right. He must be even more confused now."

"Cats are very adaptable. He'll be fine once he sees you."

At the last minute, Phoebe had remembered the cat, who she knew would get upset with a herd of police officers in her apartment, tearing through everything. Detective Mossbacher had been pretty understanding about that, Maggie thought. He even helped them catch the cat and close him up in a carton. Before meeting Phoebe at the police station, Maggie had swung by her house and dropped off the cat, along with his necessities.

She hoped Van Gogh had not succumbed to a cat panic attack and shredded things or hidden himself in some inaccessible place. Phoebe would be glad to see that familiar furry face, that was for sure. Some small distraction from her bad day.

It felt good to be home, Maggie thought as she unlocked her front door. The house was quiet and still, its familiar warmth and scents reaching out to comfort her.

"Van Gogh? Are you all right? Where are you, kitty?"

Phoebe walked into the living room and looked around. There was no sign of the cat. While Phoebe continued looking, Maggie went into the kitchen, took out a can opener and a can of tuna.

"Here, kitty. Dinner," she said blandly.

The cat darted out from beneath the sofa and ran straight to her. Phoebe followed. "Good trick, Mag."

Maggie shrugged. "Not really. Pets and men are pretty much the same. Food rarely fails to bring them running."

The cat's dinner was easily solved. But Maggie wasn't sure what to do about herself and Phoebe. She was overdue for a visit to the grocery store, but thought she could rustle up something. Neither of them was very hungry.

She wasn't sure why she'd turned on the TV. Force of habit, she concluded. She always watched the local news when she happened to be home at this hour and had clicked on the set right before peering into her nearly bare refrigerator.

There was a dour synchronicity to their timing. The screen filled with a video of the shop swarming with police. Chelsea Porter was on the scene once more, with her white down jacket and matching teeth.

Phoebe gasped and pointed. She couldn't even speak.

"In Plum Harbor today, police searched the floor above the Black Sheep Knitting Shop, a residential apartment and the home of Phoebe Meyers, the shop's assistant, in connection to the murder of a local college student, whose body was discovered late Sunday night in off-campus student housing. Officials are not releasing any further details about the crime or their investigation.

"But they were here for quite a few hours, searching for clues to this tragedy. We are told that Maggie Messina, shop owner, is not a target of investigators. But Phoebe Meyers, who works in the shop and lives above the store, may be a person of interest in the case. Both Messina and Meyers could not be reached for comment."

"'Could not be reached for comment'? That makes it sound like we were purposely ducking them," Maggie sputtered. "We couldn't be reached because we were with the police, helping them solve the crime. I'm going to call and demand a retraction. Or a correction . . . or whatever they're supposed to do."

"Maybe they called the shop phone or our home numbers?" Phoebe offered.

"Maybe . . . I haven't checked the messages yet. Maybe I wouldn't have even called them back," she admitted.

"I'm so sorry, Maggie. This really stinks. It's such bad publicity for you . . ."

Maggie secretly felt the same but just shrugged and forced a smile. "Oh, you know what they say, 'Any publicity is good publicity.'"

Maggie didn't really believe that. A news video of her shop in connection with a murder investigation could not be twisted into some positive interpretation, no matter how she tried. But Phoebe already felt bad enough. Wringing her hands wasn't going to change a thing.

"Come on, Maggie. The only thing worse would be if the police found a body in your store."

"Heaven forfend . . . that would be worse," Maggie agreed. "Little chance of that happening . . . I hope."

She had tried again to make a joke. A small, dumb joke, granted. Phoebe didn't even try to smile. Just sat with her long, skinny legs folded beneath her and picked bits of lint off her sweater sleeve.

"Okay, it's bad. I won't say it's not. But by next week, no one will remember. They'll be on to the next disaster, believe me," she promised Phoebe. "The shop survived worse than this when I was hauled off to jail and the police searched it from top to bottom. Don't you remember?"

Phoebe finally met her glance again and nodded. "That was bad. I do remember."

"But I got through it, right? All of you had to remind me that people in town have much shorter memories than we give them credit for. And you just can't worry so much about what people think. If we need to blame somebody, let's blame the police . . . Better yet, let's blame whoever killed Beth Shelton."

Phoebe didn't reply but at least looked a tiny bit comforted by Maggie's words. Van Gogh jumped up on Phoebe's lap, then managed to walk in circles, hoping to be petted. Phoebe quickly complied.

Maggie's phone rang, and she saw Lucy's name on the caller ID, though she had already guessed it would be one of their friends. As Maggie had expected after she called Dana, told her what had happened, and asked for some advice, all of their friends soon knew that Phoebe was being questioned again. They had all offered to come to the police station and wait with Maggie. But she hadn't seen the purpose in that.

Lucy was calling now for an update. Maggie was too tired to talk but picked up anyway.

"Did you see channel 25 news tonight?" Lucy asked in a cautious tone.

"Fame is a fickle mistress. What can you do? One minute I'm their needlework expert—and the next, the shop is a hot-bed of evidence in a murder investigation."

"They didn't go that far . . . thank goodness."

"I wish they had. I could sue for slander. Right now, it's just an implied smear. Newspeople are very cagey that way."

Lucy didn't encourage her, Maggie noticed. She knew better by now. "How's Phoebe holding up?" she asked, changing the subject.

"She's very tired. We both are. It was a hard day."

"I'm sure. I guess you don't want any company tonight. Have you had dinner? I could bring you a pizza or something."

"Sweet of you to offer, but I think we're better off turning in early. There will probably be an impressive mess in Phoebe's place . . . If you have a few minutes tomorrow morning, she might need help cleaning up."

"I'm there. What time?"

"I'd better get there by eight. You don't have to come that early, though."

"I'll see how it goes. See you tomorrow."

They said good night, and Maggie turned her attention back to Phoebe. She'd shut off the TV and seemed to be in sort of a daze, petting the cat, who now lay on her lap, posed like the Sphinx, his eyes closed to narrow slits.

Maggie walked over and sat next to them, then patted Phoebe's free hand. "I know how you feel. But the police will soon eliminate you as a suspect. They've got to be following other leads, too. And you aren't even a real member of the Knit Kats. You didn't even get a call back."

"Saved by my subpar needlework. I might be sitting in a jail cell right now if those crazy weirdos had liked my knitting," Phoebe agreed glumly.

"They would be truly crazy not to love your knitting," she insisted. "I hope you're not feeling bad about that, too?"

Phoebe didn't answer, just looked back down at the cat. Maggie knew she did feel bad. How ironic.

"Your knitting is first-rate. I would have never hired you otherwise," she reminded her. "Nobody is going to put you in jail. I simply won't let that happen. The only thing the police can accuse you of is being such a loyal friend to Charlotte. It was just unfortunate you were the one to find Beth's body."

"I guess . . . but I should have told them right away about the Knit Kats thing," Phoebe admitted. "Keeping it secret just made me look bad. And I should have told you, Maggie . . . and everyone else," she added. "Even if the Knit Kats said they'd make trouble for me."

Maggie wasn't sure what to say. "I respect people who can keep a confidence. And I admire you for trying to protect Charlotte, I really do. But sometimes, what seems like the wrong thing to do can be the right thing. Not very often, but it does happen." Maggie shrugged. "That's just a call we each have to make."

Phoebe nodded. Van Gogh was purring now. The sound was surprisingly soothing.

Phoebe sighed. She looked up at Maggie. "Thanks for helping me, Mags. And waiting for me all day. You totally didn't have to do that."

Maggie smiled at her. "Are you crazy? I couldn't leave you there all alone. I want to help you, Phoebe. We all do. If something else comes up that you need to talk about . . . whatever it is, please don't be afraid to tell me. Or Dana or Lucy—or even Suzanne, though we all know how dramatic she gets." Maggie rolled her eyes, finally making Phoebe laugh. "You're like totally *not* alone, kiddo," she added, teasing her a bit more. "We are all going to help you get through this."

Phoebe's dark eyes were wide and wet with tears again. She sniffed and nodded. "Thanks."

Maggie felt a lump in her throat and couldn't reply. She leaned over and gave Phoebe a hug and felt Phoebe hug her back.

She really was so young and didn't have anyone but her friends to help her now. Maggie was determined to be there for her. Her own daughter was just about Phoebe's age, and Maggie couldn't imagine Julie facing a situation like this all alone, with no concerned adult to support her. She had great affection for Phoebe . . . they all did. As independent as she was, Phoebe needed some mothering from time to time. Especially at a time like this.

"I don't know about you, but I'm happy to keep the television off tonight and just sit here and knit. Why don't we forget about Chelsea Porter and real life for a while?"

Phoebe seemed in perfect agreement with that plan. "No arguments here. Reality is like . . . so overrated."

As always, knitting was the perfect way to de-stress and unwind after their hard day. But there was no avoiding reality the next morning.

And no avoiding their friends. Suzanne and Dana sent text messages before Maggie had even downed her first cup of coffee. Lucy was already waiting at the shop when she pulled up, sitting on the porch steps. Sans dogs, Maggie noticed. Perhaps she thought it best to avoid another skirmish with the cat. That was the last thing they needed this morning.

"Hey, Mag . . . where's Phoebe?"

"Oh, she was so tired and worn out. I told her to get a little more sleep. She'll be along in a while."

"How are you doing? You look a little tired, too," Lucy observed cautiously.

"Oh, I'm all right. Considering my shop was all over the news last night, the scene of a murder investigation." Without Phoebe around, Maggie felt able to vent freely. "How's that for free advertising?"

"You never know. People are so nosy these days. You might draw some new customers who want to poke around such a notorious knitting shop."

Maggie had to laugh at that theory. Trust Lucy to find any possible upside. She climbed the porch steps and stuck the key in the shop door.

"I suppose it's possible," she said with a sigh.

She pulled open the door, then entered the shop and left her knitting bag on the front counter and headed for the storeroom. "Well . . . everything looks the same. I was afraid the police started tossing things around down here, too."

She set up the coffeemaker as she spoke. Lucy stood in the doorway and slipped off her jacket. "What were they looking for? Did they say?"

"Anything that might help their investigation. At least they give you a receipt for things they confiscate. I know they took her computer and all of her yarn. They're trying to match fibers with the wrapping on Beth Shelton's body."

Lucy took in a quick, sharp breath. "I thought they were only bothering Phoebe because she'd been in touch with the Knit Kats. They can't possibly consider her a suspect."

Maggie sighed and shrugged. "They called her a person of interest. But they sometimes don't use the term 'suspect' until they've built a case."

"But there's no motivation. Phoebe hardly knew Beth Shelton . . . and she loves Charlotte. She's been trying to protect her."

The coffee had dripped down, and Maggie poured out two mugs. "Yes . . . I know. But once the police saw her on that video, it opened Pandora's box. Or maybe Pandora's knitting bag."

A weak jest, but the best Maggie could muster. The idea of Phoebe becoming a real suspect in this case was just unthinkable. She didn't want to sound negative, but she was honestly worried. "Let's hope that now that they've questioned her twice, searched her apartment . . . even taken a DNA sample—"

"They did?" Lucy stared at her, looking concerned.

"She didn't have to. But her attorney advised her to do it voluntarily." Maggie paused, trying to keep her thoughts straight. This was so distressing to talk about. "What I'm trying to say is, now that the police have all the information they can possibly want, maybe they can rule her out."

"I hope so." Lucy took a testing sip of her coffee. Maggie could see it was still too hot to drink. Lucy took her coffee black, and Maggie could never figure out how she didn't burn her mouth every morning. "How is she doing otherwise?"

"Better than most people would be. I know she doesn't look it, but she's a strong girl."

"I'm sure you've been a big help."

"I try. It's not over yet," Maggie answered in a softer tone.

They went out to the oak table and sat down. The construction paper and doilies from the interrupted window-decorating project were still on the table. Maggie pushed them aside. The front window was a mess and would just have to stay that way for a while.

Lucy didn't speak for a long time. "Didn't they see anyone else on those videos? There had to be other Knit Kats creeping around that night."

"I wondered about the same thing. The detectives wouldn't say. Only that they're still looking at the tapes and it takes time. Maybe Dana knows more about that. And where in the world is Charlotte?" Maggie added in a hushed but emphatic tone. "I have a feeling she knows plenty. Phoebe has really put her neck out, trying to protect her. I wonder if

Charlotte would be so loyal. If Phoebe's situation gets more complicated, I wonder if Charlotte will come back to help her."

"Oh now . . . let's not get carried away," Lucy insisted. "The police have to rule Phoebe out. She didn't do anything," she pointed out emphatically.

Maggie sighed. "Yes, of course she didn't. I'd still like to know where Charlotte is and what she knows. I have a feeling she's all right. Just hiding somewhere."

"I'm not sure why, but I feel the same," Lucy said. "Have the police said anything more about tracking her? Beyond the train ticket in New Jersey?"

"Not to me or Phoebe. But perhaps they know more. I hope they do," Maggie added. "At first I thought she was running away from Quentin. But now it seems it's definitely something more."

"I think so, too." Lucy took a sip of her coffee. "I can see Quentin losing his temper so badly that he could do mortal harm to someone. In an angry rage. I can even accept that he might mistake Beth for Charlotte in the dark because his head was so fogged by his feelings. But covering the body in knitted material? Not an afghan he grabbed off the bed but real fiber art? Why would he do that? Where would he even find it?"

"I agree." Maggie nodded. "If I was a detective, I would have to rule Quentin out of this. Or at least put him on the back suspect burner. Unless Charlotte had a big piece of her artwork in her apartment and he was trying to make a statement of some kind?" Maggie sighed and shook her head. "I don't know. It's all so confusing. I just hate to see the way

Phoebe's being dragged into the whole mess. It seems so unfair."

They both heard the shop door open and Suzanne's dulcet tones before the sassy brunette came into view. "How's our girl? Is she all right? I couldn't sleep a wink, thinking of her at the police station. Where is she? I picked up her favorite breakfast."

Suzanne walked to the back of the shop, waving a white bakery bag. In a dark-red peacoat, jeans, and knee-high black boots that laced in back, she looked like some sort of regal messenger, Maggie thought.

"She's still at Maggie's. She needed a little more sleep before facing the apartment," Lucy explained.

"Oh, right . . . Is it a huge mess up there?"

"We don't know. She asked me not to look before she got here." Maggie poured Suzanne a cup of coffee and set it on the table.

"What did you bring her, a carrot muffin?" Lucy asked. Everyone knew how much Phoebe liked carrot muffins from the bakery that was down near the harbor.

Suzanne gave Lucy a look. "A plain old muffin? At a time like this? It's a red velvet cupcake. I said 'favorite.' Not 'default setting.'"

"For breakfast?" Maggie asked.

"It's an emergency. I want to cheer her up. I didn't think a muffin was going to cut it. I can't even imagine what that child went through."

"Very thoughtful," Lucy said, hiding a grin.

Maggie had no comment. Suzanne could be absurd at times. But the cupcake actually might cheer Phoebe up.

And by the time she got to the shop, it could be time for lunch.

"Thank goodness they didn't charge her with anything and put her in jail." Suzanne sat down and opened her jacket.

"We can thank Phoebe's lawyer. She got the police to drop the vandalism and littering charges in exchange for cooperating," Maggie told her. "But Phoebe's attorney was concerned that the connection to the Knit Kats and the direction of the investigation made for some hot water. After all, she's the only Knit Kat they've managed to get hold of."

"So far," Suzanne added. "I still can't believe she auditioned for them. They must have an eye on this shop. Maybe they even know about our knitting group, especially after you were on TV. And that weird meow call. You told the police about that, right?" Suzanne had taken her own cup of coffee and a croissant out of the bakery bag and started on her breakfast.

"Yes, I did. Don't worry . . . Besides, Phoebe told the police that Charlotte was her connection. Charlotte knew the group was looking for a new member and asked Phoebe if she wanted to try out."

Lucy had been paging through a knitting magazine and now looked up at Maggie. "Is Charlotte a Knit Kat? You never would have known, sitting with her while we watched that news clip about the parking meters. If she is in the group, she's a pretty good actress."

Maggie had been unpacking a special order but sat down at the table again with her friends. "Phoebe had a feeling she was connected to them. Or knows who they are."

"There is a face crossed out on the website page with

their photos," Lucy reminded them. "Maybe that's Charlotte's photo."

"Maybe . . . I hope it wasn't Beth Shelton's. That might imply that Knit Kats X-ed her out in real life as well," Maggie told her friends. "But the thought that the Knit Kats are cold-blooded killers chills me to the bone. I don't know why. I don't even know them."

"I know what you mean," Lucy agreed. "They've always seemed so clever and playful. That dark side would be like a horror movie—when all the house pets grow long, gruesome fangs and attack their owners."

"*Eeew*, yes . . . creepy," Suzanne agreed around a mouthful of croissant. "Maybe Charlotte was invited to join the Knit Kats but didn't. That's how she knew the group was looking."

"That could be. Impossible to say at this point. Charlotte did know that the Knit Kats submitted work to the art exhibit. But it was rejected. Phoebe isn't sure how she knew, and Charlotte made her swear not to tell anyone."

"Interesting." Lucy frowned. Maggie thought of it as her "thinking cap" expression. "Isn't that sort of information kept confidential? Though there is a lot of gossip in art departments . . . well, any department at a college," Lucy added.

"Almost as much as in a real-estate office. And that's saying something." Suzanne glanced at Maggie. "Hey, could the Knit Kats have gotten so jealous they wanted to kill Charlotte because her work was chosen and theirs was tossed aside? It seems too extreme, and insane," Suzanne added, answering her own question. "Even for people who run around in the middle of the night, wrapping yarn around public property."

Maggie looked at her. "Hard to say. The way you describe

it, the two seem fairly equal on the obsessive-and-insane scale . . . don't you think, Lucy?"

"I wouldn't rule it out. Maybe there were other more serious issues, and this rejection pushed them over the top. By the way, what happened after Phoebe drank the Kool-Aid? Did they try to bring her into the cat coven?"

"No, thank goodness. After she did their bidding—and got caught on candid security camera—she never heard from them. She even tried to get in touch, but the e-mail address didn't work anymore."

"Really? That's spooky, too." Suzanne was wearing a white cowl-neck sweater but still rubbed her arms for warmth.

Lucy laughed. "It sounds like a bad first date. You think you did everything right. Then the guy never calls you."

Maggie nodded. "Something like that. Which is often a blessing in disguise. Not that you have to worry about that anymore." She glanced back at Lucy, who had taken her punches on the singles scene—or avoided it altogether—until she'd met Matt.

"Yes, it was a blessing Phoebe didn't get a call back," Suzanne agreed. "If the police are badgering her this much for just trying out, imagine how bad it would be if she'd been a dues-paying member."

"I don't even want to think about it," Maggie said quickly. They all heard the shop door open. Lucy had the best view and took the others in with a sweeping glance.

"It's Phoebe," she silently mouthed.

"Hey, Phoebe," Suzanne called out. "We're back here. I brought you a surprise."

"A surprise? Is it good?" Phoebe walked to the back of the shop, carrying a big box. Maggie knew Van Gogh was inside.

The others could probably guess from the scratching sounds and faint meows.

"Why is your cat in there?" Suzanne asked.

"He was at Maggie's. While the police were here," she added reluctantly. "I didn't want him to get scared and run away or anything."

Then have to explain that to Charlotte when she got back, Maggie knew she meant. Maggie hoped Charlotte *did* come back. Pronto. She could answer a lot of questions and help Phoebe out of this jam.

But Maggie was certain now she wouldn't insist that Phoebe return Van Gogh. Not after she'd seen how the cat's mere purring presence had brought Phoebe so much comfort last night. Pets do have an amazing power to care for and nurture human beings, though we get all the credit for taking care of them, Maggie thought.

"Maybe he should stay down here until you see what happened upstairs," Maggie suggested. "In his box, I mean."

Her "no cats in the store" rule remained ironclad. No question.

"Good point." Phoebe put the box down and put her big purse on top to keep the clever creature from opening the flaps.

Maggie could tell she was reluctant to go upstairs. Understandably.

"Want some coffee? There's plenty left."

"No . . . I'm okay. I already had some at your house. I don't want to get too wired." She looked like she was readying herself to face the mess, then suddenly turned to Suzanne. "Where's my surprise?"

"I have it right here . . ." Suzanne handed her the bakery bag. Phoebe quickly opened it and peeked inside. She smiled and sighed with gratitude. "A red velvet cupcake? Suzanne . . . it's beautiful."

Suzanne sat back and smiled with satisfaction. "I thought it might cheer you up a little. You don't have to eat it now," she added, glancing at her friends with an "I told you so" look.

"Right. I'll save it for lunch," Phoebe agreed, carefully closing the bag. She looked up again, taking them all in with a glance, her expression serious. And sheepish, Maggie noticed.

"I don't think I even deserve a cupcake . . . I mean, after the way I lied to all of you last week. Acting like I didn't know a thing about the parking meter covers. I feel like such an idiot. I thought being part of the Knit Kats would be so cool. I should have realized I already have the coolest knitting friends in the entire universe. Why would I ever need new ones?"

Maggie had not expected this heartfelt apology. She could see that the others were taken by surprise as well.

"You don't have to apologize. We understand." Lucy stood beside Phoebe and patted her shoulder. "I can see why the secret society stuff would be tempting . . . and the Knit Kats are real artists, just like you."

Suzanne smiled and carefully patted her lips with a paper napkin. "It's flattering when a new clique asks you to hang out. We know you'd never ditch us."

"Well . . . thanks for being so understanding. I'll make it up to you guys. I promise."

Phoebe set the bag with the cupcake on the table, then sighed. Everyone else sat back, watching her. Maggie knew what they were all thinking. There was nothing left now for Phoebe to say or do but go up to her apartment.

Lucy stood up from her seat. "Want me to go upstairs with you, Phoebe? Come on. Let's go together."

Phoebe glanced at her. "It's going to be pretty bad. I know they took my computer. I mean, why not just pull my little wings off, right? Who knows what else they took . . ."

She looked about to cry. Maggie's heart went out to her.

Suzanne stood up, too. "I'll go up with you. Messes are my life. You guys should see my house on the weekend, when everyone is home for two days straight. It looks like the FBI was searching our TV room for Jimmy Hoffa. Guess who has to clean that up by her little old self?"

"Yeah, it's a small world—unless you have to clean it," Lucy added.

"How true." Maggie stood up, too. "All right, let's go. We may as well face this together."

"Wait . . . where are you all going? I just got here . . ."

Dana had come into the shop, but no one had heard her. They'd all been so focused on Phoebe, Maggie realized.

"Up to Phoebe's apartment. To help her clean. If necessary," Maggie added. It was possible that the police had not made a shambles of the place. Possible, though not likely.

"Oh, I see." Dana shrugged her coat off, set it on a chair with her handbag, then leaned over and gave Phoebe a hug. She left her arm around Phoebe's shoulder.

"Well, are you ready? It's totally up to you," Dana reminded her . . . and her other friends, Maggie realized.

Phoebe seemed to be thinking about it a moment, then nodded. "Let's just do this thing."

"That's the spirit. You know cleaning can be fun . . . when it's done," Suzanne said cheerfully. She fell into step behind Dana and Phoebe as they led the way up to the apartment.

Lucy was next in line, and Maggie brought up the rear. It was possible that a customer might wander in while they were all upstairs, but Maggie didn't care. It was more important right now to be there for Phoebe.

Phoebe entered her apartment and let out a piercing scream.

The line stopped, and Maggie was stuck in the stairwell. She heard Suzanne scream next, and then Lucy said, "What in the world?" in an astonished but revolted tone.

Finally Maggie reached the top of the steps and quickly stared around. It looked as if the tidy, charming place had been turned upside down and vigorously shaken. Then, for good measure, stirred.

What had they been looking for?

What had they found?

Phoebe darted around, picking up random belongings and putting them down again. She was shouting and crying. "Look at my stuff! Look at all my stuff! It's wrecked. It's ruined . . ."

She ran over to a wooden cupboard near the couch. The doors hung ajar, and she pulled them open. The cupboard looked fairly empty, with only a few shoeboxes on the top shelf, marked "buttons," "needles," "thread."

"They took my entire stash! All my yarn . . . stuff I'd been saving for years. It's gone!" She turned to the others, crying harder now. "Why did they do that? I didn't do anything, guys, honest . . ."

Dana caught up with her and held her close, stopping her in her tracks, though she resisted. Suzanne quickly came to stand on Phoebe's other side and rubbed her back in a soothing motion.

"We know, Phoebe. This is totally unfair." Dana spoke softly. "You have a perfect right to be upset and angry . . . but we can fix this. We'll all work together and help you clean up," Dana promised.

"Don't worry, honey. We'll put this place back together in no time. Or we can add a few empty beer bottles and a box of cold pizza, and rent it out to some college guys."

Suzanne was exaggerating, of course. But trying to strike a lighter note.

"The police will return the yarn and the computer and everything they confiscated, eventually," Maggie told her. "In the meantime, there's plenty of yarn right downstairs. And you can use my computer anytime you need it. Just help yourself."

Maggie knew Phoebe would need a computer for schoolwork—that was annoying. And it wasn't just losing the yarn. It was the fact that a knitter's stash was such personal territory. Phoebe just stared back at the empty cabinet like a character in a fairy tale discovering that some evil troll had stolen her treasure chest. Maggie had a shop full of yarn but would have hated it if anyone had stolen her stash, stored safely back at home. She would have hated knowing strangers had pawed through all of her personal belongings.

This whole mess was fixable. But it felt like such a violation. That was the real reason Phoebe was so upset.

Lucy stood in Phoebe's kitchen, gazing at the cupboards, which all hung open, obviously searched. Some of the dishes, bowls, and cups stood on the counter . . . along with boxes of cereal, crackers, and whatever else was stored there, which had been emptied out into the trash. Some of it spilling on the floor.

"I'll start in here." She'd found a big trash bag and snapped it open.

Dana and Phoebe started cleaning up the living room, where pillows had been tossed off of the couch and chair, opened and examined, and every book and knickknack removed from a set of shelves. Suzanne started in Phoebe's bedroom area, which was obscured by a curtain. Maggie could only guess what she'd find back there.

"I'll get the big vacuum cleaner downstairs," Maggie offered. She knew Phoebe got by with a small electric broom. Heavy equipment was needed today.

All the king's horses and all the king's men could not put poor Humpty Dumpty back together. But she and her friends could put Phoebe's apartment back together. Maggie felt sure of it.

Still, the fact that the police had gone through Phoebe's place with a fine-tooth comb was worrisome. It was not a good sign in Maggie's book. Not a good sign at all.

CHAPTER NINE

Many hands make light work—that's what her mother used to say. With so many hands on the job, Phoebe's apartment was back in order faster than Maggie had expected. It had been generous of her friends to give up prime-time morning hours, Maggie had to grant them all that.

Phoebe was very grateful and promised to make everyone dinner as a thank-you. Sometime after the investigation was over, Maggie guessed. When things settled back to normal.

"Did you have any customers yet today?" Phoebe had stayed up in her apartment after the cleanup, but finally came down around noon

A fair question, considering last night's dreadful publicity.

"A few." Maggie kept her gaze on the packets of buttons she'd been sorting. She'd only seen two customers so far. Was that "a few"? Or did the expression mean three or more? When Phoebe didn't reply, she added, "It's still early. Maybe we should work on the window again . . ." Maggie heard steps on the porch and paused. "Wait, there's someone."

They both looked at the shop door. Maggie felt a sudden lump in her throat. She hoped it wasn't the police again. Dear God, please . . . no more of that, she silently prayed.

It was not the police, thank goodness. But the visitor did catch her by surprise. It was Sonya Finch, the art professor who had run the reception at the gallery.

"Hello, Phoebe." Professor Finch strolled in with a smile. "I had to come this way for a lunch date and wanted to see how you're doing. I got so worried when I saw the news last night. Are you all right?"

"Oh, sure . . . I'm okay." Phoebe shrugged. She looked embarrassed. She had two classes at school today, one of them in Professor Finch's studio, but she'd decided to skip both. Understandably, Maggie thought.

"Hello, Professor. Nice of you to stop by," Maggie said.

"No problem. I couldn't believe it. Poor Phoebe . . . Did the police really search your apartment?"

"Yeah, they did. Every inch," Phoebe added.

"It was totally voluntary. Phoebe has nothing to hide," Maggie quickly added.

"I don't understand." Professor Finch tilted her head back. "Why would they bother you? Because you and Charlotte are friends and she's run away? Seems a slim connection."

Phoebe didn't answer for a moment. Maggie wondered what she was going to say. Finally, she shook her head, gazing at the floor.

"No . . . that's not why. They had some video from a security camera on Main Street. They saw me covering the parking meters last Thursday morning."

"Covering the parking meters? Oh . . . right. I saw that on

the news, too. You mean, with the Knitted Kats?" Dr. Finch looked very surprised. Her green eyes grew wide. "Are you a Knitted Kat, Phoebe?"

"No! Absolutely not." Phoebe's tone was emphatic.

"The name is actually *Knit* Kat," Maggie quietly corrected. "And she's not either."

"But I was dumb enough to think I wanted to be. I made some of the cat faces and covered the meters. As sort of an audition to be in the group. But they never got back in touch with me."

"Oh . . . I see . . . I had no idea. No wonder the police were here." Dr. Finch nodded, her lips a tense, thin line.

Oh dear . . . was Phoebe going to be thrown out of school over this? Maggie guessed it was possible.

"Is Phoebe going to be in trouble at Whitaker?" she asked quickly. "She wasn't charged with anything. Only questioned. The police are just bothering her because they have no other leads."

"I understand." Dr. Finch looked over at Phoebe again. "Don't worry. If it comes up at school, I'll take care of it for you. I know that you're a very serious student. "

"You would? That would be great. Thanks, Dr. Finch. I guess I'm a little worried about what Professor Healey is going to say."

"Don't worry about him. Didn't you hear? He's going on a leave of absence soon. To Italy, to research a book. Maybe before the end of the semester," she added.

"Really? I didn't know that." Phoebe sounded surprised and a little disappointed. Maggie knew she would miss her favorite teacher and had planned on working with him on special projects this year. "Will he be gone long?"

"I'm not sure . . . He's set no firm date for his return. I know that. He's aiming for a book contract, and it's publish or perish for our kind," she added quickly.

Phoebe looked even glummer at this news. Maggie felt obliged to pull up the conversational slack.

"I wish knitting-shop owners could get book contracts and do research in Italy. Maybe I could—if I found someone to watch over the business," she added, answering her own complaint.

Dr. Finch smiled. She had a very nice smile, Maggie noticed. Even teeth and two deep dimples. She was a bit overweight. But her smoky eye makeup emphasized her large eyes, and her hairstyle and outfit were very hip and stylish. Maggie thought she was still attractive, and at one time, Sonya Finch had been very pretty.

"Don't feel so bad. Someone has to stay behind and watch over the art department, too. Quite ironic that I'll be acting chairperson soon. It was my husband, Owen, who really wanted that job," she added in a wistful tone. "Funny how life works out. Meanwhile, Professor Healey hasn't been in the hot seat very long. And off he goes . . ."

She shrugged and smiled again—though Maggie sensed a darker feeling beneath that amiable gesture, neither cheerful nor resigned.

Professor Finch suddenly turned to Phoebe. "But I didn't come to dish about department politics. I just wanted to see you, dear, and make sure you were all right. Did the police keep you very long?"

"It felt like forever. But it was only a few hours, I guess."

"A few hours? That's awful . . ." She walked over to the

velvet love seat near the window and sat down. Maggie noticed again that her gait was stiff and she carried herself with a slight limp. "Were they badgering you with questions all that time?"

"Not exactly . . . there's a lot of waiting around. They try to psych you out. Get under your skin," Phoebe tried to explain. "But I had an attorney there . . . and Maggie," she added, glancing at Maggie with a grateful smile.

"At least you had some support. The whole ordeal sounds positively medieval. And they searched your apartment, too?"

"Turned it inside out," Maggie cut in. She hadn't meant to interrupt but couldn't stop herself.

"It was pretty bad. I just finished cleaning up."

"You've been through the mill since Sunday, haven't you? But what were they looking for? Did they say?"

"I'm not sure. We think they're trying to track down the rest of Knit Kats. They think the group could be connected to the murder."

"I see. Did they find any more of them? I heard there are a few."

"I don't know . . . They didn't tell me," Phoebe replied.

"I suppose we'll hear about it on the news if they do," Maggie offered.

"Right . . . very true. But you just said you weren't really a Knit Kat, didn't you?" she asked Phoebe. "You were just trying out or something? Like pledging for a sorority?"

"Something like that. I only had one or two e-mails with them. I never met them face-to-face."

Sonya Finch looked surprised again. "Really? How fascinating. I suppose people can disguise themselves completely these days on the Internet. It's very . . . disconcerting."

"Yes, it is," Maggie cut in. She tried to catch Phoebe's eye. The police had told Phoebe not to discuss the details of the case. But maybe Phoebe was so worried about getting into trouble at school, she'd forgotten about that warning. Or put it aside for a while.

Professor Finch looked dismayed. "So much concealment and deceit. Some people can really take advantage. And has anyone heard from Charlotte? Do the police have any idea where that poor girl has gone? . . . Or if she's even safe?"

"They have a few clues, but they haven't found her yet. They say that they think she's all right." Maggie wasn't sure she could say how investigators knew this. She had actually heard it through Dana. She glanced at Phoebe, hoping she wouldn't give away any more information, either. They didn't need to get into any more trouble with the police.

Dr. Finch was very curious, but Maggie guessed that the entire campus was buzzing about the murder and everyone wanted to know these details. Maggie had a feeling anything Professor Finch learned here would be quickly circulated at Whitaker.

"And how about Beth Shelton's parents? How are they managing? I heard they were in town. Dean Klug visited with them, to offer our consolation," she added in a sympathetic tone.

"What a tragedy. An unthinkable heartbreak," Maggie replied. "I imagine they'll take her remains back to Maine for the funeral. But I don't think the police have released her body yet."

Sonya nodded. "I've heard these things take time. It's only been, what . . . two days since the murder?"

Phoebe nodded, her eyes wide and glassy. Maggie sensed she was eager to get off this topic before she started crying. Maggie was wondering how to change the subject when suddenly Professor Finch did.

"This is a lovely shop. I love looking at all your yarns—all the colors and textures. So pleasing to the eye. I've often noticed this store. But I don't think I've ever been inside," she added.

Maggie didn't think so, either. She would have remembered Sonya Finch. She had a very notable personality.

"Do you knit, Professor?" Maggie was glad to change the subject.

"Call me Sonya, please. No reason to be so formal," she said with another smile. "No . . . not really. I learned as a child but have pretty much forgotten. Coming in here does make me want to try again."

"Phoebe can teach you. Or you can take a class. It's very relaxing . . . a great outlet for creative energy," Maggie added.

"I'm sure it is. But I won't have time for hobbies this semester once I take over Professor Healey's work. Maybe I'll come back in the summer. When school is over."

"We'd love to see you anytime," Maggie said politely.

"Thank you, I'll remember the invitation." Sonya turned to Phoebe. "I'll be happy to see you back in class soon. But not before you're ready. Take your time. Rest a day or two. I post the assignments on the virtual blackboard every week, and if you have any questions, just come see me during office hours."

"Thanks, Professor. But I'm not going to be a total slacker. That's not going to help anything."

Help figure out who killed Beth Shelton or help them find Charlotte, Maggie knew Phoebe meant.

"Good for you." Professor Finch offered an approving nod, then turned to Maggie. "So young and strong. So resilient. That's why I love being around students. Isn't it wonderful?"

"Yes, it is. Makes you more . . . optimistic," Maggie agreed.

Sonya Finch picked up her handbag and gloves and said good-bye. For someone who had a lunch date, she had not seemed in a great hurry, Maggie thought.

Oh well . . . who knows. Some people are not as uptight about being punctual as I am.

Maggie and Phoebe took a moment to remember what they'd been talking about before the interruption, then started to work on the window. Maggie had saved all the cutout hearts and doilies and other arts-and-crafts materials, and set them out on the table. Phoebe got to work with her scissors and fine-point markers, while Maggie assembled baskets of yarns in valentine colors and knitted pieces for display.

"It was thoughtful of Professor Finch to check on you," Maggie said finally.

"Yes, it was. This is the first course I've taken with her. I don't know her very well."

"Really?" Maggie had been under the impression that Phoebe's relationship with Professor Finch was closer than that. "Maybe since she's an administrator in the department, she made a special effort to be in touch."

"Maybe . . . Charlotte knows her much better. She's had her for a few studios. She's the one who told me to take her class this semester."

"Do you like the course? Is she a good teacher?"

"It's hard to tell. The semester just started. She's okay, I guess. It is weird that she might turn out to chair the department. Her husband, Owen Finch, was a teacher there, too, and he really, really wanted to be the chairman. But he was competing with Professor Healey. Healey is more laid-back. He knows how to deal with the dean and all that."

"Good at office politics?" Maggie asked.

"Yeah, that's what I mean. Professor Healey knows how to handle people. Owen Finch was more of an artist. I think he just took up teaching on the side. For steady income. His work is in museums and like all over the place. He's got a zillion pages on Google. He was a good teacher, too . . . but sort of rough around the edges. Kids liked him. But people said he drank a lot. And had a lot of opinions about the way the school was run. Sort of a problem child. Dean Klug likes Healey. So it would have been hard for Finch to win."

"Win how? Is there some sort of election?" Maggie asked curiously.

"Oh yeah. All the other tenured professors in the department vote. I think you get like two or three years a term or something. I don't know who was there before. Someone who retired."

"So obviously Professor Healey was elected, right?"

"Right. But it turns out Owen Finch got really bummed out when he lost. He couldn't paint or anything. Then he crashed his car one night because he'd been drinking. That's how he died."

"Oh dear . . . how awful." Maggie had had a feeling this story was not going to end well, but she hadn't expected it would be this bad. "How awful for his wife. No wonder she feels odd taking over the job he wanted."

"Yeah, weird, right? She was in the car, too. That's why she limps. Her leg got all banged up, and that's the best they could fix it."

"That's very sad. She's constantly reminded. It must be very hard for her. But she seems so . . . even-tempered and pleasant."

Phoebe nodded, focused on the shape she was cutting. "She is pretty easygoing. She's very laid-back in class, and she's not walking around the campus, grinding her teeth and sticking pins in a little voodoo doll shaped like Professor Healey."

"Though if she did, no one would blame her. Is that what you're trying to say?" Maggie glanced at Phoebe, who was now gluing shapes together.

Phoebe shrugged. "Yeah, well . . . it's not Professor Healey's fault Owen Finch got plastered and crashed his car. But some people could see it that way."

"Yes, some people could," Maggie agreed. "His wife, for instance."

Phoebe shrugged without looking up. "That's all I'm trying to say. And Professor Healey is great. But he can rub some people the wrong way. Like now he's going off to Italy to research a book. He never even mentioned that to me, and I was supposed to do an independent-study project with him this semester. He can be sort of intense and get carried away by his ideas sometimes."

"Selfish" and "self-absorbed" would be other terms for that sort of behavior. But Maggie didn't interrupt her.

"It's hard not to feel sorry for Professor Finch," Phoebe added. "She's always like in his shadow."

"So there's a real soap opera going on in the art department. Who told you all this juicy gossip? How do you even know it's true?"

"Charlotte, mostly. But everybody knows the story about the Finches," Phoebe promised.

Charlotte again. The last few days, Maggie sometimes felt she could see her out of the corner of her eye. But every time she turned her head, no matter how quickly, Charlotte would dart away. Long legs taking long strides. Her blond hair streaming out behind her like a flag. She'd flash by for an instant . . . and disappear.

Just like the night of the art show. The last time anyone had seen her.

But Maggie did believe Charlotte Blackburn was alive and well somewhere. She suspected Charlotte was hiding, to protect herself. She just hoped that the police—and the FBI, who were also investigating now—found Charlotte before the faceless menace the girl ran from caught up with her.

Phoebe was not quite ready to return to her classes on Wednesday, or again on Thursday. Maggie didn't blame her. She did come down to work promptly, and they had a quiet day in the shop.

She wasn't sure if the slow business was due to the time of year or the bad publicity. But knitters needed yarn and needles sooner or later. And her shop was pretty much the only game in town. Business would pick up soon. In the meantime, she was determined to make good use of the downtime by finishing the front-window display and straightening out her inventory.

There were still many weeks of winter to go, even if the groundhog did see his shadow tomorrow. But spring inventory—the bright, cheerful colored yarns that recalled a garden in bloom—would soon arrive at the shop and fill the shelves and baskets. Something to look forward to, Maggie thought.

Thursday was knitting-group night, and it was Lucy's turn to host the meeting. Maggie was eager to spend the evening with her friends.

Lucy lived in a neighborhood of Plum Harbor called the Marshes, bordered by the beach and filled with stretches of marshland and tall grass—wide-open space, unsuitable for building, that gave the neighborhood a wild and beachy edge.

Many of the homes were small, basic cottages built as modest summer homes back in the 1940s and 1950s. Winterized and expanded, they now served as perfect starter homes for young families or retirement retreats for empty nesters scaling down. So many had been drastically remodeled or knocked down, the neighborhood was almost losing its character, Maggie thought wistfully.

Everything changes. That's the only thing we can really count on in life, she knew.

She parked her car behind Suzanne's huge SUV, which was almost as large as Lucy's house, and noticed Dana's sleek Volvo there, too, just in front of Phoebe's VW.

Last to arrive. She hoped she hadn't missed anything. Dana had hinted in a text that Jack had passed along more tidbits about the investigation. But she would wait until they were together tonight to tell everyone.

Maggie walked up the short path from the street. The cottage was small, not quite two stories, with a screened-in porch and dormer windows that stuck out from the roofline. Only two bedrooms upstairs, Maggie recalled. But large enough for Lucy and Matt and their two dogs. And there would be room for a nursery, she thought . . . if the two lazy lovebirds ever got around to that.

Lucy is happy. That's the most important thing, Maggie reminded herself. She had long ago sworn off giving friends unsolicited advice. Now she just heard them out and sympathized when necessary.

The wiser course, for sure.

The door was unlocked, and she walked into the living room. Her friends sat in a circle, some on the couch and some in chairs, gathered around the coffee table where Lucy had set out platters of hors d'oeuvres. They were too engrossed in the discussion of a recipe to even notice her arrival. Lucy was explaining a recipe, and Maggie didn't want to interrupt.

"It's really easy. You just mix the artichoke hearts with lots of fattening ingredients—cream and grated cheese and some bread crumbs on top—and bake it a while."

"Absolutely delicious. Total comfort food," Suzanne said around a mouthful of . . . something. Maggie didn't know yet what it was.

"It's smells very good, too." Maggie left her coat on the rack near the front door and walked in.

Everyone turned and greeted her.

"Did I miss anything?"

"Just the artichoke dip. We pretty much inhaled it. I think there are a few bites left." Lucy whisked the dish off the table, rescuing the last crackerful for Maggie.

Maggie took an empty seat on the couch between Phoebe and Dana, though she wasn't ready to take out her knitting. She tasted the baked concoction with a plastic fork. "Mmm. This *is* good," she agreed. "But I was really wondering if I missed any . . . news."

She glanced over at Dana, but Suzanne replied, "Dirt about the investigation, you mean? We didn't start dishing yet."

"I was waiting until you got here. But I'm dying to start," Dana admitted. She took a breath and sat up taller in her chair. A big fan of yoga, she sat with admirable posture—reminding Maggie she should be more mindful, and less of a slouch.

Before Dana could begin, Phoebe said, "Did they find out anything else about Charlotte? Have they found any trail?"

"She's been smart about covering her tracks. She hasn't used a credit card since the train ticket in New Jersey. And there's been no activity on her phone, either. She may have picked up some cheap, pay-as-you-go phone somewhere. Or is doing without one. But the police are pretty sure she switched trains in Philadelphia and is headed toward Pittsburgh."

"Pittsburgh?" Suzanne acted as if Dana had said Charlotte was headed toward the moon. "How do they know that?"

"They spotted her face on a security-camera video with some high-tech face-detection program. The FBI did," Dana clarified. "She cut her hair on the first train and even dyed it brown somehow. But they saw her buy another ticket at a machine and board a train headed west. That machine took cash," she added.

"She must have a suitcase full of money with her if she's been able to go on the run without using credit cards. I can't even walk down the block without whipping out some plastic." Suzanne laughed.

"You should carry a little cash, Suzanne. You might need it someday for an emergency," Maggie advised.

"I try . . . but my kids walk by my wallet and suck the bills out like little Dirt Devils. It's scary."

"She might be using someone else's credit cards," Lucy said. "Maybe she's not traveling alone?"

"That's possible. But she disappeared so abruptly. She didn't even go back to her apartment to get clothes," Dana reminded them. "She hasn't used any cash machines, either. But when the police opened her locker at school, they found a backpack full of cash. Almost fifty thousand dollars. I think the exact sum is forty-nine thousand? They're speculating there was more, but she took some out before she left town."

"I know Charlotte," Phoebe insisted. "I know it looks bad, having all that money in her locker. But that still doesn't mean she had anything to do with the murder. But that money probably does have to do with why she's scared and ran away," Phoebe added. "And if she took any of it . . . well, maybe she needed a little to get out of town."

"That could be, Phoebe." Dana's tone was comforting. They could all see Phoebe striving to defend her friend.

"I say way to go, Charlotte." Suzanne smiled and blinked. "Wonder where that little rainy-day fund came from?"

"She had a part-time job for a law firm in Boston," Phoebe cut in. "The pay was good. But no way could she have saved that much."

Maggie laughed. "If the salary is that good, I might take up the work myself. What did she do there?"

"Proofreading. She reviewed legal documents and worked really odd hours. She didn't have to go into the office that much. Only once in a while. They e-mailed most of the jobs, and she did them at her apartment and sent them back."

"What was the name of the law firm? Do you remember?" Lucy asked.

Phoebe thought for a moment. "I'm not sure I do . . . It was like three names together, and there was something funny about it . . ."

Dana looked up with a puzzled face. She was almost done with her bear, Maggie noticed. It had come out very well, in a rich pink yarn. "Funny? How?"

"It was the combination . . . we used to joke about it. Oh, right. It was like Garland, Dylan . . . and somebody. I can't remember. But one night Charlotte and I were saying, imagine if Bob Dylan and Judy Garland did one of those dumb duet albums? And he was like singing 'Somewhere Over the Rainbow' in that creaky, nasal voice?" Phoebe took a breath, then started to do her Bob Dylan imitation. "Some-where . . . oh-vah the rain-bow . . ."

Maggie sat up, taking deep offense. "Wait a second, young lady. As practically a first-generation Dylan fan, I object to you disrespecting one of my most revered icons."

Dana and Lucy were laughing—but trying hard not to insult her, too, Maggie noticed.

Suzanne, however, looked very serious. "Hey, kid, don't you

dare mock Judy . . . or that song. I love that movie. I watch it alone at night whenever I'm stressed out."

"Oh, well . . . that explains a lot." Dana rolled her eyes. Maggie grinned, too. Suzanne did have a very sunny Dorothy-in-Oz attitude most of the time, come to think about it. Had she brainwashed herself? Maggie took a breath, quelling her mirth.

"Dissing Judy aside, Charlotte's job sounds pretty boring to me," Suzanne said decidedly. "I'd probably fall asleep on the job. And my spelling is atrocious. I don't even know how to spell 'atrocious' . . . come to think of it."

Phoebe had taken out her knitting. She was working on a Valentine's Day project, a red cup warmer with a white heart in the middle. "She said it was boring, but it paid the bills. Charlotte doesn't have much family. Her parents divorced when she was really young, and her mother died when she was in high school. Her father lives out in Arizona somewhere, with a new wife and kids, and she hardly ever sees him. I think she said she has a grandma somewhere. But it's not exactly a Hallmark card group, if you know what I mean."

Maggie did. And was reminded again that Charlotte's background was a lot like Phoebe's. That must have been another reason the young women were drawn to each other. And part of the reason Phoebe remained so loyal to her?

"I'd been wondering about that," Dana said. "I mean, no one's mentioned any parents or family members coming to Plum Harbor to talk to the police. The girl has been missing several days now. Her father must have been contacted. He must be dealing with investigators by phone."

"Probably. Maybe they've told him there's nothing he can

really do here," Maggie said. Though if it had been her child, she would have come anyway. "Unless Charlotte's been in touch with him and he knows that she's safe," she added.

Dana nodded. "That could be. I never thought of it."

"But let's get back to the murder," Lucy said suddenly. "Forgetting about the money a minute, we had that theory that the Knit Kats were jealous because Charlotte's work was featured in the art show while theirs was rejected. But that's such a lame motive. Even for a crazy knitting group. There must have been something else, some serious disagreement between all of them. Or maybe Charlotte knew some damaging information about the Knit Kats and they wanted to keep her quiet . . ."

"But ended up silencing poor Beth instead," Suzanne finished for her.

"Yes, poor Beth. Jack heard that her body was released today. Her parents took her back to Maine for the funeral. I feel so bad for them," Dana added.

"It's a parent's worst nightmare, no question," Maggie replied quietly. "I know that we don't know her or the family, but perhaps we should send flowers or something?"

She wasn't sure how this idea would go over with her friends. She didn't want to seem intrusive to the Shelton family. But she did want to reach out to them in some way.

"That's a good idea, Maggie. I was going to send something myself." Phoebe glanced at her friends. "I could find out the information and send flowers from all of us."

Everyone nodded and thanked her for taking care of it. "Just let us know our share, and we'll all chip in," Lucy said finally, mindful of Phoebe's tight student budget.

Phoebe agreed. Maggie was glad it was settled. If only they could figure out the rest of this puzzle so easily.

"So, getting back to figuring out why poor Beth lost her life," Lucy continued, "we were saying that perhaps Charlotte knew something damaging about the Knit Kats and they wanted to silence her but killed Beth instead."

"Something that ties in with that knapsack of money," Suzanne added. "Fifty grand can buy a lot of cat chow."

Phoebe shook her head. "Do you really think they're that awful? You guys make those Knit Kats sound so scary . . . like a witches' coven."

"A sinister sisterhood?" Maggie asked.

"Good one, Mag. I like it." Suzanne looked up and nodded.

"'Mocking the meters' is still my favorite," Lucy noted. "But 'sinister sisterhood' is right up there."

Maggie laughed. "Thank you, ladies. I'll save it for my next interview. Clever turns of phrase aside, I agree with Suzanne. Maybe that's how the money ties in."

Suzanne had started a pair of Eleanor Roosevelt mittens, Maggie noticed, and was checking the stitching. "Absolutely. We can't just ignore all that loot, girls."

"Right, there must be some connection between Charlotte's stash of cash and this mess. It's just so hard to connect the dots . . . and it's time for dinner," Lucy said as she headed back to the kitchen.

Lucy had set up a buffet on the countertop in her kitchen. The cottage didn't have a dining room, and the kitchen was too small to fit everyone around the table. She'd made an interesting dish, mixing oven-roasted zucchini and grape tomatoes with grilled shrimp, pasta, and a touch of pesto—though she had thoughtfully set it out separately to accommodate her friends who might be dieting or gluten-free and skipping the pasta.

Maggie's nutrition priorities fell in neither category. She had skipped lunch and helped herself to a generous portion.

"Mmm . . . this is yummy." Suzanne was the first to praise the recipe. "You're a good cook, Lucy. I hope Matt appreciates that," she added with a sly glance.

"He does . . . don't worry. Though we've both put on a few pounds since we started living together."

"That's what happened to me and Kevin. Then once we got engaged and set the date, I had to practically kill myself to look good at the wedding." Suzanne laughed, remembering—until Dana gave her a look and she suddenly seemed self-conscious. A rare moment, but it did happen, Maggie noted.

"You're comfortable together. That's good," Dana said simply.

Maggie knew she and her friends were all thinking the same thing: Lucy and Matt had been living together for almost a year and dating for even longer than that. Wasn't it time for the relationship to move on to the next level?

"I'm not saying you and Matt have to get engaged, Lucy," Suzanne clarified. "I was just telling a story. I guess with Valentine's Day coming, you're feeling the pressure, right?"

Now Suzanne was trying to get all sympathetic and therapeutic. Maggie practically groaned aloud. The first faux pas was bad enough.

Lucy looked up from her dish, seeming surprised. "Um . . . no."

"Good. That's very good," Dana said quickly, beating

Suzanne to the punch. "These holidays are so commercialized. They make everyone think they have to feel a certain way on some certain day. And it just isn't so."

"Dana's right. You guys seem totally happy. You've both been down this road before, too. Just go at your own pace." Suzanne waved her hand in a sort of blessing. She tasted another forkful, then said, "But don't drag it out too long. That's my advice. I've seen couples just wait soooo long, it's not fun and romantic anymore. Everything has cooled off, like a piece of leftover toast. All the butter congealed and everything. Yuck." She shivered and shook her head. "You should definitely get married before the cold-toast stage sets in. Then he can't wriggle out of it so easily . . ."

"Suzanne! What are you talking about?" Dana put her dish down on the coffee table and dabbed her mouth with a napkin.

"I think you've given Lucy enough relationship advice for one night," Maggie cut in. She glanced at Lucy. Luckily, she was laughing.

"That's all right, Suzanne. I know you only say such bizarre things because you care," Lucy said kindly.

Suzanne shrugged and gazed around at the circle of friends. "What's the matter? What did I say?" she insisted. "I think she has to give Dr. Dolittle a little push in the right direction, that's all. Hey, nothing says 'Be My Valentine' like a diamond solitaire. Believe me."

Maggie knew Lucy didn't like diamonds. She thought they were cold. She preferred colored stones like rubies or sapphires, but she didn't bother to correct Suzanne—though Maggie did hope Matt knew his beloved's jewelry preferences by now. Perhaps he would secretly consult her good friends when the time came?

Now you're getting as bad as Suzanne. And Lucy's face was beet-red, Maggie noticed. Not from cooking, either.

"Speaking of Valentine's Day . . . has anyone finished their projects?" Maggie gazed around at the group, hoping to change the subject.

"I'm almost done with a bear. I just have to make her arms . . . and stuff her up." Dana held up the knitting and arranged it so everyone could get an idea. Even without the filling, the toy was adorable and had come out very well, Maggie thought. "I have some white voile ribbon. I'm going to give her a big bow and sew on some eyes and a nose. In white yarn, or a different shade of pink. Though the pattern shows black."

"I think you should stitch a little heart on her chest, to make her a real Valentine's bear," Phoebe suggested.

"Good idea. That will be perfect." Dana slipped on her glasses. "This was a quickie. I might make another. But I'm making ear warmers for Jack first. He can wear them when he plays golf in the winter . . ." Dana's phone sounded with a musical ringtone. She dug into her purse and checked the number.

"Speaking of my husband's ears, they must have been ringing," she murmured just before she pressed the phone to her own ear. "Hi, honey . . . what's up?" she greeted him cheerfully.

Dana's expression suddenly flipped from warm and relaxed to surprised and excited. Maggie wondered what news had penetrated her typically unshakable calm.

"Really? . . . Wow . . . We'll put it on right now. Talk to you later."

She looked over at her friends, her blue eyes wide as saucers as she put her phone down. "The police have taken Sonya Finch in for questioning. It's on the news right now. They think she's connected to the Knit Kats."

"Sonya Finch is a Knit Kat? I knew it!" Suzanne dropped her knitting and tossed her hands in the air.

"The thought crossed my mind . . . but I found just as many reasons to dismiss it," Maggie admitted.

Lucy led the way to the family room and grabbed the remote. "Is it channel 25?"

"*News Alive 25!*" Dana said, finishing the jingle. "Maybe we'll even get to see Chelsea Porter again."

"Won't that be a treat," Maggie said drily.

She and Phoebe straggled behind a bit. Maggie quietly considered the update for a moment.

"For some strange reason, I'm not that surprised. Though when she came to the shop, Professor Finch claimed she barely knows how to knit," Maggie told her friends.

Phoebe, however, was definitely surprised. "She acted as if she didn't know anything about the Knit Kats. As if she didn't even know their name. And she asked me like a million questions."

"I noticed that, too. She was fishing for information, obviously. Trying to figure out what you'd told the police and if she was going to be picked up next," Maggie said succinctly.

"Yeah . . . that was the only reason she stopped by, to snoop," Phoebe added sharply. "What a big phony."

"If it's any consolation, Phoebe, I went for the bait, too," Maggie told her honestly. "Looks like there's more bad publicity for Whitaker College and the art department. Unfortunately."

The television was on by the time Maggie and Phoebe reached the family room, which was just off the kitchen. Maggie saw Chelsea Porter on the screen, front and center, and in the background, the big gray building at Whitaker College where they had visited the art exhibit . . . and chased Charlotte and Quentin through the maze of studios.

"*. . . a possible break in the murder investigation of college student Beth Shelton. Police have begun searching the office and home of Professor Sonya Finch, a teacher here at Whitaker College. As seen in this video from earlier this evening, Professor Finch was escorted from her campus office by homicide detectives presiding over the case.*"

The TV showed a distant shot of Sonya Finch, with a big hood pulled up over her white hair and most of her pretty face covered by a scarf. She left the art department building beside Detective Reyes and was helped into the back of a dark sedan by uniformed police officers.

"*College officials were taken by surprise. We interviewed art department chairman Professor Alex Healey, who gave a statement to the media.*"

Professor Healey suddenly appeared, a microphone thrust into his bearded face. He stood alone in the art gallery, where one of Charlotte's pieces could be seen in the background. He looked nervous and tense, his face shining with sweat. Maggie noticed he wore the same tweed sports jacket he'd had on at the art exhibit opening, but this time it covered a plain cotton T-shirt. As if he'd been caught by surprise without his dress shirt and tie.

"*We are shocked and saddened by the recent events off campus, the senseless murder of Beth Shelton,*" he said sincerely.

"Whitaker College is fully cooperating with the investigation. Professor Finch is cooperating as well, and hopes to help the police in any way that she can. We support her totally, and do not believe she has any connection to this heinous crime."

Chelsea Porter returned to the screen. *"While Professor Finch is not charged with any crime, she has been deemed a person of interest in the case. Sources close to the investigation tell us that she is primarily being questioned in regard to her connection with the Knit Kats, an underground graffiti knitting group that has recently made its presence known in this area and may be involved in some way with this crime."*

Phoebe made a glum face. Maggie could tell she still felt annoyed at being "played" by the professor the other day. "Think of it this way, Phoebe. She was fishing, but you didn't give her anything useful."

Phoebe sighed. "I hope not."

". . . Police are releasing very little information due to the sensitive nature of this case. But you can see they are definitely gathering more evidence and clues . . ." Chelsea stepped aside so that the cameraman could get a good shot of police officers marching in and out of the building, like a line of worker ants, Maggie thought.

Practically the same footage had been shown the night police searched Phoebe's apartment. She hoped this time their efforts would yield solid information.

The news continued with other stories, and Lucy waved the remote and shut off the TV. "That is big news. I hope this lets you off the hook, Phoebe. It sounds like Sonya might be a real Knit Kat. Not just auditioning."

"Maybe even the top Kat. The police will be much happier

with the real thing," Suzanne agreed. "I wonder how they caught up with her. Maybe with more security video?"

"Jack heard there was more. But it was taking a long time to review. She must have been well disguised. She's done it before and never gotten caught. But maybe her limp gave her away?" Dana added.

"That could very well be. The police may have questioned her early on and then someone recognized her on the video— her body type and uneven gait," Maggie suggested.

"So if Sonya's a Knit Kat, who do you think are the other two?" Dana asked.

"Good question," Lucy replied. "I have an even better one. If Sonya was on the selection committee for that exhibit, why couldn't she just pick the Knit Kats' work for the show?"

"It wasn't just up to her. I think Charlotte said Professor Healey was the one who nixed the Knit Kats' entries," Phoebe recalled. "He said he didn't believe in anonymous group projects. And they weren't 'real' artists. Just playing around, and giving fiber art a bad name. Making it seem frivolous and not worthy of serious consideration."

Suzanne had started on her knitting again. "Whoa . . . He takes this stuff very seriously, doesn't he?"

"He's a serious guy," Phoebe added. "He's mainly a sculptor but does some work with fiber. He puts together these macho-looking things, not really knitting, more like weavings or something. With different kinds of ropes and knots and bolts and stuff hanging down."

"Sounds like macramé on steroids," Suzanne replied without looking up. "Remember all those plant holders and wall hangings people used to decorate with?"

"I still have a few of those," Maggie admitted. "His version sounds interesting." She didn't like to dismiss anyone's artwork without seeing it firsthand.

Lucy had disappeared briefly but now returned with a tray of coffee cups, a pot of coffee, and a plate of cookies that looked homemade.

She set the confections on the low wooden table by the TV and started filling mugs with coffee. "So without realizing it, Professor Healey was rejecting and insulting Professor Finch's work. But she couldn't complain about it, or she'd reveal her extracurricular activities. Interesting."

"It is interesting," Maggie agreed. "Makes you wonder why the Knit Kats didn't try to get back at Healey. He was the one who had dismissed and belittled them. Not Charlotte."

Suzanne leaned forward and grabbed a mug of coffee. "I'll tell you what doesn't make sense to me. If I was a Knit Kat and wanted to get rid of someone, why would I give myself away and throw my whole gang under the bus? Wrap the body in yarn graffiti? Duh . . . that's not exactly covering your tracks," she stated flatly.

Lucy sat down to join them again. She had her knitting, too, and was working on a red scarf. "Maybe they're just so full of themselves, they did it as sort of an in-your-face statement? Maybe they think they're so clever and anonymous, no one would find them?"

"Not in this day and age. No one is anonymous for very long. Case in point, the police have already tracked down one member and will likely figure out the others soon," Dana reminded her.

"And they found the dumbbell who tried out for the

vacancy," Phoebe reminded them. "I agree with Suzanne. I don't think the Knit Kats killed Beth. Even mistaking her for Charlotte. That just doesn't make sense . . . It had to be someone trying to frame them."

"Copycats . . . No pun intended," Lucy added quickly, glancing at Maggie.

"Yeah, copycats. Exactly," Phoebe agreed. "Someone who had a problem with the Knit Kats . . . and with Charlotte. That's who the police should be looking for."

Lucy reached out and passed the plate of cookies around. Maggie was full from the delicious dinner but took a small one. Home-baked chocolate chip cookies were her favorite, and Lucy's were first-rate.

"How about someone who has a problem with Sonya Finch?" Lucy added as she walked by. "She's the one spending the evening with Detectives Reyes and Mossbacher right now. Maybe someone is trying to frame her?"

"Very possible," Dana agreed. "It will be interesting to hear what she tells the detectives." She brushed a few crumbs from her fingers. "So far, it sounds like the Whitaker College art department has more passion and pathos than the season finale of *Real Housewives*."

"Oh please . . . those women are so plastic. Their personalities and their body parts . . . I just can't watch it anymore." Suzanne crinkled her nose in distaste.

"Did you *ever* really watch it?" Maggie asked in amazement.

Suzanne looked up from her knitting, her face as rosy as her Valentine's Day project. Everyone waited for her answer.

"I refuse to answer on the grounds it will definitely make

me the butt of too many jokes around here. Don't I get a phone call?"

Maggie laughed, but also wondered if Sonya Finch was delivering the same line to her interrogators.

But the news had reported that she was cooperating with police, and she did seem the talkative type. Maggie knew for a fact that Detective Reyes could be a very attentive listener.

CHAPTER TEN

Phoebe dreaded returning to her classes on Friday. But she dragged herself out of bed, got dressed, filled her Hello Kitty travel mug with coffee, and headed out.

Just like she'd told Maggie and Professor Finch, she didn't see how hiding in her apartment was going to help anything. She had meant that, too. Though saying it had been a heck of a lot easier than actually doing it.

As she drove toward school, she knew she couldn't quite deal with classes yet, seeing her teachers and other students, who would all ask a zillion questions. She decided to compromise with herself by just picking up her assignments and maybe hitting the library for a while.

She'd already fallen behind and had a lot of work to make up. Especially in Professor Finch's studio course. Even if Finch didn't show up—which was highly likely—there would be a substitute.

Phoebe knew she couldn't handle setting up her easel in her usual place and seeing a big blank spot next to her, where

Charlotte always set up, too. Or, worse yet, seeing some insensitive clod move in. As if Charlotte didn't even exist anymore.

You can cut that class. Finch probably won't even be there. For one thing, she'll be too embarrassed to show her face on campus so soon after being dragged away by the police. For another, she might even still be at the station . . . in a jail cell.

That thought was surprising. And possible.

Though it was more likely that the detectives had gone through the same routine they'd used with her, Phoebe thought. Questions for hours, police picking apart her house and office but finally letting her go because they didn't have enough evidence yet to do more.

Phoebe doubted Professor Finch had been behind the dirty deed. She wasn't sure why, she just did. Though she didn't trust her any farther than she could throw her. Which was . . . not at all, come to think of it. That expression was so dumb and meaningless, Phoebe wasn't even sure why it had popped into her brain. Maggie's antique way of talking was rubbing off on her . . . not good.

Had people ever walked around picking each other up and heaving them into the air? Was it some sort of bizarre tradition or ritual somewhere? She made a mental sticky to ask her anthropology professor sometime.

The gated entrance of the Whitaker campus came into view. Phoebe turned in and followed the campus road back to the Stimson Art Center. She parked in the lot and grabbed her knapsack, then headed toward the building.

She'd arrived between classes, and the lot and quad were quiet, nearly empty. Perfect timing. Everyone was in class.

She slipped into the building and headed for her locker, just outside the ceramics studio, which was empty, she noticed.

And so was her locker, she realized, as she yanked open the door, which was missing its lock.

She stood there, staring into the empty black space. Then double-checked the number. Even the art postcards and interesting pictures she'd cut from magazines and pasted on the inside of the door were gone. All she saw in their place were wads of old tape.

Where the heck was her stuff? Her big black sketchbooks and pastels, paint box . . . brushes, pencils . . .

The police. They'd been here. They'd gone into Charlotte's locker, too, Dana had told them all last night. The police had found a pile of money in there . . . but what did they want with her stupid art supplies? That pile of stuff had cost her a small fortune . . . money she didn't have right now to replace it.

Phoebe kicked the door closed in frustration. Detective Reyes had never shown her a warrant for this. Or if she had, Phoebe didn't remember. But maybe the college had given permission. It was on their property. And Professor Healey had kept repeating how the college was *cooperating*. He'd repeated the word more times than an episode of *Sesame Street*.

Well, they must have cooperated about giving all my stuff away. Phoebe felt so mad she was shaking. She thought about calling Maggie or Lucy but decided to march into the art department office first and ask Professor Healey about this, before she took the edge off her explosion by venting to her friends.

How dare the police just . . . just grab all her stuff. She had a ton of good artwork in there . . . assignments and everything.

When would she ever get it back? Try *never* . . . It wasn't right. Somebody should have at least called her and let her know what was going on.

Phoebe turned the corner in the long corridor and saw the office doors of art department professors and the department's main office across the hallway.

The main office was empty. The secretary's desk looked neat and bare, as if no one had been there all morning. But out in the hallway again, she heard Professor Healey's voice behind the closed door of his office, talking to someone, probably a student.

She decided to wait and snag him when the door opened. He was a pain about seeing students if they had not made an appointment. But this was an emergency. Maybe he could help her get her stuff back.

Just thinking about her empty locker made her upset all over again. The burst of energy she'd felt moments ago suddenly drained away. Phoebe slid down the cool wall and sat on the linoleum, her knees hugged up to her chest.

She suddenly heard another voice in the office, a woman's voice. It sounded like Professor Finch. She sure had a lot of guts to show up here today.

But it didn't sound as if Finch was getting any points for good attendance. More like Professor Healey was firing her. Whoops . . . that is a bad hair day.

"How many ways do I have to say it? What part of the word 'resign' don't you understand?" Professor Healey's voice grew even louder.

"You can't do this, Healey. I have tenure. I'll go to Dean Klug . . . I know people on the board of trustees . . . and the union."

"Klug knows all about it. He's the one who insisted. Listen, Sonya," he said in a milder tone, "we go way back. I know how it is. I tried to fight for you . . . but there are grounds here. Even you can't deny that."

"Ha! The hell you did. You're only interested in saving your own neck, Healey. I don't believe a word of that."

"All right. Gloves off. Did you really think you could weather this . . . this crap storm you've brought on? We simply can't afford this publicity. Especially the art department. We're hanging on by a *thread* . . . A student murdered off campus, another one on the run, wanted by the FBI . . ."

"But how can you blame me? It's not my fault at all . . . There's not a shred of evidence against me. If there was, do you think I'd be standing here? I'd be stuck in a jail cell somewhere."

"That's just what I mean. This isn't over, Sonya. Who knows what will happen next? Do we have to turn on the TV and see you escorted to a police car every night of the week?"

"Ha! Very amusing. They'll be coming for you next," she warned him. "Ever think of that?"

Phoebe couldn't hear Professor Healey's reply. Professor Finch's loud, brassy laugh, which Phoebe had always liked, drowned him out. This morning Professor Finch sounded like a cackling witch. It gave Phoebe chills.

"This all started with your little pet, Charlotte. Not me," she goaded him. "I know all about the two of you. I told the police, too. Believe me, I gave them an earful."

"Told them what? That I'm her adviser? Her mentor? I'd never in my life get involved with a student. And risk my entire career and credibility?"

"Save it, Alex. That line might placate your wife, but it

doesn't wash with me. I know what goes on in that studio of yours. And if your artwork is any indication of your prowess as a lover, I pity that girl even more." She laughed again, but this time Phoebe could hear his comeback.

"You are insane. Certifiably. Is this your only defense for your outrageous behavior? Do you think pointing a figure at me is really going to get you out of this mess?"

"The truth will out, Healey. I'm not worried. What about your own behavior? Of course my work wasn't good enough for this two-bit gallery. You knew it would eclipse your little princess. But she used you, didn't she? . . . Then dumped you."

"You're mad. I'm surprised the police didn't bring you straight to a mental hospital. Charlotte was . . . is . . . a very talented artist. Yes, she's young and very . . . attractive. But any attention and support from this department was well deserved."

"Well deserved? Ha! The fix was in, my friend. Anyone could see that. Hey, it didn't matter to me if you took the Knit Kats work or not. I was just curious to see if you'd show a little spunk. A little manhood. If you'd color out of the lines for once in your pathetic life."

"How dare *you* call me pathetic. How about hiding behind a mask and a comic-book identity? *That's* pathetic. Your dress-up games have cost us plenty. Not just this department . . . the entire college. A tenured professor, in line to be the chair, spends her nights sneaking around in a cat costume. Vandalizing public property . . ."

"The Knit Kats make a statement. We open minds. Real art takes courage. Real art is radical, Healey. It challenges the status quo. But you wouldn't know anything about that."

"That's quite enough. You have no idea of what I know or—"

"Did you know that your sweet little Charlotte was a Knit Kat? Dressed in costume, a mask, and devised her own—what did you call it?—comic-book identity?"

Phoebe sucked in a sharp breath. Charlotte had been a Knit Kat? Why didn't she just tell me? She knew I thought it was cool. At the time.

Professor Healey's voice shouted back, drowning out her rambling thoughts. "That's a lie! Why would she do a stupid thing like that? You're just saying that to—"

Professor Finch's braying laugh made it hard to hear him again. "Oh, to see your face . . . priceless. Yes, I know it's hard to hear someone so dear has deceived you. It's a blow. Cuts like a hot blade, right to the heart," she added, her voice dripping fake sympathy.

"You're vile . . . a vile, wicked woman. I hope the police put you behind bars for—"

Healey was saying more, but Finch shouted over him. "And you are a petty, pompous, soulless slug, Healey. With an epic ego and zero imagination. A very bad combination. My husband had more talent and artistic spirit in his little toe than you do in your entire—"

"Are you quite done?" he shouted. "Or do I need to have you dragged out of here kicking and screaming? You'd love that, wouldn't you? More drama and attention. Providing another fine endorsement of Whitaker on the evening news!"

It was suddenly quiet. Phoebe thought she could hear someone breathing heavily, exhausted from the emotional explosion, then realized the sound might have been her own breath. Her heart was pounding, and her legs were weak as water. She suddenly noticed she'd come to her feet, her back plastered flat to the wall.

One or both of them were going to come out of the office any second now, and she didn't want them to know she'd been sitting here and had heard every word of their argument.

Phoebe grabbed her big bag and slipped lightly down the hallway, then turned at the next corridor. She quickly ran to the metal door at the end of the hallway and opened it.

She suddenly found herself in the gallery. Sun streamed through the long, tall windows that covered one wall, the pure winter light bouncing off the white walls, ceiling, and floor.

She took a few deep breaths to calm her nerves. Was security really going to drag Professor Finch out of her office and off the campus? Phoebe wasn't sure why, but she felt sorry for Professor Finch. But Healey had been right. There was something pathetic about a middle-aged woman who ran around in a costume with this make-believe Knit Kat identity.

The gallery was empty, and she wandered a moment, looking at the artwork, then found herself in Charlotte's section. Her work was so good, Phoebe felt a twang of envy, but pride, too.

The last few days she'd had to wonder if she really knew Charlotte as well as she thought she did. Charlotte had some heavy stuff going on that she'd never talked about. Why else would she run away or have a big stash of money in her locker?

Was there some clue in Charlotte's artwork about this whole stupid mess? Some sign of where she'd gone? Phoebe studied each piece carefully, looking for a message. Maybe something Charlotte didn't even realize she'd revealed?

She was standing in front of the sculpture called *Date Night*, gazing at the gag around the mannequin's mouth, when she heard quick light footsteps coming closer. She turned to see Professor Healey's wife, Gena, walking through the gallery.

It took a minute to recognize her. She looked like another student from a distance. The outfit helped—a short down jacket, jeans, tall brown boots, and a pale peach-colored scarf slung around her neck, a delicate, knitted-lace pattern that caught Phoebe's eye. She was pulling it off, even the trendy accessories. She was younger than Professor Healey. That helped.

Phoebe had heard she'd been his grad assistant or something and they'd had this wild thing. And he left his first wife for her. Gena had also taught in the department. But now that they had kids, two little boys, she was staying home to do the Mom routine for a while.

She seemed really focused and hardly noticed Phoebe as she strode past. Phoebe wasn't sure whether or not to bother her, then just blurted out a greeting.

"Hey, Mrs. Healey."

Gena turned toward her, looking surprised, then smiled politely. "Oh, hello . . . It's Phoebe, right?"

She looked eager to get the name right. She probably met so many of her husband's students, it was hard to keep them all straight.

"Yeah . . . that's right. We met at the opening. Hard to believe it wasn't even a week ago."

"Yes, I know." Her expression turned serious again. She shook her head regretfully, pushing back her glossy hair with her hand. "It's so awful about that poor girl who was killed.

And about Charlotte Blackburn . . . I hope the police find her soon, and she's all right."

"I do, too," Phoebe said quietly.

"It's caused quite a commotion here. Professor Healey has his hands full," she confided.

"Oh, I bet." Phoebe nodded again, thinking about the wild argument she'd just overheard.

Then suddenly she wondered if Mrs. Healey had seen her on TV, too, the night the police had come to search her apartment. If she had, she was polite enough not to say.

"Have you seen Professor Healey? He won't pick up his phone. I was just heading for his office."

Phoebe wasn't sure what to say. She didn't want to lie . . . but didn't want anyone to know she'd been outside his office a few minutes ago, eavesdropping.

"I think he's around," she said vaguely. "I don't think he's teaching a class right now."

"Thanks." Gena smiled briefly. "I'll run and catch him. He's a fast-moving target these days," she joked. "Nice to see you again."

"Same here." Phoebe turned to watch her go. She moved with a fast, swinging gait. She looked very fit, as if she worked out a lot. The opposite of her husband, who was getting that middle-aged doughy look, Phoebe thought. Though some of the girls she knew thought he was hot.

She liked guys her own age. She didn't have a Daddy thing.

She walked toward the front entrance of the gallery and out to the campus. The campus seemed quiet, the sun slipping in and out from behind puffy clouds. It seemed colder out now, and Phoebe flipped up the collar of her coat.

No sign of Professor Finch, or any security cars outside the building. No TV crews, either. She sort of doubted that Professor Healey had gotten his way. For all his bluster.

Professor Finch was one tough bird. No doubt about it. Phoebe had no idea if she was involved in Beth's murder or not. She was swaying mostly toward a vote of "not involved" right now. Even though Professor Finch was a Knit Kat.

But she and Charlotte must have been closer than either of them had ever let on—if Charlotte had really been a Knit Kat. Had Professor Finch just said that to get under Healey's skin? She definitely knew how to push his buttons.

Something deep in Phoebe's gut told her it was true. She wasn't sure how she knew, she just did. Charlotte had been a Knit Kat and had dropped out of the group. Maybe it was her picture that had been X-ed out on the website.

She felt shocked and hurt. Maybe Professor Healey felt that way a little, too. Charlotte was sort of his pet. But she still didn't feel that angry at her friend. If Charlotte was going to so much trouble now to hide, she must have a very good reason and, like Maggie said, maybe telling all this stuff would have been really stupid-dangerous for her. Maybe even for me, Phoebe realized.

Nah, she wasn't mad at Charlotte. She just wanted to know where she'd gone . . . and if she was safe.

As she walked across the parking lot toward her car, she heard someone shouting her name.

"Phoebe! Hey . . . wait up . . ."

She looked across the lot and saw Quentin Gibbs. He wasn't on his motorcycle, just on foot, and he began running toward her.

Phoebe froze for a moment, then made a dash for her car. When Quentin realized she was trying to get away, he put on the speed and came toward her even faster.

"Hey . . . give me a break, man . . . I just want to flipping talk to you . . ."

He shouted a few expletives that did not persuade Phoebe to stay and chat with him. In fact, his angry shouts only made her more frightened, and her hands shook as she clicked open her car door and jumped in.

She immediately hit the lock button and started the engine. Her car was old and finicky and sometimes didn't turn over at the first try. Especially in cold weather. She jiggled the key and tried again. Quentin got nearer, his angry red face shouting at her, barely muffled by her car windows.

He waved his fists in the air, his leather jacket flapping like big dark wings. He had reached the car and banged his fist on the front hood.

"Hey! I'm *talking* to you! Don't you blow me off like this . . . you scrawny little . . ."

The engine turned over. Phoebe shifted into reverse and hit the gas, speeding backward. Quentin lurched forward but caught his balance without falling down. He stumbled around the parking space a minute while she put the car in drive and raced out of the lot, hitting speed bump after speed bump that made her teeth rattle and her head hit the upholstered roof of the car.

Quentin chased her on foot a few seconds, then gave up. Phoebe saw his face, full of rage, in the rearview mirror.

Then stared straight ahead as she drove back to the village.

Why did I go back to school today?

Phoebe couldn't remember.

Fridays could be busy in the shop. Sometimes as busy as Saturdays. Maggie had never been able to figure out why. She taught a class on Friday, too. She tried to schedule the classes around Phoebe's schedule at school, but that didn't always work out. Phoebe had gone to school today, and it was hard to teach, help students one-on-one with their work, and keep an eye on customers.

Finally, around noon, the store magically emptied out. Maggie sat at the stool behind the counter and took a deep breath and then checked the day's receipts to see how she was doing and catch up on the inventory book. The lull would not last very long, but she cherished the little slice of downtime.

She wondered how Phoebe had managed today at school. She hoped no one had confronted her about her apartment being searched or being questioned by the police. Maybe people would be a little kinder than to bother her, or were more interested in the fate of Sonya Finch now and her connection to the murder.

Not that Maggie wished Sonya Finch any ill will—well, not unless she was the murderer—but now that the police had focused on the professor, Maggie hoped they would cross Phoebe off their list.

But like a wise man once said, "It ain't over till it's over." Maggie had a feeling there were many more threads to unravel before this story was done.

She realized later that it was funny she'd had that thought

just at the moment Detective Mossbacher walked into the shop. She looked up from a new knitting pattern she was studying and slipped off her glasses. He smiled at her briefly and removed his hat.

"Mrs. Messina, how are you today?"

"I can't complain, Detective. What brings you this way?" She tried to hide an edgy note but wasn't very successful.

He lifted his hands, a universal sign of harmlessness. "Just wandering around town. I have a question for you, actually. I thought you might be able to help us. Being a . . . What did they call you on the news? A knitting expert?"

Maggie's mouth puckered a moment, as if she'd bit into a lemon. "Needlework expert, actually. And I don't claim to be either. Though I do know my fair share."

"Your fair share is plenty." He had a pleasant smile, she noticed, even white teeth, and smooth skin for a man his age . . . which was about her age, she guessed. He looked fit, as if he kept himself in shape. But law officers usually did.

"So . . . what's your question?" She tilted her head to one side, curious now.

"I have some photos. We have people looking at them back at the station. But I wondered if you'd take a look, too, and give us your opinion." He was carrying a manila envelope and took out a few sheets of slick photo paper.

She didn't even realize she was shrinking back until he glanced up at her. "Don't worry. It's not from the murder scene."

She wouldn't see the victim, he meant. Thank goodness. She put her glasses on again and looked down at the pictures, three close-ups of knitted patches. The strands were many different types of yarn. Sometimes doubled and sometimes single. Cut and tied, a few rows in a thick weight, the next in a very thin one, random and unpredictable, with many long snipped strands hanging down here and there, like crazy sorts of tassels or fringe.

"What am I looking at again?" she asked curiously.

"I didn't say." He gave her a look, as if she'd been trying to trick him into explaining. "And if I told you, it would ruin everything. This is sort of a blind test. Just knitting samples. That's all you need to know. What can you tell me? Anything that comes to mind."

A blind test? Like in a food commercial? Was she supposed to pick the new and improved brand as opposed to the standard favorite? Maggie smiled, snapping her mind back to the task at hand.

"Oh, well . . . okay." She looked back down at the photos. "Well . . . all the photos are fairly typical of pieces of fiber art. That's all about mixing texture and color, with abstract patterns emerging from the random blend."

"The Knit Kats, they call themselves fiber artists, right?"

Maggie nodded. "Yes, they do. This is very similar to the type of wrapping they've used on big projects. Like covering a statue. But you must know that by now."

He nodded. "Do you think the same person could have done all this knitting?"

"Hard to say. But knitters do have characteristic styles. You can give five people in a class the same pattern, and each finished product will come out very different."

"How do you mean?"

"Oh, some people knit very tight stitches, some looser. Some give the yarn a twist here and there. It's almost like . . . hand-writing. Though maybe not quite that distinctive," she clarified. "I don't know if it would hold up in a court of law," she added playfully.

"Doesn't have to. But it might help us. Go on."

Detective Mossbacher's expression didn't change on his fairly deadpan police-officer face. But his dark eyes lit up a bit. As if this information was encouraging. "So what do you think of the photos?"

Maggie held the pictures up to give them a closer look. She felt Detective Mossbacher looking at her but didn't meet his gaze. She put the pictures down and took off her glasses again.

"I don't see many similarities. This one is consistently tight. This one is much looser. And this is sort of . . . in between. The person who knit this last one drops a lot of stitches. Maybe on purpose, to give the fiber art more texture? But maybe just because they're a sloppy knitter. Three different knitters, I'd say." She shrugged. "I'm sorry. That's all I can guess."

He nodded. "No need to apologize. That was very helpful."

Maggie nodded. She wasn't sure if Detective Mossbacher cared at all what she really thought, beyond looking over this knitting. But she decided to share her opinion anyway.

"Frankly, Detective, I know that you have to explore every lead. But the Knit Kats being behind this crime doesn't make sense to me. If I were going to murder someone, would I smother them with yarn?"

The detective's large brown eyes grew wide, his mouth twisting in a surprised smile. "I don't know, Mrs. Messina. You might use anything handy . . . and you have plenty of yarn around here."

Maggie shook her head. His smile was . . . distracting.

"This is not a situation where a murderer grabbed anything handy. This attack was planned. Everyone knows I'm a knitter, so why be so obvious? I'd be much smarter to knock the victim out with a golf club . . . or a bowling ball. Because I don't like either of those hobbies."

"You don't like bowling?" He seemed surprised—and to take it personally in some way. She gave him a puzzled look. But before she could comment he said, "I get your point. Of course, we've considered that someone might be trying to frame the Knit Kats, or Charlotte Blackburn. Or just staging a ploy to distract attention. But you said it yourself, we have to investigate all the possible scenarios and eliminate them, one by one."

"I understand. Sorry to be telling you your business."

He shrugged and smiled. "You aren't the first person . . . and won't be the last. I'll tell Detective Reyes what you said about the photos. I'm sure she'll be interested."

The comment was flattering. "I'm happy to help. Anytime."

He picked up the photos and stuck them back in the envelope, then put his hat back on, preparing to go.

"You have a very nice shop. Very comfortable. My wife would have liked this place. She liked to knit."

Past tense. He was a widower. The expression in his eyes confirmed it. Maggie met his gaze a moment. "I'm sorry . . . How long has it been?"

"Two years, in April."

"It's hard," she said sincerely. "I lost my husband, Bill, almost five years ago. That's part of the reason I started this business. For something new to do. I was a high school art teacher before that."

"Somehow that doesn't surprise me." Her expression must have shown that she wasn't sure how he meant that. "Everything is . . . eye-catching and artistic."

"Thank you. We try. Phoebe is a big help. She's very creative." She paused, not knowing if she should say more. "You don't really think Phoebe is mixed up in this, Detective . . . do you? I mean, she's not seriously a suspect?"

Mossbacher looked put on the spot. He seemed about to answer, then pressed his lips together and stared at her. Finally, just when he was about to answer, the shop door flew open.

"Maggie . . . you won't believe what just happened to me . . ."

Phoebe slumped forward, looking breathless, bedraggled, and quite dramatic. Maggie could tell she was about to launch into a long story . . . or would have, if Detective Mossbacher had not been there.

He turned and greeted Phoebe with a nod. "Hello, Phoebe. How are you doing?"

Phoebe pulled back and squared her shoulders, then stared him down. "Pretty awful, that's how I'm doing. You . . . you went into my locker at school and took *all* my stuff—my sketchbook and . . . and everything. That's not right. That's not fair! . . . I didn't even know!"

"Calm down. It's all right . . ." He made a conciliatory gesture, then glanced at Maggie for support.

She quickly came out from behind the counter. "Oh dear, is that what happened? Your locker was searched?" She'd wondered about that when they'd heard from Dana last night that Charlotte's locker at school had been searched. She'd guessed Phoebe's would be, too.

"It was like . . . gutted. I didn't even know . . ."

Detective Mossbacher looked contrite. "I'm sorry, you should have been told, Phoebe. That was an oversight. Technically, the locker is college property so you didn't have to sign a warrant. I guess they gave the voucher to someone at the college."

"And I won't get anything back until you're all done and the investigation is closed, right?"

"That's pretty much the way it goes. It does depend a bit on what you want back. Ask your lawyer to contact the district attorney's office and see if they'll return the sketchbook and art supplies. If they don't think it's evidence in the case, they'll probably give it back."

Phoebe looked greatly relieved. Maggie felt grateful to him. "Thanks, Detective. That helps. Right, Phoebe?"

She nodded quickly. "My computer? . . . A hamster's chance in Hades, right?"

"Sorry . . . you'll have to wait on that."

"Whatever . . ." Phoebe seemed mad and glum but was trying hard to hold her temper. "Are you guys watching my e-mails to see if Charlotte gets in touch?"

Whoa . . . now she'd gone a little far, Maggie thought. But he didn't seem offended. More like mildly amused.

"Not personally. The FBI probably is. Your friend is wanted for questioning in a homicide." He tugged his hat down over his brow. "Besides, Phoebe, we don't need your computer to do that."

Maggie sighed. How true. Even Google ogled e-mails to see what sort of advertising they should sic on you.

Phoebe just twisted her mouth to the side.

"Has there been any further sign of Charlotte?" Maggie couldn't help asking, though she doubted she'd get a straight answer.

"Further than what?" He tilted his head to one side, looking curious about her answer.

Maggie suddenly remembered that the information Dana had passed on was not common knowledge and she really wasn't supposed to know.

"We heard she bought a train ticket in New Jersey. And the train was headed to Baltimore. That's all." She shrugged. "It's a knitting shop. I hear a lot of gossip. Almost as bad as a beauty salon," she added.

He didn't reply for a long moment, as if measuring his words. "We believe Ms. Blackburn has not come to any harm. I can't tell you any more than that."

He glanced at Phoebe, and she looked down at her boots. It suddenly occurred to Maggie that Detective Mossbacher might think Phoebe was in touch with Charlotte, by some super-secret means, and was keeping her apprised of the investigation.

"Well . . . that's something, I guess," Phoebe mumbled.

"You're welcome," he replied, though she hadn't really thanked him. "So long, ladies. Have a good day."

Thank goodness he left, Maggie thought. Phoebe was so feisty today. She nearly smart-talked her way back to the police station.

Maggie was about to tell Phoebe that, too, when she heard her assistant give out an unholy gasp just as the door closed behind Mossbacher.

"You won't believe what I heard at school! . . . Charlotte was a Knit Kat!"

Maggie wasn't surprised. "I suspected that when you told us that she put the group in touch with you. But I guess it is a shock to hear it confirmed. I guess it's her photo that's crossed out?"

"I bet it is . . . but of course it's hard to check with my computer being *confiscated*."

"Mine is right here. Let's take another look." Maggie walked over to the counter and flipped open her computer, then searched for the Knit Kats website. But all she got was a page with an error message.

"Oh dear . . . I've messed it up somehow. You try."

She turned the computer around so Phoebe could use the keyboard. But a moment later, Phoebe glanced up at her, looking annoyed.

"The website is gone. Someone took it down."

Maggie wasn't sure how these things actually worked. "Took it down? You mean . . . like a billboard or something?"

Phoebe nodded. "It's gone. Maybe Professor Finch took it down, after she was outed . . . Oh, more big news. I was waiting to see Professor Healey, to complain about my locker being searched, and I overheard a shouting match between him and Professor Finch. It sounded like he was trying to fire her . . . but she wasn't getting the message."

"I'm sure she understood him. She just wouldn't accept it," Maggie clarified. She wasn't surprised at that, either. "I think it would be hard to get rid of a tenured professor. And no one has accused her of a crime yet . . . a real crime, I mean, not just vandalism or littering."

"Yeah, that's what I thought. But Healey sounded like he has everyone at the school against her now—Dean Klug and the whole board of trustees. He thinks it's going to get worse for her, with the police . . . like maybe she's really the *one*." Maggie knew it was hard for Phoebe to say it more directly—the one who killed Beth Shelton. Phoebe looked worried, her dark brows drawn together in a frown. "Professor Finch always acted all sweet and supportive to Charlotte. But today it sounded like she really hates her guts. As if she's jealous of her or something."

"Charlotte was starting to get some attention for her artwork. And she's young and beautiful," Maggie added. "That scores high on the jealousy meter, in my book."

"Enough to want to kill her?" Phoebe asked bluntly.

Maggie shook her head. "I get your point. But you just said Charlotte was a Knit Kat. Maybe there was some intense issue between them because of that."

"Yeah . . . could be. Professor Finch kept calling Charlotte Healey's little pet and talking like they had something going on."

"Like . . . an affair? That type of thing?"

Phoebe nodded. Maggie could tell it was very hard for her to talk about Charlotte this way—and all the secrets she'd kept.

"That sort of freaked me out, too," Phoebe admitted. "Charlotte told me she'd started seeing someone, after Quentin. But she never told me the guy's name or much about him. When I asked her the other day how it was going, she sort of shrugged and said that it was over. He'd turned out to be a big nothing. A real jerk, not at all what she thought."

"'A big nothing' . . . that's a good one." The brief phrase conveyed a lot. "So you're wondering now if she was talking about Professor Healey?"

Phoebe shrugged. "I don't know . . . He kept saying it wasn't true and calling Finch insane. Which was also true. I thought she was going to stroke out."

"Professor Finch might have heard gossip. It doesn't mean it's true. But she must have told the police and it's the perfect way to discredit him and turn their attention his way."

"Oh yeah . . . she had that all figured out. She said something like, 'They'll be coming for you next, Healey.'" Phoebe sighed and picked a bit of cat hair off one of her gloves. "I wish Charlotte was around and I could just ask her."

"That's just the trouble," Maggie said quietly. "There are a lot of people who want to talk to your friend Charlotte."

Phoebe nodded. Maggie hoped she hadn't made her feel bad. That had not been her intention at all.

She suddenly looked up again. "Something else weird happened, too."

"Really? You had some day."

"I'll say. I started with my empty locker and ended with being chased by Quentin Gibbs."

"Quentin?" Maggie's pulse quickened. "He chased you? Where?"

"Across the parking lot near the art department building. He kept shouting that he wanted to talk to me . . . but I do *not* want to talk to him."

"I'll say you don't. You need to stay miles away from that guy." Maggie didn't know how to say it in a stronger way. "He's not stable . . . or rational," she said simply.

He could very well blame Phoebe in some way for Charlotte escaping his pursuit the other night, when they all chased one another through the studios. In fact, she wasn't even sure the police had totally eliminated him as a suspect in Beth Shelton's murder.

"I think you should tell the police he tried to confront you, and then come home with me tonight." Maggie tried to catch Phoebe's gaze, but she could see her young friend wasn't persuaded. "I'd be too worried about you alone here, Phoebe. Honestly."

"Don't be silly. I'll be fine. He's not going to bother me. Besides, I have a guard cat now."

The joke fell flat. Maggie stared Phoebe down. "He's a very persistent . . . obsessive personality. We don't know what he's capable of. And don't tell me that he doesn't know where you live. I'm sure he does by now."

It had been all over the news the other night, just in case he had any trouble finding Phoebe's address. Maggie didn't say that. She didn't want to rub it in.

Phoebe rolled her eyes. Before she could protest again, Maggie said, "Humor me on this. We'll have fun. I'll make waffles. We'll play Scrabble or something."

"Waffles? What kind?"

Maggie was pleased to catch her attention. "Apple. Banana. Whatever you like."

"Okay, deal. But no Scrabble. You pound me with your forty-point words. I'll just bring my knitting."

Maggie smiled. "Sounds even better to me."

Phoebe and Maggie closed the shop at six and left in separate cars. Phoebe had to pick up a new sketchbook and some other supplies at Alice's Arts & Crafts, on the turnpike. She liked to shop for her art supplies in a smaller store, an authentic art-supply store that was up in Newburyport—one that was frequented by working artists and didn't display rows of glitter stickers and plastic fruit in every other aisle.

But Alice's was an easy option for a quick, basic purchase. She really hoped the police would give her back her art stuff. She'd bought a ton of supplies for this semester's courses. It was so stupid and pointless that they took it.

Phoebe could feel her hair practically catching fire just thinking about it. She focused on her list, looking for the few items she needed most. She picked up a big sketchbook and some soft charcoal sticks. The sepia pencils she preferred, which gave her sketches a sort of Leonardo look, she thought. A gummy eraser and a box of pastels.

Maggie had been nice enough to give her a bunch of store coupons, so she still had a little money after checking out to make a stop at Pet Palace, which was right next door

For a little cat, Van Gogh could eat a lot, and the food was way cheaper at the big discount store than at the supermarket. She filled her cart with cans and two bags of fish-shaped nuggets, and tossed in a few cat toys, a scratching post, and a bed that she found in the mark-down bin.

When she reached her car and put all the bags in, Phoebe realized part of her must really believe that Charlotte was not coming back. Or why would she be buying all this stuff for Van Gogh? As if he was her cat now?

Charlotte is fine, she reminded herself. Mossbacher said so. Or almost said so.

She left the parking lot and headed for Maggie's house.

When Charlotte comes back, I'll just give her all Van Gogh's new things. Or maybe she'll let me keep him. She has about a million more cats. Maybe she won't miss one.

It was a cold, clear night. The kind of frigid, dry air that cut to the bone and was a little painful to breathe. Phoebe couldn't help wondering what was going on with Charlotte's cats. Was anybody putting out food for them?

How many days had it been since Beth's body was found and Charlotte had disappeared? Phoebe counted back. Five days. The art show had been on Sunday, so it wasn't quite a week yet.

They were outdoor cats mainly and used to catching their own "fast food" in the wild. But Phoebe knew she'd promised herself to come by and check on them when she'd taken Van Gogh. She felt guilty about that now and headed for Charlotte's house, which was not far from Maggie's and not out of her way at all.

Here I am with a carload of cat food, besides. Yes, it was getting late and Maggie was probably firing up the waffle iron by now. And it was colder than a penguin's butt out there. But "a job begun is a job half done." That's what Maggie always said. It would only take two seconds to put out cat food and find a dish for some water. She definitely had a bottle or two in her knapsack.

Phoebe pulled up to Charlotte's house and parked in the driveway. The windows of the front apartment were dark, though the light by the front door was on. She walked toward the back of the house, to the little porch at the entrance of Charlotte's apartment. Yellow crime-scene tape was still strung around the porch railing, like sagging strips of crepe paper left over from a party.

Phoebe hesitated a moment, then decided not to cross the tape and go up on the porch. She was getting so spooked out from this whole miserable deal, and already felt like her every move was being watched. Especially after what Mossbacher had told her today about police looking at e-mails and Facebook and all that stuff. They could have a camera hidden out there, waiting to see if the culprit returned to the scene of the crime. Didn't that always happen in the movies?

Well, let them watch. All she was doing was putting out cat food. That wasn't a crime yet . . . was it?

The question was where to put it. She didn't want some helpful dumb person coming back here and cleaning it up before the cats could find it. Charlotte's pals probably wandered around behind the house mostly, out of view. Or maybe even around the unattached garage that stood at the end of the drive. Both spots would be good places to set up the feline smorgasbord.

With grocery bags full of pull-top cans and water dangling from each hand, Phoebe made her way around the corner of the building, to the backyard. It was a small square of property, partially covered by snow and bordered by a high wooden fence. A feeble outdoor lamp, hanging above the garage doors, cast a bit of light. She saw a broken-down wooden picnic table with a bench underneath and a few beer cans scattered on the ground, reminding her again that this was off-campus housing.

It was so dark she could hardly find the pull tops on the cans of cat food.

204 / Anne Canadeo

She pulled opened one can and then another, carefully saving the metal lids for the recycle bin at Maggie's. She was working on a third when she heard a rustling sound in the dry, bare bushes at the fence. She looked up to see Picasso trot out of the darkness. He boldly jumped on the table and began gulping down the tuna—chewing loudly, Phoebe thought.

"Hey, guy. Good to see you. Glad you could stop by for a bite," she said quietly.

Another light-footed form darted out of the shadows from some hidden space behind the garage. So the cats do hang out there, Phoebe thought. Good guess. I'll hit that spot next.

A sleek calico ran up to the table. Frida Kahlo. Another one of Phoebe's favorites. Frida jumped on the picnic bench and rubbed herself on Phoebe's jacket.

"Hello, sweet girl. I should have taken you home, too, right?" Phoebe reached down and gently stroked her head. "Do you want some food? What a question . . ."

She set another can on the bench for Frida and was about to take out the water bottles when she heard heavy footsteps just behind her.

Phoebe turned quickly, expecting to see someone who lived in the building. Or maybe even a police officer who'd come back to check the house.

But it was Quentin. His intense expression horrified her.

"AAAAaaaaa! . . ." Phoebe's thin voice trailed off on a ter-rified note as she turned to run. She was quick. But he was faster and totally focused on her.

She'd barely made it to the fence when she felt a big hand come around her head and cover her mouth. One big arm wrapped her middle like a steel band, and they fell together onto the ground. Phoebe kicked and struggled. She tried to slam her knee into his groin or kick his shin, as she'd learned in a self-defense course. But Quentin's heavy leg easily kept her own legs pressed to the ground. Tears filled her eyes as she tried to scream and then bit down on his hand. He cursed, but his hold only tightened. With her strength ebbing, Phoebe sadly realized that even had she been three times her size, Quentin still would have been stronger and she had no chance of getting away from him.

"Give it up, Phoebe . . . I've got you now," he hissed into her ear.

CHAPTER ELEVEN

*I*t was Quentin, after all. He killed Beth in some crazed, angry rage . . . mistaking her for Charlotte . . . and now he's going to kill me!

The truth crystallized in Phoebe's mind in a single, horrifying instant as she lay with her head pressed to the ground, her eyes bugging out. Quentin's big hand remained plastered over her mouth.

A surreal feeling dropped over her, like a heavy mist. As if she were trapped in a dream—her worst nightmare. Quentin loomed above her, blocking out the meager light from the lamp on the garage.

"Stop fighting me . . . You're like a squirming little bug. I could snap your bones with a flick of my wrist, don't you get it? So just shut up and listen to me!" he shouted down at her.

But I haven't been talking! You have your hand over my mouth, remember? she wanted to scream back. But maybe in his head, she *had* been talking?

Phoebe stared up at him. Her head was about to burst with

all the words she wanted to shout into his stupid face. Finally, she stopped struggling and just nodded, her chin bobbing up and down like a little doll.

She saw his expression relax a bit, and so did his grip. He still held her down, but he wasn't hurting her anymore.

"I need to talk to you about Charlotte . . ."

Phoebe gulped. Was he going to make some sort of confession now . . . about killing Beth? She didn't think she could stand hearing that. She squeezed her eyes shut, but he kept talking. She had no choice but to listen.

"Do you know where Charlotte is? Did she get in touch with you?"

Phoebe shook her head, trying to say no.

"You'd better not lie to me, Phoebe. You're the only person she'd get in touch with. She must have tried, a text or Instagram or something?"

Phoebe didn't know how to indicate "I'm not lying!" while being unable to speak. She stared back at him, her eyes bugging out of her head.

"Okay, listen . . . the night I chased her, at the gallery, I wasn't going to hurt her. I knew she was in trouble with some guy she'd been seeing after me. That's who killed Beth Shelton. He was trying to get Charlotte and I wanted to help her. To protect her . . . but she wouldn't let me. I told that to the police," he added, "but they didn't believe me. So now you have to tell them. Understand?"

Phoebe blinked. She really didn't understand. She mumbled against his hand.

"All right . . . all right. I'll take my hand off your mouth . . . but you'd better not scream. Or try to get away. I'm warning you."

His tone was so severe, any thought of calling out for help immediately dissolved.

When he finally took his hand away, Phoebe gasped for air.

"So talk already," he said impatiently.

"I don't get it . . . You want me to lie to the police and tell them Charlotte told me something that she really didn't say? That she's in trouble with some boyfriend?"

"It's not a lie. It's the truth. It could save her freaking life. Don't you want to save her life?" he practically screamed at her. "Hey, this dude is powerful. He knows people. He knows how to find someone and shut them up for good. He can hunt someone down as good as the police. Even better."

So . . . Quentin Gibbs was paranoid, too, on top of all his other quirks? That figured.

Phoebe quickly nodded, mainly to calm him down. Making Quentin more excited and angry was not a good idea. He had loosened his grip considerably, though he still held her to the ground.

She tried hard to focus and keep her voice calm.

"I'm sorry . . . I still don't get it. What do you want me to tell them?"

Quentin seemed frustrated, his skin flushed right up to his scalp and the edge of his Mohawk.

"You just say like . . . you suddenly remembered something. Charlotte told you she had some guy, an older dude. And you think he's out to get her for some reason. I'm thinking now it's a guy from that law firm in Boston. Where she had the proofreading job. That's who wants to get her . . . I just don't know why."

"The law firm?" Phoebe had never thought of that. When he'd said "older dude," she'd immediately thought of Professor

Healey. But all that money in her locker . . . Some big corpo-
rate lawyer would be rolling in dough. A lawyer made more
sense than a college professor once you figured in the stash of
cash. Still, Phoebe wanted to know why Quentin thought so.

"What makes you say the law firm?"

"I'm a freaking fortune-teller, okay? . . . And I've been keeping an eye on her. Ever since we broke up," he admitted. "I followed her to the train station a few times—her car is like always
in that lot. Even overnight. And I know her. Inside out. All right?"

Phoebe decided it was not smart to ask any more questions. "Just wondering," she mumbled.

Charlotte went into the city from time to time, just like
everyone else. Maybe even more so, to visit galleries and go to
the law office. Seeing her car at the station didn't mean much,
Phoebe thought.

So on top of being paranoid, he'd also read too many John
Grisham novels? No . . . check that. Seen the movies. He probably had not read a book without pictures for a few years now.

Her lips felt bruised and swollen from being smashed by
his hand for so long. Maggie was going to think she'd stopped
off for some quickie Botox injections.

Quentin's voice broke into her wandering thoughts. "So . . .
are you going to do it or what?"

"Or what" was not the answer he was looking for. Phoebe
knew that.

"Okay . . . I'll do it. I mean, what the heck. The police are
fairly clueless, if you ask me. They should look into any leads
they get. I don't know why they ignored you." It was hard to
deliver that last line with a straight face, but somehow she
managed.

"That's what I thought. But they laughed me off. Like I was just pushing the blame on someone else to save my own skin. Hey, I didn't kill Beth Shelton . . . and I'd never hurt a hair on Charlotte's head . . ."

Right . . . that's why she had to get a court order to keep you away, Phoebe wanted to remind him. Skip that reply.

"I love Charlotte. And she loves me . . . deep in her heart. We're soul mates. When she comes back, she's going to face that, and we'll be together again."

His tone was matter-of-fact. And totally deluded. Phoebe didn't dare challenge him. If Charlotte did return, she'd need more than a restraining order to keep this guy away.

Phoebe sucked in the sharp cold air, but it was hard to get a full breath with Quentin's arm still wrapped across her body, holding her down.

Are we done here? she wanted to ask. But she wouldn't dare. She stared into his cold blue eyes. He looked like a deranged husky dog . . . except for the stiff strip of hair sticking up on his head. A crystal stud earring in one ear glinted in the darkness and a multicolored tattoo curled up his neck. She couldn't tell what it said. She realized she didn't want to know.

"So . . . did you follow me here or something?" she ventured to ask.

Thick brows knit together. "I came here for the same reason you did. To feed the cats. Catching up to you was just a lucky break."

Yeah, my lucky day, too, Phoebe thought.

"Nice," she managed. "Charlotte's probably wondering if anybody's watching them."

"I thought so, too." He stared at her, as if wondering if

she was making fun of him or not. She hoped he decided the latter.

She took a breath and decided to make her move. His mood could flip any second.

"So . . . can you let me up now? . . . I'm like morphing into an ice pop ."

He didn't seem to hear her at first. Just stared down into her face, his expression angry, scared, lonely, crazy, and desperate all at once. She wondered if he only felt control of his own feelings when he had someone else under control.

Finally, he took his arm away and she was able to sit up.

She gasped and rubbed her face with her hands. She wanted to cry but didn't want to waste a single second getting away from Quentin. Save it for the car, Phoebe, she told herself.

Quentin had already stood up and extended his hand down to her.

She looked at it but didn't make a move to touch him again.

"Go on. I'll pull you up. You just said your legs are numb." Before she could answer, he grabbed her arm and pulled her to her feet.

Phoebe wobbled from side to side and grabbed the edge of the table.

"Need help getting back to your car?"

"Seriously? . . . You want to *help* me to my car? After you nearly squeezed the living juice out of me?"

He shrugged, looking a tiny bit sheepish. "Hey . . . you're all right, aren't you? If you'd just talked to me the other day, I wouldn't have had to grab you like that. It's your own fault," he added.

"Right . . . you nearly maim me for life, and it's my fault?" The guy has more twists than a hot pretzel. Phoebe knew it was totally stupid to stand here arguing with him. But she was so enraged, she couldn't help it.

"Hey . . . if I wanted to put a hurt on you, Phoebe, I could have done better than that."

"Yeah . . . well . . . you need help, Quentin. Seriously." She mumbled the parting advice, half hoping he didn't hear.

"Hey, I heard that! You just remember, I'll know if you don't keep your promise and tell the cops what I told you to say. As far as anybody needs to know, we just had a nice little talk back here. If you complain to anybody about me, I won't go so easy the next time . . . You hear me?"

Phoebe ached all over but managed to run the last few steps to her car. A wave of nausea rose up, nearly overtaking her.

She slipped behind the driver's seat, slammed the door, and flipped the lock switch. She looked back at the yard, to make sure Quentin had not chased her. He was still standing there, by the picnic table.

Then she saw all the unopened cans of cat food that had spilled out of the bags, the shiny tops of the cans catching the light.

Phoebe sighed, feeling frustrated. All that food. It would do no good now. Cats did not have opposable thumbs . . . possibly the only reason their kind did not rule the universe. But no way was she going back out there. That was for sure.

But Quentin had noticed, too, and started picking up the cans, opening them, and carefully setting them out around the yard. A cat appeared and started eating. He crouched down and gently petted its head.

Wow, was he bizarre. Her mind could not contain the extent of his weirdness.

She started up her car, wincing at the aches and pains as she backed out of the driveway. Maggie was probably worried about her now.

Worse yet, she'll freak out when hears this story, Phoebe realized. But I have to tell her . . . and tell Detective Reyes what Quentin said, too.

Phoebe was almost afraid to ring Maggie's doorbell. She had even considered going back to her apartment and making some excuse about deciding to sleep in her own apartment tonight.

The truth was, Quentin had caught up to her, and she was positive he wouldn't bother again. Not tonight anyway. He'd had his fun, she thought, as she rubbed her aching wrist.

But Maggie saw her from the living room window and came to the door before she could sneak away. "What happened to you? I tried your cell . . . and your jacket's covered with dirt. So are your jeans." Maggie looked her over, her mouth hanging slack.

Phoebe shook her head. She unzipped her black parka and winced a bit, turning her arm to get it off.

"Phoebe . . . you're hurt. Did you have an accident?" Maggie quickly glanced outside at Phoebe's car as she closed the door. "Did you fall down somewhere?"

"Yeah, I fell . . . well, I was pushed down actually. I stopped at Charlotte's house. To feed her cats. And I ran into Quentin."

"Quentin?" Maggie practically gasped repeating his name. She stood closer to Phoebe, facing her squarely. "I knew he was going to bother you . . . Did he follow you there?"

"He says he didn't. He said he came to feed the cats, too . . .

Maggie, he has this wild theory that Charlotte is being hunted down by some sleazy attorney from that law firm where she did proofreading . . . and he wants me to tell the police that she said that to me. Because he tried to tell them, and he says they just blew him off."

Maggie gently touched her arm. "Slow down, I don't understand . . . Did he hurt you?"

Phoebe realized she sounded a little hysterical. A lot hysterical, actually.

She took a breath and shook her head. Tears welled up in her eyes. "Scared me . . . a lot," she managed. "I ran when I saw him. But he caught me and pushed me down . . . and sort of made me listen to him."

Maggie's expression melted. Phoebe saw her friend's chin tremble. "You poor thing . . . He must have terrified you."

"He's insane. You have no idea. I was stuck on the frozen ground for like forever while he spun these bizarre theories about Charlotte . . . and told me they were soul mates. Can you believe that insanity? I'm so cold, I've got like goose bumps on my goose bumps."

Maggie turned Phoebe gently toward the staircase. "You go up and take a long, hot shower and put on some dry clothes. Pajamas would be a good idea at this point. Did you bring everything you need?"

Phoebe nodded and picked up her knapsack. "Right here."

"Good. I'll fix some tea and you can tell me the whole story. When you're ready."

Phoebe nodded thankfully. She slung the knapsack over her shoulder and headed up to the guest room. Maggie watched her from the foot of the stairs. Halfway up, Phoebe paused.

"Are we still having waffles?"

"Absolutely. The batter is all ready."

Phoebe sighed. For some reason, that made her feel a whole lot better.

A short time later, Phoebe sat at the table in Maggie's cozy kitchen, wearing flannel pajamas printed with penguins and thick fuzzy slipper socks she'd knit for herself. She'd forgotten her robe, but Maggie had given her a soft white afghan.

Comfortably wrapped, she sipped a cup of chamomile tea, described her encounter with Quentin in full detail, and explained his wild theory while Maggie made their waffles.

"It sounds like he's seen too many evil-lawyer conspiracy movies. You know, the ones where all the witnesses die in mysterious accidents? He's so screwed up. No wonder the police didn't take him seriously," Phoebe concluded.

"Well, we don't know that for sure. Maybe the police did follow up on the lead, but nothing came of it." Maggie set a pot of hot tea on the table and took her seat.

Phoebe smashed a few banana slices on her waffle with her fork and sprinkled on some cinnamon. "Maybe . . . but I was thinking in the shower, what if it *is* true? It sort of explains a few things, like why Charlotte had all that money. If this evil lawyer was close to Charlotte, he could have known she was a Knit Kat and figured that was a good direction to throw the blame."

"All right, I'll buy that. But if he was close to Charlotte, he would have known it wasn't her, it was Beth."

"These guys don't get down and dirty, Mag. They call Creeps for Hire and find some sleazeball who just sees a picture of the person he's supposed to kill, in a dark bar or an underground parking garage. Someplace like that."

"Now it sounds like you've seen too many of those movies." Maggie speared a bite of waffle with her fork. "So you think Quentin is on to something and the police didn't listen to him? I guess that could be true. Even a broken clock is right twice a day."

"In his case, a broken cuckoo clock. I'm going to tell Detective Reyes what he said. I'm just not going to lie and say *Charlotte* told me all that stuff and I just remembered. I don't want to get in any more trouble, either."

"Good point, and good plan. But what about filing a complaint against Quentin? He twisted your arm, pushed you to the ground, held his hand over your face. I bet you have bruises . . . do you?"

Phoebe twisted her mouth to the side, a dumb habit she had when she didn't want to answer. "Not really. Just a few red spots. They're going away."

"Phoebe . . . I know you're afraid of him. But I think you have to report this. Even if you don't press charges, the police will have a talk with him. He can't walk around thinking he can behave like that and get away with it."

"I know . . . but I don't want to think about it anymore. I'll ask Detective Reyes and see what she says I should do. I'll call her right after we eat, okay?"

Maggie nodded. "Fair enough. Do you want another waffle?" she asked, noticing Phoebe's empty plate.

"Yes, please . . . that was really good. Thanks."

Maggie glanced at her as she walked back to the waffle maker. "I haven't made these in a while. I think they came out pretty good."

"Pretty good? These waffles are awesome . . . and thanks for making me come here tonight. I would have been a total mess alone at home. You must be psychic or something."

Maggie laughed. "Probably just 'or something.' But I have my moments."

After their wafflefest, Phoebe followed through on her plan and called Detective Reyes. She told her Quentin's theory about the mysterious ex-boyfriend, an evil lawyer who was out to get Charlotte for some unknown reason. It sounded even wilder and more deranged when she was repeating it to a law officer than Phoebe had imagined.

To her credit, Detective Reyes listened patiently and didn't laugh out loud. "I believe he told us something like that during his interview. I believe someone followed up. I'll look back in my notes and check."

Phoebe thanked her, then told her about the way Quentin had persuaded her to deliver his message and asked her advice about filing a complaint.

"Did he have a weapon?" she asked quickly.

"No . . . it wasn't like that. He just sort of tackled me and held his hand over my mouth a while."

"He assaulted you," Detective Reyes said succinctly. "And I'm sure he threatened you. Said if you told us how he cornered you, he'd come after you again, right?"

"Something like that," Phoebe mumbled.

"Phoebe, just the fact that you've told me this gives us grounds to investigate. If he did that to you, he'll do it again. To someone else. Another woman. The Quentins of the world never take on anyone who can fight back and win."

Phoebe knew that was true but was still trying to weigh

the pros and cons. "I hear you. But I mean, there were no witnesses. It's just going to be like my word against his. And even if I file a complaint, is that really going to stop him? It could make life a lot worse for me."

Detective Reyes sounded suddenly weary. "I know you're scared. But I encourage you to come here tomorrow and report this officially. You don't have to press charges. You can wait on that, or never do it. But we have more reason to keep an eye on Quentin Gibbs and, possibly, lock him up the next time if there is more documentation of his bad behavior." When Phoebe didn't answer, she added, "There's going to be a next time, Phoebe. The next woman might not be as lucky as you were."

Phoebe knew that was true. She felt as if she'd had a brush with mortality today. "All right. I'll do it. What do you think of his idea, though, really?"

She didn't expect Detective Reyes to answer. She was the original zipper lip. But she thought she'd give it a try.

"We can't discount anything. But there have been some new developments in the case that lead in another direction."

"Really? What kind of developments?"

Detective Reyes laughed. How rare was that?

"I can't tell you that, Phoebe. But you might want to watch the news tonight. I think that will answer some of your questions."

After they hung up, Phoebe ran down to the family room, where Maggie was knitting. The television was on, the channel set to a quiz show. Phoebe bet Maggie knew all the answers. Or most of them.

"Oh, there you are." Maggie put her knitting down and put the set on mute. "So how did it go? Did you talk to Detective Reyes?"

"Yes, I told her everything. I'm going to file a report about Quentin's conversation skills. She convinced me it was the right thing to do."

"I think it is, too," Maggie agreed. "Did she seem interested in that evil-attorney idea?"

"Not really." Phoebe flopped on the couch. "She said there were new developments in the case and we should watch the news tonight."

"Oh . . . that's important. Why didn't you say something?" Maggie picked up the remote and quickly changed the channel to *News Alive 25!* It had become her favorite program, Phoebe realized.

"A three-car pileup on Route 1A today left passengers with only minor injuries, but made the rush-hour commute a real headache," the news anchor said. There was an aerial photo of a car accident.

"I have the best commute . . . except for Lucy," Phoebe said.

The next story was about a blood drive at a high school. Phoebe and Maggie were about to switch the channel when the news anchor said, *"Coming up next, a break for investigators in the ongoing investigation of the murder of college student Beth Shelton. We go to Chelsea Porter, who was on the campus of Whitaker College earlier this evening."*

"Oh boy . . . here we go again," Maggie murmured, her gaze fixed on the TV as Chelsea Porter came into view.

Chelsea stood in front of the art department building once more, a familiar grave expression on her pretty face.

"Here at Whitaker College, new and shocking allegations in the investigation of the murder of college student Beth Shelton. Police have turned their attention once more to a prominent

faculty member, Professor Alexander P. Healey, chairman of the art department—teacher, administrator, and acclaimed sculptor."

"Finch called it. She told him, 'They'll be coming for you next,'" Phoebe reminded Maggie.

"She probably engineered it, too," Maggie murmured. "Let's hear what Chelsea has to say."

"Police questioned Professor Healey in his office, then escorted him to the Essex County police headquarters, where he is presently being interviewed in depth. Police say that at this time, he is cooperating voluntarily with the investigation and is considered a person of interest in the case. Yet just a short time ago, a judge issued a warrant permitting the search of his office, home, and art studio. As you can see, evidence in this case is now being collected."

Once again a team of uniformed police officers and a few in plainclothes were seen in long shot, going in and out of the art department building, carrying boxes and trash bags.

"Give me a break. The police have enough supplies now to open their own art school. Do you think that's their secret plan?" Phoebe asked.

"Reyes and Mossbacher don't look like art lovers to me. They're just looking for a needle in a haystack right now." Maggie turned to Phoebe. "I wouldn't switch jobs with either of them."

"Me, either," Phoebe agreed. "Detective Reyes sounded tired. No wonder she didn't get excited about Quentin's evil-attorney theory. She already had an evil art professor in the bag."

"We don't know if he's evil yet. Allegedly evil, I think, is the official terminology. Maybe the police really don't suspect

Healey of the murder but just want him for questioning, now that Sonya Finch put out the possibility that he and Charlotte are involved. Anyone connected to Charlotte has to be questioned," she added. "But we already know that."

"Maybe Healey knows where Charlotte is. Wouldn't that be great?"

"The police will be even happier than you, if that's at all possible. Healey might be the key to this whole mess."

"Yeah . . . but too bad in a way. That evil-attorney theory was starting to grow on me. And I hate the idea that Professor Healey might be guilty," Phoebe admitted. "He hasn't been showing his best side lately. But I still, well . . . think he's a good guy. I'm going to Google the law firm anyway. Can I use your laptop?" She knew Maggie wouldn't mind, but she wanted to be a polite houseguest.

"It's right on the kitchen counter. Help yourself."

Phoebe brought the computer back to the couch and booted it up. "I think I'll send an update to everyone. In case they missed the news. But I can't tell them the whole story about Quentin in an e-mail."

"Don't worry. They'll all march into the shop tomorrow morning, bright and early, and demand a full report. By the way, while you were in the kitchen, I just heard that they've identified the other Knit Kat: a woman who used to teach literature at Tufts. She's been wintering down in Florida since Christmas, so they doubt she's involved."

"So Professor Finch was sort of a one-woman band after Charlotte left the Knit Kats. No wonder she was looking for fresh meat."

"That's true. She had some Knit Kats vacancies to fill.

There are a lot of moving parts in this puzzle now, Phoebe. And there will be a lot more theories spun before we're done."

Maggie was usually right. But this time, Phoebe hoped she was wrong.

Phoebe hoped now that the police had gotten around to Professor Healey, the case would be solved quickly. She just wanted Charlotte to come back, but she had a feeling her friend wouldn't feel safe until the police nabbed Beth Shelton's killer. Nabbed them and locked them up in a jail cell somewhere.

CHAPTER TWELVE

"**D**o you want me to come with you? I don't have to open the shop until ten. That should be plenty of time." Maggie was putting the breakfast dishes in the dishwasher, her purse and knitting bag on the table, packed and ready to go.

Phoebe had decided to head straight to the police station to file a report on Quentin. She could have gone in the afternoon, but why put it off? She'd woken up with a waffle hangover, or just a nervous stomach, and was starting the day with just coffee this morning.

"That's okay. I'm just going to do this and get it over with. It shouldn't take long. I don't really have that much to say. He grabbed me, held me down. And is a total psycho idiot."

Maggie nodded and pulled on her down coat. "That about covers it. If the gang arrives, we'll try to wait for you. I have a feeling Dana is going to be chock-full of news about Healey."

Phoebe thought so, too. Another reason she wanted to be quick at the police station.

Maggie paused and looked over at her. "I'm proud of you, Phoebe, for filing this report. It takes courage to face up to a bully like Quentin."

Phoebe shrugged. Maggie's compliment made her feel good, but she wasn't sure what to say. "Well . . . a wise person once told me that you have to do the thing you fear most . . . or something like that."

Maggie smiled. "Yes, I did tell you that. But Eleanor Roosevelt said it first," she added with a smile. "She was wiser than me—along with being a good knitter. Good luck. Call me if you need me."

Phoebe appreciated the offer but hoped that wouldn't be necessary.

She had been inside the station once or twice before. But the empty entrance area and big glass window were always unsettling. A uniformed officer with a stocky build and a reddish-blond crew cut sat behind the desk. A brusque and short-tempered attitude was obviously part of his official duties.

Or maybe he didn't approve of Phoebe's streaked hair, or the tiny hoop earring in her nose. Should have expected that around here, she realized.

"I want to file a complaint about . . . someone. I spoke to Detective Reyes last night. She told me to come in."

Detective Reyes's name caught his attention. "Aw-right. Door to the left. First desk. Officer will help you."

Phoebe nodded and headed for a door to the left of the window. An incredibly loud buzzer echoed in the small space, and she nearly put her hands up to cover her ears.

The door led to a large open office space with rows of metal desks. She saw some uniformed officers and some with regular clothes working here and there. Many of the desks were empty, though.

She scanned the room but didn't see Detective Reyes or Mossbacher.

The desk facing the door was unoccupied, too, but a young officer in uniform appeared and walked behind it. He set down a pile of folders on the desk along with a cup of coffee

"Can I help you, miss?" he asked before sitting down.

Phoebe nodded, trying to hide a sudden attack of nerves. "I want to report someone. An incident," she added, using the words Detective Reyes had. "Someone, this guy I sort of know, sort of grabbed me yesterday and pushed me to the ground."

Yeah, and there must have been some brain damage . . . because you sound like a babbling idiot, Phoebe.

If he agreed, or disapproved of the way she looked—like the guy outside—he didn't show it. "Please have a seat." He offered her a plastic-and-metal chair beside the desk and sat down himself. "So you want to make a report about the event?"

Phoebe nodded. "I spoke to Detective Reyes last night. She told me to come in."

"Detective Reyes is busy right now. But I can help you." He was being super polite, but Phoebe realized that Detective Reyes was probably trying to solve Beth Shelton's murder. She didn't have time to fill out petty reports about head cases like Quentin Gibbs.

Speaking of head cases, she suddenly noticed two policemen escorting a rough-looking man in handcuffs down a corridor behind a glass partition. The guy in cuffs looked like he could belong to some Quentin Gibbs Club. Phoebe couldn't help but think of the threat Gibbs had made to her.

"Yeah, sure . . . whatever. Is this going to take long? I have to like get back to work." That wasn't exactly true, but Phoebe felt like she was getting cold feet.

"Not long at all. Let me pull up the form and we'll start."

He turned to his computer and began asking her questions, the usual stuff at first—name, address, contact phone numbers. Once she got rolling with her story, it wasn't as hard as she'd expected. The police officer didn't say much. But she could tell he agreed that Quentin Gibbs was out of control and she'd done the right thing.

When they were done, he printed out the form. Phoebe read it over, signed her name on the bottom, and took a copy for herself.

"I guess Detective Reyes explained that, since Gibbs didn't have a weapon and this was not a robbery or sexual assault, this is not the type of complaint we follow up on automatically. You would have to press charges for the police to determine if the incident requires further action."

"I understand . . . I'm good with the report for now. I don't know about the other thing."

"All right. But if Gibbs bothers you again, call right away. Don't wait," he said firmly. "That makes it harder for us to pick him up if we have to."

"I get it." She had waited, more than twelve hours, but at least she'd come in. She'd done the right thing.

"You're all done. Thanks for coming in, Ms. Meyers." He'd been taught to say that, she guessed. But he still seemed like a nice guy.

Phoebe smiled back briefly and grabbed her big bag. "Great. Thanks. That was . . . weird."

He smiled briefly but didn't reply.

Phoebe felt so relieved, she practically flew out of the police station. She pushed through the first door and came out into the lobby, then quickly headed for the next doors that led to the parking lot. A woman was walking just ahead of her. She pushed open the doors and left them to slam in Phoebe's face.

Nice . . . thanks a lot, Phoebe nearly said aloud. But the rude one had already pulled a big hood up over her head and Phoebe doubted she'd even hear her.

Outside in the lot, the hooded woman ran toward the rows of parked cars. She was carrying a big overloaded bag, along with a manila envelope, and a pile of loose papers under her arm. A few of the papers fluttered out from the pile, and she didn't seem to notice. Phoebe ran to pick them up, stomping on one or two with her boot toe to keep them from blowing away.

"Hey . . . wait up. You dropped something," Phoebe called out.

The woman didn't stop. She walked briskly toward the cars. But when she was only halfway there, Phoebe heard a shout from the far side of the lot, the entrance near the road. She turned to see a swarm of reporters holding microphones and video cameras, charging toward the building.

"There she is . . ." someone called out.

"Hey . . . Mrs. Healey . . . how's your husband doing?"

"Gena . . . how's it going in there? Will Alex be out on bail?"

The object of their attention suddenly ducked her head and turned, running back toward the building. Phoebe still couldn't see her face, but called out anyway.

"Mrs. Healey! It's me, Phoebe Meyers. From school."

When Gena Healey finally looked her way, her face was half covered by big sunglasses. Phoebe barely recognized her. She was all in a state. Who wouldn't be?

Mrs. Healey met her gaze and ran straight toward her. The reporters were getting closer. "Phoebe . . . thank goodness. Is your car nearby? Can you get me out of here?"

"Yeah . . . sure . . . it's right over here. The orange Bug." Phoebe led the way to her car, which was parked in the front aisle, close to the entrance.

Just as Phoebe was about to open the driver's side, Gena Healey dropped the manila folder and more of the papers she was holding. As she crouched down, her big leather bag spilled out on the ground. Phoebe ran over to help her pick everything up. Her body was shaking, and Phoebe could tell the woman was crying.

"No worries, I got this," Phoebe said.

"Forgive me. I'm just . . . having a total meltdown right now." She shook her head, and her hood fell off. Phoebe couldn't tell if she was crying or laughing. A bit of both—just plain hysterical.

Phoebe didn't take time to answer. She focused on picking up the belongings that had spilled from the bag. More papers, a wallet, a makeup case, a magazine—*Vogue Knitting*. There was also a plastic truck, a rubber ball, and a child's knitted hat shaped like a bear. It looked handmade, and well used. Phoebe dumped the items back in the leather tote along with the papers she'd picked up.

Then she quickly unlocked the passenger-side door of her car and ran to the other side. "Get in, they're getting closer."

She slammed her door shut and started the engine. The reporters were close now, a small knot blocking the way out of their parking aisle. Phoebe tricked them by driving in reverse all the way down the aisle, pulling a U-turn, and heading out in the opposite direction.

Gena Healey's mouth hung open. "Wow . . . that was some driving."

Phoebe tried not to gloat. "I saw it in a movie once. I always wanted to try it."

Gena Healey sat back and sighed as they drove past the exit and out onto the street. "Thank you. Thank you so much," she said sincerely. "I've been up all night. Waiting to hear about Alex . . . Professor Healey," she corrected.

Phoebe nodded. Her high spirits quickly deflated. This was serious stuff. "How is he doing?"

"I don't know . . . They won't even let me see him yet. We found a good attorney, though. That should help. He told me to go home and wait. Wait for what? To hear that Alex murdered someone and is going to be sent to jail for the rest of his life?" Her voice was bordering on hysteria now. She hardly seemed to know Phoebe was even there. "Sorry . . . I don't mean to burden you. I need some rest. I don't know what else to do . . ."

Phoebe handed Gena a box of tissues. "Thanks." She took a handful and dried her eyes.

Phoebe had a vague idea where the Healeys lived, in a section of Plum Harbor with stately old homes and long green lawns called Shady Hills, where many of the faculty owned homes. She headed in that direction.

She decided not to talk unless Gena did. She didn't want

to bother her with a lot of questions . . . though her brain buzzed with more than a few.

Gena stared out the passenger-side window and let out a long sigh. "It's been a nightmare. You have no idea."

"Yeah, I'm sure it's been awful," Phoebe replied quietly.

"Alex and I . . . we have our differences, but I hate to see him like this. Locked up in jail . . . You know what he's like . . . It's just . . . unthinkable."

She cried into the handful of tissues again. "I'm sorry, every time I think of our boys . . . He is a good father. No matter what else they try to say about him."

"I'm sure," Phoebe murmured, glancing over at her passenger a moment. "The police questioned me," she admitted. "They searched my apartment and my locker at school and took all my stuff. But they didn't find anything and they finally left me alone. Maybe it will go like that for Professor Healey."

Gena turned to her with a sad smile. "I'd love to think that . . . but it's gone too far the other way," she said quietly

Phoebe looked over at her. "What do you mean? Did they find something?"

Gena took a breath and nodded, staring straight ahead. Phoebe didn't think she was going to answer but finally she said, "You'll probably hear this is on the news tonight anyway, so I guess I can talk about it. The police say they found some yarn in Alex's studio that matches . . . ." She paused and swallowed hard. "That matches the wrapping on Beth Shelton's body. And some shoes . . . The tread and the dirt match footprints they found outside a window . . . where they say the murderer broke into Charlotte Blackburn's apartment." Gena gasped and covered her mouth with a wad of tissues.

"They did?" Phoebe looked over at Gena again, then reminded herself to keep her eyes on the road. Holy enchiladas. That was bad news . . . the very worst.

Phoebe felt a giant lump in her throat. She suddenly felt like crying, too. How could this be? How could good old Professor Healey be a murderer? Pompous and full of himself, yes. A bit of a lech? Definitely. But capable of killing somebody, a girl like Beth Shelton? No way . . . she just couldn't get her brain around that.

"I'm so sorry, Mrs. Healey. I don't care what the police say. I just don't think Professor Healey is the guy. No way could he ever do anything like that. He's just not . . . not that type of person."

Gena nodded and blinked, trying to smile, her large eyes full of tears. She touched Phoebe's arm lightly. "I don't think my husband could ever do anything like that, either. But . . . there's more. More reasons the police say it's got to be him." She paused and sighed, then stared out the side window again, covering her mouth with a tissue. "I really can't talk about it."

Phoebe didn't want to ask her more questions, either. She could guess what some of those reasons might be. He was having an affair with Charlotte, for one thing. She sure wasn't going to ask Gena Healey about that. If there was something else, well . . . Dana would fill in the blanks later at the shop, she thought.

"We're going to stick by him. And fight," Gena said finally. "I don't know what else to do."

"I'm sure a lot of people at Whitaker will help you," Phoebe said sincerely.

"I hope so . . . Oh dear, I forgot to tell you where to turn.

It's the next left, Birch Way. Third house on the left," she added.

Phoebe made the turn and quickly noticed the *News Alive 25!* van and two others like it parked on the street in front of the Healeys' house.

"Oh . . . no. They won't leave us alone. It's not right." Gena was about to start crying again. Phoebe wasn't sure what to do.

"Put your head down, I'll just drive by," she said. Gena did as she was told, and Phoebe hit the gas, cruising by the news van. There were a few media people standing near the vans and near the front lawn, but no one paid attention to her car.

She turned at the first corner, and Gena sat up. "Just go around the block and stop at that white house," she instructed as they came down the street. "My neighbor who lives behind us will let me go through her backyard. I'll get in that way."

Good plan, Phoebe thought. She pulled up to a white Victorian, and Gena pulled her hood up and put on her sunglasses again. Then she jumped out and grabbed her bag and papers from the backseat.

She stood with her arms full and looked inside the car. "Thank you so much, Phoebe. It was so good of you to go out of your way like this to help me . . ."

"No big deal. I . . . I hope things improve for Professor Healey. You never know. It could totally turn around again," she offered, trying to sound hopeful.

Gena Healey didn't seem encouraged. Her expression bleak, she nodded quickly. "I appreciate your concern . . . thanks again."

She closed the car door and quickly turned to walk up the

path that led to the backyard. Phoebe felt a pang in her chest. Wow, what a big mess that family was in now.

It did look bad for Professor Healey. Real bad.

"There you are. Was it difficult to file the report? They must have asked you a million questions." Maggie was relieved to see Phoebe. She'd encouraged her to report Quentin and now worried the process had been an ordeal.

And they'd been waiting for Phoebe to return—she, Lucy, and Suzanne. Dana had taken a yoga class but had just sent a text that she was on the way.

They sat in the small alcove near the front of the shop, a cozy knitting niche Maggie had set up for small classes and customers who wanted to knit and chat, and make new friends. There was a camelback love seat, two armchairs, and a velvet-covered rocker, with a low marble-topped table in between.

"It wasn't so bad. But I didn't come straight back to the village. Guess who I met at the police station and then ended up giving a ride home?" Phoebe sat down in the velvet rocker and dumped her big bag on the floor. She smiled mysteriously. "And she gave me the inside scoop on Professor Healey."

"Detective Reyes?" Maggie guessed.

"Nope . . . why would I give her a ride? She has like a whole parking lot of police cruisers at her command," Phoebe reminded her.

"Oh, right." Maggie hadn't thought of that. It was early. She needed more coffee.

"I got it . . . Gena Healey." Suzanne pointed her finger at Phoebe.

"You are good, Suzanne. Winner, winner, chicken dinner," Phoebe recited, sounding silly.

Lucy gave her a look. "Are you all right?"

"Never mind that, how did you end up as Gena Healey's driver?" Suzanne followed up.

"Long story. She came out of the station ahead of me and started dropping all her stuff. And crying all over the place."

"Poor woman, anybody would be unhinged in her place," Maggie said.

"Once we got outside, a pack of news hounds came stampeding across the lot, badgering her. So we jumped in my car and I did this amazing super-reverse move and like nobody could even follow us. I could be like a stunt driver in the movies after that."

"That sounds like quite an adventure," Maggie commented. "Oh, look . . . here's Dana. Let's wait until she gets in before you tell us the rest."

Phoebe shrugged. "No problem. It gets even better."

Maggie smiled. For once Phoebe had the inside story. But she didn't think Dana would mind at all. It was a refreshing change.

"Good, I'm glad you're here," Maggie greeted Dana. "Phoebe had to visit the police station this morning and ended up giving Gena Healey a ride home. She got an earful, too."

"Really? Let's hear what the wife has to say before I tell you what Jack found out."

Dana quickly slipped into an empty chair and took out her usual breakfast, a big green smoothie. She set it on the table and unwrapped the straw.

"Well, we get in my car and she just starts talking," Phoebe began. "She was like hysterical. She used up a whole box of tissues. The back of the car looks like a wastepaper basket." Maggie wanted to laugh but didn't want to miss any of the story. "Having your husband in a jail, being questioned about a murder, and being all over TV is bad enough. But the worst part is that the police told him this morning they found yarn in his studio that matches the covering on Beth Shelton's body, and his shoes match footprints from the yard. So . . . they think they've got him. And," Phoebe added, "Gena Healey says that's not the only thing they've got on him. She says there's more, but she couldn't tell me."

"More? Isn't that enough to put him away for a long time?" Suzanne shook her head and flipped the lid of a tall paper cup. Maggie spotted milky foam, Suzanne's usual latte.

"There *is* more," Dana told them. "He doesn't have a good alibi for the night of the murder."

"Where was he Sunday night? The reception ended at eight," Suzanne recalled. "Didn't he go home with his wife?"

"That's just it. Seems there have been some tensions in the Healey household. Healey has been having an affair with Charlotte, and he's been sleeping in his studio the last week or so."

"So it is true. That's what Professor Finch said, but he kept denying it," Phoebe told her friends.

She sounded disappointed, Maggie thought. A bit disillusioned with Charlotte, perhaps, as well as her mentor.

Dana had picked up Phoebe's reaction, too, Maggie realized. "If it's any comfort to you, Phoebe, the relationship didn't last very long. He told the police that Charlotte broke up with him a week or so before the art show. After the reception, he said, he went to the studio alone and went straight to bed. Well, to his futon. He thought Charlotte might go there, to hide from Quentin. But she never did. And he doesn't have anyone to confirm that he was there. Especially at the time of Beth's murder."

"Where is the studio, someplace on campus?" Suzanne asked.

"No, it's in the village. Not too far from the train station. But there's not much on that road, an old warehouse and a storage place. The area is very deserted at night, and there aren't any security cameras at the entrance or anything like that."

"So he's sort of stuck trying to prove he was there all night," Lucy said. "Why did he think Charlotte would go there for protection—did he say?"

"Just a fantasy, I think. He thought they would get back together again after the art show and she'd just been overwhelmed by the pressure." Dana took a sip of her green drink. "But of course, Charlotte vanished. So we don't know if that's true."

"I have a good guess." Phoebe put down her own yogurt-and-berry smoothie and sat up in the armchair. "Healey must be the guy she told me about. No way Charlotte was getting back with him. She called him a big nothing and said he'd just used her. Talk about optimistic. Maybe just egotistic."

Now Phoebe sounded angry and disillusioned with Healey. It was hard to see the secret, unseemly side of people you admire, mentors and role models. Like turning over a beautiful stone and seeing all the squirming bugs underneath.

But everyone had their squirming-bug side. That didn't

negate the whole person. It didn't mean his teaching had been without value. But it would take time for her to realize that, Maggie knew. A long time, perhaps, and this saga wasn't over yet.

"I agree," Maggie said finally. "I think Professor Healey is the man Charlotte was talking about. If we discount Quentin's villainous-lawyer theory," she added.

Maggie had already told the others about Phoebe's confrontation with Quentin and his theory about Charlotte being chased by nefarious attorneys from Dylan, Garland & Doyle. It had seemed plausible last night, but faded to the background now, in light of Healey's apprehension.

"So his wife knew about Charlotte?" Maggie asked Dana.

"No, he claims the marriage had other problems and had not been happy for a long time. Wait . . . he used this great euphemism—I have to remember it for my practice—he said they suffered from 'perennial tensions and anguish.'"

"Oh brother. Sounds like one of those ailments you never knew you had, and they describe all the symptoms in a drug commercial? Twitching eyelids, restless legs, vertigo, rashes . . ." Suzanne put her cup down and was left with a foam mustache.

Everyone laughed quietly.

"What? What did I say?" she asked, gazing around. "It wasn't that funny."

Maggie made a motion at her lip. "You have a little . . . froth."

"Mustachioed-lady latte thing? I hate that." She whisked it away with a napkin. "I never drink a cappuccino with a client . . . or eat spinach," she added. "So? What else did Healey say?"

"He said the breakup wasn't about Charlotte at all. He said his wife didn't even know about the affair. Though she probably does now," Dana added.

"I couldn't tell one way or the other," Phoebe cut in. "She never mentioned Charlotte."

"Oh, puh-leaze . . . of course she knew. Women can sense these things. We can sniff it out. He might have a huge vocabulary, but he's still a dumbbell." Suzanne went back to her cup, patting her mouth with a napkin after each sip.

"He wouldn't be the first man—or woman—to think he was fooling his spouse." Maggie picked up her knitting and sat back against the love seat. "So, along with the yarn they found in his studio, his goose is cooked."

"Not entirely . . . but the DA likes this guy," Dana noted. "Healey has no alibi and a strong motive for the murder with Charlotte breaking up with him. His bad blood with Sonya Finch gives him a reason to frame the Knit Kats, too. He was close to Charlotte and must have known she was a Knit Kat. Maybe he tried to make it look like the group turned on her? And if that's not enough, he's done some fiber art. You already told us that, remember, Phoebe?"

"Yeah, that's right. He's mainly a sculptor. But he's done these big wall hangings. But it's not really knitting," she pointed out.

"I'm not sure the prosecutor is going to worry about whether it's knitting or weaving . . . or plastic lanyards that kids make at day camp." Dana slipped her glasses on and took out her knitting. "So far, Healey is the best they can come up with. And they've connected him to the crime scene."

Maggie checked the time. On Saturdays she didn't open until ten. They still had a few minutes before customers came in. She wanted to hear the rest about Healey.

"Is he still in custody?" she asked.

"Last I heard. The police can hold him for twenty-four hours without charging him. But he has a good lawyer, Richard Scherer, who's trying to get him out."

"Gena Healey mentioned that—she seemed to trust the lawyer they found," Phoebe added.

"How about Gena? Is she going to stand by her man? Or let him swing in the wind? She must be in total shock from all these nasty revelations about her husband. Even if they were estranged." The latte was drained, the cup covered with the plastic cap again. Suzanne took out a slim compact and began reapplying lipstick with the aid of a tiny mirror.

"She was flipping between hysteria and staring into space," Phoebe recalled, "so it's hard to tell. She did say she was going to stick with him and fight. But she didn't seem very hopeful."

"There isn't much to be hopeful about right now." Maggie sighed and counted out the stitches on the top row of her work. She wasn't sure she'd reduced this row properly, she'd gotten so distracted by the conversation.

"They have kids, right?" Lucy asked.

"Two boys," Phoebe replied.

"That's too bad. It's always hardest on the children." Suzanne shook her head as she put her lipstick away.

"Yes, it is." Dana's tone echoed Suzanne's sympathy. "Some new information may come to light. But it's hard to see how Healey can talk his way out of this now."

Maggie was about to speak when she heard someone's phone ring, playing lilting bars of classical music. One of the Goldberg Variations? A speedy one, though she couldn't identify it by number.

Dana pulled her phone out of her pocket and checked the screen. "A text from Jack." She opened it and read it quickly, then looked up at her friends, her expression somber. "'Latex glove found at crime scene matches Healey's DNA. Police due to charge H. soon.'"

Suzanne gasped. "Game over."

Lucy seemed less surprised. "You called it, Dana. You said they needed to find physical evidence that ties him to the crime scene. I can't see how he'll talk his way out of this now."

"Now a glove? Gee . . . I'm like blown away," Phoebe admitted. "I know it might be him. I mean, it sort of makes sense. But I can't believe it. He was always so nice and encouraging . . . and so . . . not that guy who would kill someone. And not in such a crazy way . . ."

Phoebe's shock and delayed reaction were understandable, Maggie realized. She knew the man personally. He was her adviser and mentor. It was hard for her to believe her mild-mannered professor was capable of murder.

Before this horrible situation, the worst offense one might have accused him of was giving a boring art history lecture. Or wearing a checkered shirt with a tweed sports coat.

"Of course you're shocked. You knew him well. He was your adviser and you saw him at school almost every day. Everyone at Whitaker is going to have the same reaction. Especially in the art department," Maggie reminded her.

Phoebe nodded, looking a little sad and confused. "It's funny, I didn't feel the same when the police were questioning Professor Finch. She has that weird laugh . . . and I always had the feeling she had a secret mean side."

Maggie could relate to that assessment. She'd felt the same about Sonya Finch ever since they'd met.

"I know the yarn thing is serious. And the shoe prints. And the glove sort of nails it," Phoebe continued. "But that evil-attorney idea caught my imagination last night, and if it's Healey, how does the money fit in?"

"I thought of the money, too," Lucy said. "I'm sure the police are wondering the same thing."

"I don't think they're done looking into his financials. Maybe they'll find a red flag there," Dana noted.

Suzanne shrugged. "Maybe the money has nothing to do with the murder. Maybe that's a whole other ball of wax and this was purely a crime of passion. A lover's revenge. If he couldn't have her, nobody could." Suzanne's dramatic tone matched her fresh slash of red lipstick. "Hell hath no fury like an art professor scorned," she declared.

"I don't think that's the *exact* quote . . . but we get the idea," Maggie said with a wry smile.

"Yeah, well . . . love really must be blind. Otherwise, why didn't he realize the blonde in the bedroom wasn't Charlotte? It was Beth. Duh? . . . That's the part I don't buy." Phoebe sat back and crossed her arms over her chest. "He should have known what Charlotte looked like by now, even in a dark bedroom . . . especially in a dark bedroom."

Her friends exchanged quick glances. Maggie was the first to reply. She could see that Phoebe still didn't want to believe

Healey was guilty, though the evidence was piling up and hearing about his secret side had been disappointing. Still, she had to agree. Healey mistaking Beth for Charlotte didn't seem logical.

"It does make you wonder . . . and it would probably make a judge or jury wonder, too."

"But if the police believe they've got their man, they're not going to look any further," Lucy pointed out. "The fiber in his studio, the footprints, and the glove . . . that's enough. Right, Dana?"

Dana nodded, focused on her knitting. "Definitely enough to charge him. They'll build a case from there."

"And if he didn't do it. And it was some crooked attorney, let's just say," Phoebe speculated out loud, "then the real killer is off the hook. Because the police aren't going to keep looking when they think they have the right guy."

"That's true, Phoebe." Dana looked up. "But there is one way we would all know for sure. There's always a chance he might confess. Professor Healey isn't a hardened criminal. He might feel guilty or give in to police pressure. He might make a deal to plead guilty to some lesser charge, in order to get a reduced sentence or avoid life in prison."

"Eek. What a fate. It all sounds pretty dreadful to me." Suzanne shook her head and picked up her purse and knitting bag. She was going to show houses today, Maggie guessed. She could predict fairly accurately from her outfits. Today Suzanne wore a striking combination, a mustard-colored wool coat with shiny black buttons, a long, multicolored scarf she'd knit herself, and black wool pants. Large sunglasses were perched on her head.

"The Whitaker campus must be in an uproar. I can think

of one person who must be happy, though." Lucy waited a moment. "Sonya Finch. She pretty much blames Healey for ruining her life. Certainly, for ruining her husband's life and making her a widow."

"A disabled one," Maggie reminded her. "Sonya Finch isn't shedding any tears over this news. She might be disgraced and even fired, but Healey's fate looks even worse right now."

Before anyone could answer, Maggie heard a tap on the window. Two early-bird customers peered in and gently smiled when they caught her eye. Maggie checked her watch and jumped up from the love seat.

"Good gravy . . . it's five past ten. I have to let a few paying customers in. Sorry, ladies. You can hang out here and dish as long as you like. You all know that."

Sometimes she wished the shop could be for her friends exclusively. But then she knew that was silly—she loved to help dedicated knitters and turn novices into true believers.

Despite the temptation to linger and solve this enigma, her friends quickly dispersed. They all had places to go and people to see this morning, too.

A few minutes later, it was just her and Phoebe . . . and the customers. Their knitting gang would return soon enough, she was sure.

Until then, it was time to get down to business. Saturday was the busiest day of the week. The bright sun and slightly warmer temperature today had brought out all the hibernating knitters. Maggie and Phoebe raced from one end of the shop to the other all morning, with barely a break.

But the revelations and questions about Professor Healey

lingered at the edge of her thoughts—and were in Phoebe's as well, Maggie guessed. Would the police find even more damning evidence? Would he confess? Or plead guilty to a lesser charge? It seemed far too early for that, Maggie thought. But sometimes, these things moved very quickly.

It really depended on how much evidence the police came up with, and how persuasive they were. And how skilled Healey's attorney was. Maybe he wouldn't let his client make a bargain no matter what the police produced. Phoebe had pointed out some interesting inconsistencies. Maggie was sure a good attorney would see them, too.

It was almost three before the flow of customers ebbed. Maggie had asked Phoebe to look up some simple scarf and hat patterns. She was going to help a customer who led a Girl Scout troop and wanted to give them knitting lessons. The woman would be in soon. Maggie had already gathered some yarn for the projects.

But when she peered over Phoebe's shoulder, she didn't see knitting patterns on the laptop screen. Phoebe was reading a news article and from a financial website, no less.

"Working on your investments? I thought you were going to find those patterns for me."

"Oh, right . . . I already did. The copies are in that folder." Phoebe pointed to a yellow folder at the end of the counter, then glued her gaze back on the computer.

"What are you looking at? I'm curious," she admitted, peering over her shoulder again.

"Well . . . sort of embarrassing to admit it, but I'm back to the evil-attorney theory. I was checking out the law firm where Charlotte worked. They have a huge website, pretty impressive.

I didn't understand half of it. Make that three-quarters," Phoebe added modestly.

"Just legal jargon. Don't be intimidated. Go on," she encouraged her.

"I was just snooping around and hit some links. They have loads of news articles posted about their big deals and high-profile cases."

"I wouldn't doubt it. Did something spark your memory? Something Charlotte told you about?"

"Yeah, sort of. A while ago, Charlotte told me about this special job her supervisor asked her to work on. She said they only asked a few of the best proofreaders and she'd get extra pay. She wasn't allowed to do it at home. She had to go into the office in Boston and sign all these privacy agreements and it like lasted all night long. But they gave her car fare and dinner, and she was going to get a lot of extra pay, so she thought it was worth it."

"So she went in and did the job?" Maggie asked.

Phoebe nodded. "Yeah, but she made some huge mistake and ended up having words with the supervisor, and he fired her on the spot. She was really upset. She'd never really screwed up before. She said it really wasn't fair. She'd liked that job—it worked out well with her classes and doing her artwork. And she really needed the money for school and all."

"Of course. What happened? Did she make an appeal and get her job back?"

"No, she didn't. But she showed me an article in the newspaper a few days later. About this big merger, two software companies in the Tech Belt up here. She said that was the legal agreement she'd been proofreading, all the documents that had to do with it. That's why it was so secret. If anyone knows about a merger like that, they can make a ton of dough on the stock market."

"Yes, I know. They say the Securities and Exchange Commission is always watching for that sort of thing. But I do think a lot of people get away with it," Maggie speculated. "Not anyone we know," she added with a laugh.

"No . . . but . . . I don't know. I just got this odd feeling when I saw the article that it had something to do with Charlotte having all that money in her locker. Like some crooked lawyer at her firm took advantage of the merger and somehow Charlotte got involved? Maybe he gave her the money to hide or something?"

Maggie considered it. "I suppose it's possible. Though there isn't much evidence to go on in that direction right now," she added.

"Yeah, too far-fetched. I'm just trying to connect dots here that don't really relate." Still, Maggie saw Phoebe hit the print button to make copies of the article and the references on the law firm's website.

Two customers were walking in, and she put on her shopkeeper's smile to greet them. She and Phoebe would talk more about this later, she thought.

The afternoon was busy enough not to be boring but not so busy that they were run ragged. Just the way Maggie liked it.

She was just getting ready to close the shop when Detective Mossbacher walked in. Maggie met his glance, and he spared a quick smile. "Mrs. Messina, how's business?"

"Life is good, Detective. It's Saturday, and everybody wanted their knitting supplies. And it's just about closing time," she added—though she didn't mean to sound like she wanted him to go. She was pleased to see him again, she realized. "What brings you back? More questions about knitting styles?"

He took his hat off and shook his head. "No, not today. I came to talk to Phoebe. Is she still here?"

"Yes . . . she just went back to the storeroom a minute." Maggie had turned around to call Phoebe when she appeared, holding a mug of tea.

"Phoebe, Detective Mossbacher's here. He wants to speak with you."

Maggie felt apprehensive, and guessed Phoebe did, too, even though today they knew for certain that Phoebe was not going to be dragged back to the station. The investigators were far too busy with Alex Healey, their latest and greatest prime suspect.

"Hey, Detective." Phoebe sounded nervous as she approached and stood near them. "What's up?"

"Not too much. But a report crossed my desk this afternoon. You filed a complaint about Quentin Gibbs this morning?"

"That's right. I did."

"Normally, I wouldn't see something like that, but since Gibbs was questioned in this investigation, the officer who took your report sent me a copy. Good police work," he noted.

"Yeah, he seemed real efficient." Phoebe took a sip of tea.

"Frankly, I was distressed to read about that incident, Phoebe. Of course, Gibbs should be detained and get counseling or treatment somewhere. But you shouldn't have been hanging around that house. It's still a crime scene," he reminded her. "Didn't you see all that yellow tape? It's a violation to cross a police line."

"There wasn't any tape across the backyard. I just went back there a minute to feed Charlotte's cats," she argued.

Detective Mossbacher took in a long, slow breath. Maggie could see he wasn't really mad at her. Just worried.

"I know, I read what you said. But it wasn't safe or smart. Especially after dark. Promise me you won't go back there."

Maggie could see Phoebe was having a hard time making that promise. Because she was thinking about the cats.

"What if I go during the day and put food near the garage? Is that part a crime scene? What if someone comes with me?" she added.

He sighed again. "Okay, near the garage and just during the day . . . and with a friend to help you. Hopefully, you won't have to babysit forever."

"Oh? Does that mean you found out something about Charlotte?" she asked eagerly.

He looked surprised at the question and then chagrined as he realized he'd slipped. "Can't say. Sorry. But we're working on it. Not just us, the FBI, too. They've got some high-tech gadgets now. Face detection, the works. It's amazing," he added.

"Amazing enough to find her?" Maggie asked tentatively.

"If they can't do it, nobody can." She almost thought he winked at her, but decided he was just squinting his eyes up a bit.

"I don't think she'll come back until she knows it's safe," Phoebe said.

"That's probably true," he agreed.

"I remembered something, Detective," she added. "I'm not sure if it's important or not. It might have nothing to do with anything . . ."

"You let us decide that. What did you remember?" He seemed suddenly alert, his focus fixed on her.

"If you read that report, you know why Quentin grabbed me. He has this idea that someone from the law firm where Charlotte worked wanted to harm her. Not Professor Healey."

"Yes, I read that. He told us that in his interview," he added. Now he didn't seem as interested anymore, Maggie noticed. "What about it?"

"Well, I was noodling around on their website . . . Dylan, Garland and Doyle. I saw a new article about a big merger they handled when Charlotte was still working there. She was called in as a proofreader. But she ended up getting fired." Phoebe paused and walked over to the counter. She had printed out the article and saved it there. She handed it to the detective. "I thought it could connect to all that money she had in her locker at school," she added.

Now he squinted . . . no, more of a real scowl at both of them. "How did you hear about that?"

"Oh . . . people in town gossip. You'd be surprised what we hear in here," Maggie said quickly, covering their tracks. "Go on with your story, Phoebe."

Phoebe explained the rest of her theory—about the sensitive information Charlotte had seen and how it could have been used by someone willing to dare to do some inside trading. Though she had no idea who, or how. If it was Charlotte or somebody out to get her now.

"It's too bizarre, right? Maybe I caught something weird from Quentin. While he was tackling me," she added, crinkling her nose.

Mossbacher didn't show any reaction. He folded the article and tucked it in his coat pocket. "We'll look into it. We did follow up on Gibbs's lead. But he didn't have any specific information. Just some wild talk. This is a little different," he added.

Interesting, Maggie thought. And true.

He soon bid them good night, and Maggie locked the door, happy to call it a day.

"It seems like he took you seriously, Phoebe," she said, walking back to the counter. "He didn't dismiss it out of hand. Just because they have Healey now."

"No, he didn't. So I did my civic duty twice today."

"Yes, you did. And if you hadn't stepped up and reported Gibbs this morning, Mossbacher would have never come here, and you wouldn't have been able to give him your information."

"Yeah . . . that's true, never thought of it." Phoebe paused and picked at her fingernail polish, sparkly blue. "It sounds like they know where Charlotte is. Or almost do."

"I thought so, too. I think that's encouraging. It will be a week tomorrow since the art show and since she disappeared. Can you believe it? It seems like so much longer," Maggie realized.

"Tell me about it. It feels more like a month than a week to me. But things are moving faster now. I wonder if Mossbacher will tell me if he digs up any dirt about that law firm."

"Oh, I don't think so. They don't work that way. But we'll know one way or the other if it leads somewhere," Maggie replied. "This stuff is like yeast. It takes a while to find out if it's live, and will make the dough rise. Speaking of dough, I'm going to try this recipe I found for flatbread tonight. I've invited Lucy and Matt. Would you like to help me make it? And eat it?"

Phoebe was smiling, but her dark eyes had narrowed. "You're just trying to get me to come over again, Maggie. You're so transparent."

"I know, but . . . it will be fun, and one more night won't hurt. Mossbacher made me worry about Quentin again. He wouldn't have come here if he didn't think the kid is dangerous." She didn't mean to scare Phoebe, but she couldn't help but be honest.

Phoebe smiled and shrugged. "All right. It's Saturday night—who wants to hang out alone? Josh has a gig here in town. I don't want to keep thinking about it. I might be tempted to go down there."

"And we don't want you to do that," Maggie said quickly. "Less temptation at my house."

"Definitely. Can I bring my new boyfriend? I feel like I've been ignoring him lately."

Maggie knew she meant the cat. She thought about it a moment. But only a moment. "Sure, we'll make him his own little bread, fish-shaped, with anchovies."

That made Phoebe laugh finally. A very pleasant sound.

CHAPTER THIRTEEN

Maggie and Phoebe decided to buy the dough ready-made for their flatbread project. They were getting a late start and needed speedy results. To Maggie's surprise, the information Phoebe had given Mossbacher yielded fast results, too.

At a little past noon on Monday, Dana walked into the shop. She found Maggie and Phoebe at the worktable, eating lunch. She put down her lunch and knitting bag, and joined them.

"Jack just called. I had to stop by. The police finally figured out the connection between the money Charlotte hid in her locker and Healey. They needed the FBI to help them . . . forensic accountants."

"Forensic accountants? I had no idea there was such a thing." Maggie paused while eating her soup.

"Oh, yes, very important work. They analyze and track financial records, offshore accounts, phony investment schemes, and tax shelters. Secret Swiss bank accounts," she added, raising her eyebrows.

"Wow . . . does Healey have one of those?" Phoebe asked.

"He has a few secret accounts. The first time the police looked at his financial records they didn't see anything unusual. But, acting on a tip," she said, glancing at Phoebe, "the team started digging. Especially around the time of a certain merger of two software companies. They came up with some offshore accounts that have a few hundred thousand altogether and some investment accounts he'd opened and used only once. Using the names and social security numbers of his deceased parents, no less. Clever, right?" she added.

"Very clever. Downright . . . shrewd," Phoebe said.

"Well, he is a PhD. Very intelligent, no question. He applied his brainpower to making some money instead of artwork, I guess."

"Profits from some inside trading on the stock market, right?" Maggie hated to steal Dana's thunder, but she couldn't help it.

Dana glanced at Phoebe again. "The lead you gave Mossbacher really panned out. Jack heard he was grateful."

"I can't really take the credit. It was Quentin's idea. But he's too crazy to follow through on anything."

"But you weren't and you did the legwork, Phoebe," Dana noted. "The police confronted Healey with all this, and he confessed—to the insider trading, but not the murder. He still claims he's totally innocent and would never have hurt Beth . . . or Charlotte.'"

Phoebe looked down at her lunch. Maggie could tell she believed Healey, despite this latest bombshell.

"What did he say about the stock market scam? How did he pull that off exactly?" Maggie asked.

"Well, he said Charlotte came to his studio one night, very upset. She'd just been fired and told him the whole story. She'd only wanted him to comfort her. But he quickly realized the information she'd passed on, while she was crying her eyes out, was valuable. The next day, he started setting up accounts and buying stock using money from retirement accounts. When the merger went through, he hit the jackpot. His plan was to hide the money and run away with Charlotte. But he says she was appalled, and that was why she broke up with him."

"But she took fifty grand anyway?" Maggie asked.

Dana shook her head. "No . . . he claims she didn't want to touch the money. But he put some in her locker, hoping it would change her mind. To her credit, Charlotte only took out one thousand dollars, enough to leave town. She must have gone into the building Sunday night sometime. Or maybe she already had it because she knew she wanted to get away."

"So he's the reason Charlotte ran away. She's afraid of getting into trouble for what *he* did." Phoebe was incensed. "No wonder she won't come back. Even less chance now, once this part hits the news."

"Maybe . . . but maybe she'll see that it's all out in the open and she can't really hide anymore," Dana said reasonably. "It could be a relief."

Phoebe didn't answer. Maggie felt sorry for her. Finally Phoebe said, "Well, at least now we understand something we didn't know before. I was trying to help him, but I guess this makes the case against Healey even stronger. If Charlotte was angry at what he'd done and didn't want to run off with him, he had even more reason to want to silence her."

Dana nodded, spooning up the last of her soup. "That's

exactly what the police think now, too. But he still claims he's totally innocent and someone is trying to frame him. He says he's a stock market swindler but not a murderer."

"While he has an even stronger motive to kill Charlotte, the question remains why he didn't realize the woman in the bedroom was Beth . . . and not his intended victim," Maggie reminded them. "He and Charlotte were lovers. He should have recognized Beth was the wrong woman."

"It's a good one," Dana conceded. "But the prosecution will try to get around it. They have a lot of other things to talk about."

Phoebe was frowning. She still looked angry and upset at this turn of news. "I still don't get that part, either. He seems totally guilty now. I feel like such a jerk for looking up to him. He was like my favorite teacher. It's like . . . who are you? And what have you done with Professor Healey?"

"I'm sure a lot of people were fooled by Professor Healey— you weren't the only one," Maggie pointed out. She turned to Dana. "With all this evidence stacked against him, don't you think he'll confess?"

Dana shrugged. She bunched up the trash bag and put it aside. "So far, he keeps saying he's innocent and claims Sonya Finch is framing him."

"Finch? That's interesting. She has plenty of reason to want to see him punished. But why would she incriminate the Knit Kats? And she also wouldn't have mistaken Beth for Charlotte."

"Healey had even less reason to do that," Phoebe pointed out.

"Yes, we've gone there before," Maggie reminded them. "That part still doesn't make sense."

"We have. And I have to run. I have a patient coming in soon, sorry." Dana glanced at her watch. "I guess we have to credit this one to the police. It seems they've got their man. At least we know that Charlotte wasn't involved in the stock market scheme. And wouldn't even take any money. That takes character," Dana reminded Phoebe. "When she comes back, she'll have some explaining to do. But she was naive and trusting, and Healey took advantage of her. She can't be punished that severely."

Phoebe nodded. "I sure hope so."

When Dana left, Maggie was alone with Phoebe. A class was coming in soon, one of Maggie's favorites, animal-face hats. Phoebe was going to help teach today. But they had some time before they had to set up.

"Well, seems like all the loose ends of this fiber piece are being tied up. What do you think now? Still feeling Professor Healey might be innocent?"

Phoebe sighed. "I don't know . . . It doesn't seem so, does it? And who would want to frame him besides Sonya Finch? And I just don't think she'd throw the Knit Kats under the bus, just to get Healey."

"I don't, either. And she's so clever, she could figure out any number of ways to incriminate him."

"Yeah, probably." Phoebe was quiet a moment. "It's hard to believe he could pull off a stock scam like that. But he's a pretty smart guy."

"Obviously," Maggie agreed.

"The only thing that still doesn't fit is him—or someone else who would stand to benefit from taking Charlotte out of the picture—mistaking Beth for Charlotte. But maybe it was really dark and he was really nervous or had on some sort of mask so he couldn't see clearly?"

"That could be," Maggie agreed. Still, she didn't think Phoebe was totally convinced. Maybe, in time, she would be.

Phoebe was feeling a little blue today for other reasons, reasons that had nothing to do with her runaway friend Charlotte, or her professor and role model who'd turned out to have feet of clay.

She'd gotten depressed again over the weekend about Josh, her ex-boyfriend with the feet of clay. She'd stayed away from his gig in Plum Harbor with admirable self-restraint. But she couldn't help looking on Facebook late that night, and found pictures he'd posted of himself at the gig, with some new girl.

Even though she'd initiated the breakup, Phoebe still felt hurt. It had barely been two weeks. "It didn't take him long," she complained to Maggie. "He can't stand to be alone. He's so insecure. A girl just has to smile at him, and he like melts in a puddle. It's pathetic. She's wrapped around him like a rash. And she looks like she shops at Sluts-R-Us."

Maggie nearly laughed at that description, but she knew this was a serious moment. "You're well rid of him, honestly. He wasn't nearly good enough for you, Phoebe. You'll do much better next time."

It was all true. But there was little more Maggie could say.

Getting over a failed romance was a roller coaster ride, up one minute, down the next. That Facebook photo had sent Phoebe plummeting again, though today, she seemed a bit better.

Maggie cleared up the lunch things, and Phoebe cleaned

off the table. For the afternoon class—"Lions and Tigers and Bears . . . Oh My!"—they'd be making animal hats for children.

Maggie brought out the yarns and needles and set up the sample hats on the table—a bear, a lion, and a tiger . . . which could also be trimmed into a cat or a dog, of course. One basic pattern was used, but many different animals could be created, depending on the colors used and the sewed-on details. And the imagination of the knitter. Simple to knit and everybody loved making them. Especially grandmas.

Phoebe picked up the bear and put it on her hand like a puppet. "So give me your honest opinion," she said to the bear. "You've heard all the evidence. Who do you think killed Beth Shelton? . . . Was it really Professor Healey? He always seemed like such a nice guy, couldn't hurt a bug . . . even though he had a shady side. What about Professor Finch . . . or Quentin Gibbs? Crazy as a bed bug." Phoebe held the bear to her ear. "Things are seldom what they seem. How true, Mr. Bear . . ."

Maggie stood back, watching this pantomime. "Are you done now?" she asked in a pointed tone.

Phoebe didn't seem to hear Maggie for a moment. Then suddenly she stared up at her and dropped the hat on the floor. Her dark eyes grew very wide and her mouth hung open a bit. As if she'd just witnessed some amazing sight.

"Yes . . . I *am* done . . . I *know* who did it, Maggie. I know who killed Beth and wants to frame Professor Healey." Phoebe's voice rose on a note of amazement and she tugged at Maggie's arm.

Maggie stood stone-still. She didn't even breathe. "Who?"

"Gena Healey. Who else could it be?"

262   /   Anne Canadeo

Maggie leaned back and shook her head doubtfully. "What made you think of that?"

Phoebe looked at the hat. "For one thing, a hat just like this fell out of her tote bag . . . and a copy of *Vogue Knitting*. So I bet she can knit. And she must have found out about her husband's affair with Charlotte and his plans to ditch her and her kids. And maybe she even knew about the money he'd taken from their retirement accounts to fund his big deal. And how he'd hidden all his profits from her. In a way, he'd stolen from their family in order to set himself up in Europe with his mistress . . . and leave her and their kids without anything. That is really low . . ."

"And definitely motive for murder," Maggie had to concede. This was making sense. "So she was the scorned wife seeking revenge on her double-crossing husband and his lover. It's classic."

"Isn't it? And I don't think Gena ever met Charlotte face-to-face. Though she'd probably seen her from far away or seen some photo of her. I remember at the art show she said something like, 'Too bad Charlotte is gone. I wanted to meet her.' Or something like that. And she easily could have planted the yarn in his studio, and even taken one of the gloves he uses when he works on his sculptures and left it at the crime scene. Ditto for the boots. Maybe she wore them herself and then put them back in his closet or something."

It could have gone like that. Maggie could not find any holes in her logic. "But where do the Knit Kats come in? Why bring them into the picture?"

"It's perfect. It makes it look as if Healey was trying to get rid of Charlotte and frame the Knit Kats. The Knit Kats are an easy target. They're mysterious and rebellious. I think it was just like a big coincidence that they staged the parking meter thing right before the murder. She must have known her husband disdained them and what he called their 'faux artwork.' But not that Charlotte was in the group," Phoebe concluded. "That was just lucky."

"But maybe she knew Sonya was a Knit Kat," Maggie reasoned. "Maybe Sonya knew that Gena liked to knit and tried to recruit her. That would have been a real coup for Sonya, getting back at Healey by bringing his wife into the secret fold that he scorned."

Phoebe nodded eagerly. "Maybe the bad history between Sonya and her husband gave Mrs. Healey the idea. That would be another perfect reason for her to pick the Knit Kats as a cover." Phoebe was breathless but elated. "Let the police take a peek in Gena Healey's knitting bag. I bet they find all the evidence they need." She picked up the bear hat again. "Hey, Bear, you're like flipping brilliant. You totally nailed this one. Professor Healey is a jerk . . . and a shifty character, for sure. But he didn't kill anybody. Which I was never buying, either."

Maggie sighed. "We'd better call Detective Reyes and tell her what you've come up with. But without the bear . . . okay?"

Phoebe nodded. "I hear you."

Phoebe was so eager to share her insights with the police that Maggie decided to close the shop early. Detective Reyes told them to meet her at the station and took them into a private interview room, along with Detective Mossbacher, who took notes again on a big legal pad.

It was hard for Phoebe to control her excitement, but she managed to talk at a semireasonable speed. She told the detectives everything she'd figured out. They asked many questions but seemed to take her seriously.

"So . . . what do you think?" Phoebe finally asked the detectives.

Detective Reyes pushed back a bit from the table. "This theory pretty much blows up the case we've built against Professor Healey. But it does answer some inconsistencies," she admitted. "We can't dismiss your information entirely, Phoebe."

"We'll look into it," Mossbacher promised in his usual flat, unenthusiastic way.

Phoebe sighed as she and Maggie left the station. Maggie could tell she felt frustrated. But Maggie was encouraged. If Gena Healey was truly the guilty party, the police would figure it out. It was out of their hands now. Where it should be.

They had been buzzed out of the station room and were out in the lobby when Detective Mossbacher caught up. "Phoebe . . . I just wanted to tell you something. About Quentin Gibbs."

Phoebe turned. She looked alarmed. "What about him?"

"He had an accident on his motorcycle last night. He was lucky, he's not badly hurt. But he'll be in the hospital a few days. He was DUI. His third offense. He's agreed to go into a treatment program in Peabody instead of serving jail time. He'll be there at least two months. Then he has to toe the line and deal with a lot of supervision if he wants to stay out of jail. I don't think he'll be bothering you again."

Phoebe had not mentioned Quentin or his threats, but Maggie could tell she was relieved. "Thanks for telling me that, Detective. Sounds like Quentin finally hit the jackpot. Couldn't have happened to a nicer person," she added.

"I'm glad to hear that, too," Maggie admitted as they walked out to Phoebe's car. "But I guess that means no more midnight waffle parties."

Phoebe smiled. "We'll still have parties, Maggie. But I will like hanging in my own apartment again . . . and getting a good night's sleep."

"I'm sure you will." Maggie patted her shoulder. Phoebe had been through so much the last week or so. But she'd handled it all so maturely. Maggie was proud of her. She was an exceptional young woman and Maggie was proud to be her friend.

Alone at home that night, Maggie sat in her favorite chair and scanned the TV for a good show. What luck, *Miss Marple* was on again. The intrepid sleuth was visiting a former schoolmate, and a dead body had already turned up in a lovely English garden.

Maggie sat back and picked up her knitting. She did miss Phoebe's company and lively chatter. But it was also good to have her space back to herself. She rarely minded being alone. Though she had to admit, she'd started to wonder if she, too, should take in a cat.

The phone was ringing, rousing her from a deep sleep. Maggie sat up in her chair, disoriented for a moment. Her knitting was on her lap, and the TV screen showed a big weather map with swirls of air-mass patterns.

She quickly found the phone, which had fallen to the floor near her feet. "Maggie? Are you still up?"

"Just barely . . ." It was Phoebe. She sounded quite excited, or maybe upset about something. "Are you all right? Is something wrong?"

"I'm fine. Turn on the news. Channel 25. The police have Gena Healey in custody. Detective Reyes really listened to us."

"Listened to *you*. You solved it all." Maggie fumbled with the remote, eager to find the channel. "I know it's late, but you'd better let Dana, Lucy, and Suzanne know about this. They'll never forgive us."

"I just sent a text and copied all of them. Here comes Chelsea Porter . . . catch you later."

"I'm going to bed. I'll catch you tomorrow at the shop. I'm sure we'll have some company."

Phoebe laughed and said good night. Maggie turned her attention to the TV. She saw a picture of Whitaker College and heard the familiar voice of her favorite reporter.

"The investigation into the death of college student Beth Shelton took a one-hundred-and-eighty-degree turn today when Gena Healey was named a person of interest. Investigators escorted the wife and mother of two to the Essex County police station for questioning, where she is still being held.

"A search of her car has already yielded important evidence—evidence that ironically has cast doubt on the guilt of her husband, Professor Alex Healey, who had been charged with the crime only two days ago and is now released on bail. Law enforcement officials are not revealing any details at this point. But it appears they now believe Gena Healey may have committed the crime and planted evidence at the scene incriminating her husband. Her motive? Her husband's affair with a student . . ."

Maggie clicked off the set. It was late, and she would hear all the details tomorrow. She already knew most of what they'd say. Thanks to Phoebe.

It still amazed her how Phoebe had figured this out. But

why *not* Phoebe? She was so creative, possessed such mental plasticity. The girl rarely gave herself enough credit.

Deep down, Phoebe could not accept that her greatly admired professor Alex Healey was really so cruel and cold-blooded. It had been a blow to hear about his bad behavior—the stock fraud and infidelity. But Phoebe had still wanted to believe he was not guilty of Beth Shelton's murder. She clung to the theory of his innocence and persevered to see him vindicated.

Hope and perseverance, always a winning formula.

I'll stitch that on a pillow, Maggie thought sleepily as she shut off the light on her nightstand. I'll give it to Phoebe for Valentine's Day.

Since Valentine's Day fell on a Thursday, the group decided to push their meeting up to Wednesday. It was not Phoebe's turn to host—it was actually Dana's—but she had asked to jump the line. She wanted to keep the promise she'd made about having everyone over for dinner after the investigation, to thank her friends for helping her clean her apartment after the police search.

"And for just sticking with me and being so nice in general," she'd added in her invitation.

Maggie and her friends wouldn't have had it any other way. But they were also happy to visit Phoebe's Wednesday night for their meeting and see what the little punked-out domestic diva would prepare.

She greeted her guests in a black minidress and lace stockings, covered with a frilly red hostess apron she'd found in a thrift store somewhere, straight from the 1950s. A red satin ribbon was tied across her forehead, trailing down into her hair.

"This is a like a Queen of Hearts dinner in honor of Valentine's Day," Phoebe announced. "Everything is red . . . starting with my special prosecco-and-pomegranate cocktail, red pepper dip, cold beet salad with goat cheese, and, for the entree, tomato sauce and meatballs . . ." Phoebe paused and sighed. "I tried to make the meatballs heart-shaped, but it didn't work out that well," she confessed.

Suzanne waved her hand. "I'm sure they taste great. What a menu! . . . What's for dessert?"

"Red velvet cake, of course. Lucy was in charge of that."

"Got it covered. I just put it in the fridge," Lucy reported as she walked in from the kitchen to join them.

"You've planned a great dinner. Not to mention these fabulous decorations." Maggie added, glancing around. There were garlands of paper hearts crisscrossing the apartment, and the table was set with a red cloth and white dishes, along with tall candles and a vase with pink roses.

"Your place looks great, Phoebe. You must have worked on this all day. You shouldn't have gone to so much trouble just for us," Lucy said, gazing around.

"Are you kidding? Valentine's Day isn't just for some stupid boyfriend you might not even want to see again. It's a day to show people you really love how much you care. And who do I love more than you guys?" she said, glancing around at the circle of friends. "Except maybe Van Gogh."

The gray cat sat between Dana and Suzanne on the red love seat. Phoebe had stuck a very un-tomcat pink bow on his collar, but he didn't seem to mind. He craned his neck and looked around, aware, it seemed, that he was being talked about.

"Did Van Gogh get his valentine from you yet?" Dana petted the cat, who curled his head into her hand.

"We shared a bagel and lox for breakfast."

"I bet I know who ate the bagel and who ate the lox." Lucy laughed. "Now that Charlotte's returned, will you keep him? Or does she want him back?"

Maggie had been wondering the same thing but had been too worried about the answer to ask. Charlotte had finally returned, about two days after Gena Healey's arrest. The police claimed that they had been very close to finding her. But Maggie believed the clever young lady had outwitted them all and had only come out of hiding when she was good and ready.

Phoebe had seen her once so far and had not shared much about that meeting. Maggie knew it had been difficult for her. Phoebe's expression darkened a bit at the mention of her friend's name, as she set a platter of dip and crusty bread bits on the table.

"Charlotte didn't mind that I had him. She was pretty relieved that one cat at least had been taken in. Her life is really unsettled now. She's found homes for a few of them. And may bring a few to a shelter."

"Okay, we've got the cats covered. But what's going to happen to Charlotte?" Suzanne asked bluntly. "Isn't she being charged for that stock trading scheme, along with Healey?"

Dana was just about to taste the dip but paused a moment. "Her lawyer worked out a deal. Most of the charges were dropped in exchange for her cooperation. She took only a very tiny portion of all that money and came back on her own. That all worked in her favor. She claims she had no part in using the information illegally—that was all Healey's idea. The police believe her. She does have to pay back the thousand dollars she took from the backpack and a hefty fine. And she'll be on probation for years."

"Poor girl. What a difficult way to start off your life. But she is young. In a few years, she'll put this all behind her." Maggie shook her head. "She really didn't do anything wrong. But she should have gone straight to the police once she knew that Alex Healey had used the information she gave him."

"I guess that's the way the police and the Securities and Exchange Commission feel about it," Suzanne chimed in. "I feel sorry for her, too, though. She was definitely exploited."

"She tried to turn Professor Healey in," Phoebe said quietly. "But she told me it was just too hard to tell on him. She could never go through with it. She'd broken off their relationship. But she still had feelings for him. And she was afraid she'd be in trouble because of what he'd done. That's one reason she ran away."

"What will happen to Healey now? Does anyone know?" Lucy looked around curiously.

"He pleaded guilty to the stock manipulation and bargained a reduced sentence," Dana told the others. "He has to serve some jail time, about a year or less, and then has to do a lot of community service. Probably teach in a prison or something like that."

"At least he'll be around for his children eventually. Gena Healey will probably be in jail a very long time. Even though she confessed and tried to use some sort of insanity defense. Temporarily unhinged due to jealous rage over her husband's betrayal," Maggie recalled. "Her planning seemed so detailed and premeditated—the glove, the boots, and planting the yarn in his studio—I don't see how she can say she was temporarily crazy."

"Love makes people crazy. It's a known fact," Dana said with a laugh. "Didn't Aristotle say love is a kind of sickness?"

"Maybe . . . but what a topic of conversation for a Valentine's Day party," Lucy said with a laugh.

"A cautionary tale," Maggie agreed with a grin. "Mainly for middle-aged husbands with beautiful young mistresses," she added. Then felt a little insensitive, knowing Phoebe was still friends with Charlotte.

Though they could never be as close again as they once were. Charlotte had betrayed Phoebe, too, in a way. Though maybe she couldn't help it, believing that her secrets were the only way to protect herself.

"Yeah, Charlotte fell for Professor Healey big-time. I'm not sure it was a sickness. But it wasn't a wellness," Phoebe had to agree. "Too bad she didn't see what a phony he was until it was too late. She never wanted to go along with his stupid plan to run off to Italy and all that." Phoebe made a face and shook her head. "She was scared of Quentin, too. Another reason to put distance between herself and Plum Harbor."

Suzanne nodded. "I totally get it. After Charlotte heard about Beth Shelton, murdered by mistake . . . well, that was another reason to run away and hide. A good one, if you ask me."

"At least she came back and took the heat. I can't believe that with all their high-tech gadgets the police couldn't find her. That was pretty cool," Phoebe added with admiration. "But I feel like a dummy. I should have guessed it right off."

"Really? How?" Lucy asked curiously. "Where was she anyway? I never heard that part."

"She was at her grandmother's house, on a farm. Out in the Pennsylvania Dutch country," Maggie explained.

"That piece in the gallery, *Granny's Parlor*. Remember?" Phoebe asked her friends.

"Oh, right . . . I remember that one." Suzanne nodded as she took another forkful of beet salad. "Why didn't the police look for her there? Didn't they realize she had a grandmother?"

"They checked in with all her relatives when Charlotte first went missing. But Charlotte's granny is very old, and a bit senile," Dana explained. "Between the time the police called and the time Charlotte showed up, Granny forgot about the instructions to get in touch if she saw her granddaughter. Charlotte was easily able to keep that part of the situation under control. And police in that area, who were told to watch the farm, didn't do a very good job," Dana added. "Charlotte was able to stay there over a week without anyone seeing her."

"They would have spotted her sooner or later," Lucy said. "Or the FBI would have figured it out. I guess that's why she just came back."

"Part of the reason," Phoebe cut in. "She said she'd been following the local news around here online and felt really bad that I was getting into so much trouble . . . and bad about Professor Healey, too. She didn't believe he'd killed Beth by mistake, either. But I don't think she suspected his wife," Phoebe added.

"None of us did . . . except you," Maggie pointed out, giving her full credit. "I suppose we all should have. Including Reyes and Mossbacher. It does seem like an obvious choice now. But there were a lot of distractions. The Knit Kats, first and foremost. What's become of Professor Finch? I read in the newspaper that she stepped down voluntarily from her position at Whitaker."

"I guess the choice was walk away in semidignity or get dragged out by campus security . . . and she didn't want to be in the news again," Phoebe decided. "I heard she's moving to Florida, to join the missing Knit Kat. Some literature professor who used to teach at Tufts and lives in . . . New Smyrna Beach? Did I get the name right? Is there such a place?" Phoebe asked her friends.

"Yes, that's right. New Smyrna Beach." Suzanne nodded. "Makes me think of a beach resort where Smurfs go on vacation. But I've heard it's really pretty and a cool place. Good real-estate values."

"Well, I hope she's happy there. A strange woman, but I felt sorry for her," Maggie admitted. "Detective Reyes told me that Sonya Finch admitted to making that prank call to the shop. She just wanted to rattle my cage a bit. And she had some vague thought of recruiting me for her cause. Can you believe that?" Maggie shook her head and took out her knitting.

"She'll have to hunt for new recruits in Florida," Lucy pointed out. "Maybe they'll start up a new chapter. The Sun and Sand Kats. No, wait . . . the Smyrna Kats?"

Phoebe stood up and signaled time-out while the rest of her friends laughed at Lucy's silly joke.

"Hey, you guys, get a grip. The pasta isn't done yet. How about we show off our Valentine's Day projects?"

Dana started digging in her knitting bag. "Good idea . . . I have a few. Two teddy bears and two pairs of socks for the shelter.

And the ear warmers for Jack. If he's embarrassed by the hearts he can just use them to keep the dust off his clubs in the winter."

Maggie had a strong feeling Jack would choose the latter. But he would surely be touched by Dana's thoughtful effort.

"I finished the Roosevelt mittens. They're definitely worthy of a titan of history . . . or my husband," Suzanne told the others. "And they were so easy. I also almost finished a teddy bear for the shelter."

"Good work, Suzanne. Very generous of you." Suzanne was usually a slow knitter and Maggie was very impressed.

"I made this cover for Matt's coffee mug." Lucy displayed a red mug cover with a pink heart. "And I'm working on some socks for the shelter. I might have at least one pair done by tomorrow," she added, holding up her needles.

"I made a few things for the shelter, too," Maggie said finally. "But my favorite is this pillow cover. Which is for a special someone." Maggie took a knitted pillow cover from her bag. She had used a dark red yarn. There was a heart in the middle and a golden border.

"I hand-stitched the lettering on this side. But I think it came out well," she added, showing her friends both sides.

"'Good friends are like stars. You can't always see them. But you know they are always there,'" Suzanne read out loud. She smiled at Maggie, her eyes shining. "Aw . . . that's so sweet . . . and true," she added quickly.

"I think so. I made it for my good friend . . . Phoebe." She smiled at their young hostess. "You'll have to be my valentine this year, Phoebe. As you know, I don't have a special guy to celebrate with tomorrow."

"Neither do I. But I have you guys. And that's plenty."

Maggie handed her the pillow cover, and Phoebe gave her a hug.

"Hey, I'm all for my women friends. But how is it that two fabulous creatures like you and Phoebe are going dateless in Plum Harbor tomorrow night?" Suzanne peered at Maggie, one of her not-letting-you-off-the-hook looks.

Maggie squirmed. Luckily, Phoebe spoke up first. "I'm taking a break from men. I need to like totally detox my brain, heart, and soul after Josh. And clean all his junk out of my apartment."

"Good plan, Phoebe," Dana said with approval.

"Oh, you know me . . ." Maggie shrugged. "I'd rather be alone than go out with just anybody . . . I do have a date for Saturday night. But it's just a first date and surely doesn't count for Valentine's Day."

All eyes turned to her. She was sorry at first that she'd let the information slip out. But she did enjoy the shocked looks on their faces.

"In your case, anything counts," Suzanne said bluntly. "And when did this happen? You held out on us, Maggie," she scolded.

"I'm telling you now, aren't I?" Maggie stared back at her, feeling her cheeks get red.

"Did you finally try PerfectDate-dot-com?" Dana had been coaxing her for months to try an online dating service that had helped a lot of her clients.

"No, I didn't," she said with satisfaction. "I did it the old-fashioned way. Meeting a real live person face-to-face."

"So who is it? Have we seen this face-to-face anyplace?" Suzanne asked eagerly.

"Yes, you have . . . It's Charles Mossbacher," she said quietly, watching for their reactions.

"Detective Mossbacher? Right under my nose!" Phoebe stared at her.

"I can see it." Dana nodded quickly. "Now that you mention it. When you told us the way he came here and asked you to compare the photos of knitting, I had a feeling something was going on. He didn't really have to do that."

"No, I guess not," Maggie admitted. "But it was interesting. I enjoyed contributing, even a tiny bit, to the investigation. I asked him about that the other day, when he called to ask me out. He said that one of the photos was a sample of Sonya Finch's knitting, another a sample of Charlotte's, and the third was the wrapping found on Beth Shelton's body."

"And you were right when you told him that none of it matched," Lucy pointed out. "No wonder he likes you. He can tell you'd be a good intellectual match for him."

"He is smart. And seems really nice," Phoebe added in a saner tone. "Even though he's a policeman."

"Well, Lucy and I haven't met him yet." Suzanne glanced at Lucy. "Can't you tell us a little more?"

Maggie shrugged. "Not much to tell. He is very smart and seems kind. And we seem to get along . . ." She also liked his eyes and his smile. Which so far had been rare, but she hoped that off duty, she'd see a bit more of it. "Much too soon to know anything more. We'll see how it goes, I guess."

Maggie did like him more than she was willing to let on. Especially to Suzanne. It really was too early to tell. Except that something about him made her feel willing to try again.

"So what do you all think? Is there hope for me yet?" she asked the group.

Phoebe patted her heartily on the shoulder. "Absolutely. I hope it works out with Chaaarrrrles . . ." She comically dragged out his name. "But you always have us, your loyal knitting pals."

"Yes, I know." Maggie met her glance and nodded. "And it's a great comfort to me. I cherish your friendship. The friendship of everyone here," she added, glancing at the others.

No one had to answer. She knew they all felt the same. And those ties went deeper that Knit Kats . . . or even boyfriends. The Black Sheep Knitters were just that important to her. And always would be.

"Happy Valentine's Day, everybody." Phoebe raised her pomegranate cocktail. "To our friendship. It doesn't get any better—or more close-knit—than this."

The Black Sheep happily clinked their glasses. No one could argue with that.

Notes from the Black Sheep Knitting Shop
Bulletin Board

Dear Friends and Fellow Knitters,

I hope you all had a wonderful Valentine's Day, sharing the love with romantic partners, family, and friends. My own knitting group whipped up some sweet little projects that made perfect gifts for V-day, and would suit just about any occasion. From ear warmers to cup cozies and teddy bears, I've posted links below to a selection of our favorites. I hope you try a few.

Adorable "You Have My Heart" Knitted Cap:

http://www.allfreeknitting.com/Knit-Hats/i-love-you-hearts
-knit-hat

Elegant Heart Pattern Scarf, with scalloped border and heart lace design:

http://www.allfreeknitting.com/Valentines-Day-Knits/hearts
-scarf-pattern .

Mrs. Roosevelt's Mittens—simple, functional, but made with love (that's what counts, right?)

http://www.allfreeknitting.com/Mittens-and-Gloves/Mrs
-Roosevelt-Mittens/ct/1

Sweetheart Mittens—cozy mittens covered with mini-hearts

http://www.allfreeknitting.com/Mittens-and-Gloves/Sweetheart-Mittens/ct/1

Valentines Mug Cozy—a mug-hugging cozy, covered with a big heart

http://www.allfreeknitting.com/Valentines-Day-Knits/valentine-mug-cozy

Take your pick between these two easy teddy bear patterns:

Bubby the Bear

http://www.allfreeknitting.com/Valentines-Day-Knits/bubby-the-bear/ct/1

One Seam Teddy Bear

http://www.allfreeknitting.com/Valentines-Day-Knits/one-seam-teddy-bear/ct/1

We also made many of these projects as gifts to donate and brought them to a shelter for homeless families, not far from Plum Harbor. It was a day for sharing the love *and* the knitting. Why wait for a holiday? We can do that every day of the year. Last but not least, thanks for continuing to visit my shop despite the news stories that seemed to link us with the infamous Knit Kats! As you know by now, there wasn't a whisker to that rumor regarding me or my wonderful assistant, Phoebe.

Funny thing is, I'm suddenly getting many requests for a

class on fiber art and even—heaven help me—knitting graffiti. Just want you all to know that I'm working on it and will announce a session soon.

I can't promise any late-night, subversive field trips—but we will have lots of fun.

As always, happy knitting!

Maggie

Dear Everybody—

You know I hate posting stuff on this board. It's so archaic. Why not just paint your message on a cave wall?

But the Valentine's Day party I gave for my knitting group was such a smash everyone's been asking me about the decorations and recipes and all that.

Hey, do I look like Martha Stewart to you? I sure hope not!

But, by popular demand, here goes. First, decorate. Loads of red, pink, and some white stuff should do it. Whatever you've got—tablecloths, napkins, ribbon, and scarves are nice, too. Especially flowery patterns, just wrap them around things. Be creative. Get the toxins out.

Lights are nice—especially little white ones. No worries if you don't have any around the house. Find some candles and candle holders, different sizes and shapes gathered together look cool. A scented candle or two is a good thing, too. It's Valentine's Day. The world should smell good.

So you gather all the stuff, and spread it around. A vase or two of fresh flowers totally nails it.

To set the mood for a really awesome party, a special cocktail to greet your guests does the trick.

Here's my original recipe for the Queen of Hearts Cocktail.

And you can make it nonalcoholic by substituting sparkling cider for the prosecco.

I'm also posting the recipe for my special appetizer, Cold Beet Salad with Goat Cheese.

Beets are really awesome. The magenta color always gets me. You can cut the slices into heart shapes, if you're super crafty (crazy?). Only kidding. :) It tastes good either way.

From my kitchen to yours!

Yeah, I know, that's a little scary. But I didn't have any leftovers. Ask my friends if you don't believe me.

XO Phoebe

Phoebe's Queen of Hearts Cocktail

One bottle prosecco sparkling wine, dry or extra dry
(Or one bottle of nonalcoholic sparkling cider)
One bottle of cranberry-pomegranate juice, regular
    or diet
3 large navel or juice oranges
Several fresh strawberries or raspberries
Long toothpicks
Ice
Large pitcher
Long-stemmed glasses (martini or margarita
    will do nicely)
Granulated sugar

First, prepare the glasses by rinsing with water and chilling in the freezer.

Mix 2 cup of cran-pom juice to 4 cups prosecco (or sparkling cider) in the large pitcher.

Squeeze two of the oranges and add juice, including some of the pulp.

Slice the third orange, and make a slit from the radius to the peel, so the slice will balance on the edge of the glass.

Clean strawberries, pat dry. Slice in half and string

on toothpicks. (Or clean raspberries and pat dry, reserve for bottom of each glass.)

Store pitcher in the fridge or freezer until you're ready to serve. Don't prepare the mix too far in advance, or the sparkling wine will go flat.

Just before serving, add several ice cubes to the pitcher and stir vigorously.

Don't allow ice to melt. Quickly remove cubes with a slotted spoon.

Just before it's time to serve, sprinkle a few tablespoons of sugar on a dish or in a soup bowl and dip the rims of each glass in the sugar. If the sugar doesn't stick, lightly wet just the edges of the glass rims and try again.

Pour the sparkling wine mixture into each glass, garnish with an orange slice and a toothpick of strawberries. Or toss a few raspberries into the bottom of each glass.

Cheers!

Cold Beet Salad with Goat Cheese

3–4 raw beets

(Or a package of whole, cooked beets, sold in some
supermarkets in the fresh produce section)

6–8 ounces of fresh goat cheese

½ cup slivered, toasted almonds

8–10 ounces of arugula

8–10 ounces of mixed greens

1 fresh lemon

2 tablespoons of white vinegar or sherry vinegar

Olive oil

1 tablespoon of Dijon mustard (optional)

Sea salt

Prep tips: Rinse and chill salad plates in the
refrigerator or freezer.

Also, best to cook the beets the day before. Or very
early the day of serving so they have to chill out in the
fridge. (Unless you're using pre-cooked beets, of course.)

When handling beets, wear rubber gloves. Especially
after they're cooked.

Enough said.

Wash and trim beets. Cut off green stems and hard
tips on bottom and top.

Cover with cold water in a large pot and bring water to a boil. Lower to a simmer and boil with a cover on the pot until the beets are soft enough to push a sharp knife through easily.

Pour off water and run the beets under cold water a few minutes to cool them off.

Drain and place in a metal or glass bowl and cool in the refrigerator.

Rinse arugula and greens, let them drain thoroughly.

Squeeze lemon and grate some of the zest into the juice.

Mix the dressing by combining the olive oil with the Dijon mustard. Add the juice of one lemon to the vinegar. Add a dash of sea salt, if desired.

In a large mixing bowl, mix greens with some of the dressing, until they are lightly covered.

Slice the beets about ½-inch thick. (At this point, you can decide if you really want to make heart shapes from the beet slices. You can use a cookie cutter, paper template from cardboard or parchment paper. Or just wing it.) Crumble the goat cheese and set it aside in a small bowl. It tastes best at room temperature.

Just before serving, remove salad plates from the fridge.

Arrange a mound of greens on each plate.

Set three or four beet slices overlapping across the greens.

Drizzle a small amount of dressing on top. Sprinkle on 2–3 tablespoons of cheese and 1–2 tablespoons of slivered almonds.